**John Dale's** first novel, *Dark Angel*, won the Ned Kelly Award for Best First Crime Novel. He lives in Sydney, edits a crime fiction magazine, *Mean Streets*, and is working on a non-fiction book.

**Also by John Dale and published by Serpent's Tail**

*Dark Angel*

# The Dogs are Barking

## JOHN DALE

Library of Congress Catalog Card Number: 98–89859

A catalogue record for this book is available from
the British Library on request

The right of John Dale to be identified as
the author of this work has been asserted by him
in accordance with the Copyright, Designs and
Patents Act 1988

Copyright © John Dale 1998

First published in Australia in 1998 by
HarperCollins Publishers Pty Limited

First published in 1999 by Serpent's Tail,
4 Blackstock Mews, London N4

The characters and events in this book are fictitious.
Any similarity to real persons, living or dead,
is coincidental and not intended by the author.

Website: www.serpentstail.com

Printed in Great Britain by Mackays of Chatham, plc

10 9 8 7 6 5 4 3 2 1

**For Nik**

*Well you've got me, I want to confess, I want to get it off my chest...*

Detective Sergeant WS14

# 1

Terry Dedovic fired combinations at the heavy bag, double jab, rip, right cross, left hook. Chin tucked in, he circled the big swinging target, left foot probing forward, shoulders hunched, keeping his right mitt up in front of his face, snapping out that left. The bag rattled on its thick chains whenever he landed a big right hand over the top. Surprising himself with the shots that he was giving, feeling the power spreading down from his thickened shoulders, snaking along his arms and wrists to converge with bulletlike precision at the end of his gloves.

"Thassa way, Vic." The gym trainer leaned on the ropes inside the ring.

Sweat ran down Dedovic's broken nose and chiselled chin. He flicked his head and droplets of sweat flew into the air. Sweat dripped from his armpits onto the slippery wooden boards underfoot. His neck, chest and thighs were covered in a wet film. The bag danced on its chain as he let rip, giving it everything he had now, clenching the mouthguard hard between his teeth.

"Time!" The trainer yelled.

Dedovic dropped his hands. His Ring Pro T-shirt was drenched, his black Puma shorts stained in a vee around his groin. He loved the feel of those toxins oozing out of him. He went over to his sports bag and towelled down, squirted iced water from the waterbottle at his mouth.

A young Turkish welterweight with Gothic red tattoos on his back was grunting over a medicine ball on a black greasy bench. All the windows in the small gym were shut, the place stank of sweaty feet and liniment. A discarded jockstrap hung over the side of the garbage bin and a poster of a former World Champion glared down from the wall.

The trainer slipped the Eveready pads on as Dedovic climbed into the ring, raising his fists high.

"Okay," he said, "let's go."

The trainer grinned, chewing on a wad of gum, eyes shining like brass buttons. A gold crucifix dangled off the thick black bed of hair that covered his chest. His body was hard and lean; not an inch of fat anywhere. The trainer looked up at the clock and then lifted his pads. "Big effort from you today."

Dedovic snorted through his nose and let fly. He felt the pain start to build in his shoulders, standing there, legs apart, his arms going like pistons.

"Everything you've got now. C'mon, work it."

The gym echoed with the sound of his grunts and the loud, steady whack of leather on leather.

"Thirty seconds. Let it burn!" The trainer called.

Face contorted, Dedovic finished with a flurry of punches and then fell back onto the ropes, sucking in the fetid gym air, arms dangling loose, panting like a dog.

The trainer stood over him. "Not bad for an old pro."

Dedovic closed his eyes, listening to the trainer masticate noisily, and then everything went quiet and even the Turkish boy stopped bouncing the heavy medicine ball on his abdominals. Dedovic wiped the salty sweat from his eyes and saw what they were staring at. She was standing by the shiny speedball, wearing an ice-blue singlet, tight mauve shorts with a pink sausage bag slung across her shoulders.

"Excuse me," she purred. "Is this the class?" Her long red hair was pinned on top of her head with a tiny plastic clip.

"Other room, love," the trainer said, not taking his eyes off her chest.

Dedovic watched her turn slowly and go out of the gym door. Tall, slender legs. He climbed off the ropes, jumped out of the ring and spat into the handbasin. He scooped up his sports bag.

"Where you going?"

"Do some skipping."

The trainer grinned, removed the piece of well-chewed gum from between his flash white teeth, stuck it on the edge of the ring post and gestured at the Turkish kid to climb into the ring.

Dedovic hurried through next door where they held the boxercise classes for yuppies and overweight businessmen. A couple of dykes were lifting hand-weights, admiring their muscles in the wall-length mirrors. One gave him the nod. He'd helped her out with some trouble in the gym car park a month ago. He got out his rope and started skipping quietly by himself in a corner. Watching the class get down to it on the floor. Five balding guys with pot bellies, three tattooed dykes and that tall, red-haired piece. A real clothes horse. Nice, well-toned figure, though her skin was too pale. He guessed she had some kind of office job. The class were doing press-ups, sets of fifty, groaning and grunting on the floor while Bert, the muscled instructor, went around exhorting them individually. "Good work,

Mona," he said to the new woman, touching her lightly on the gluteus.

Dedovic skipped a little faster, the rope whirring around his head, one eye on Mona on the floor, his cock flopping about inside his Pumas. Bert glanced over at him as if he knew what was going down. She had to know he was giving her the hard eye now, but for all she let on, he might've been watching her on video. Miss Cool. Down on the floor doing forty-five stomach crunches, hardly even perspiring while the older males around her went scarlet in the face, bluish veins bulging out the sides of their scraggy necks.

He stopped skipping, stood holding the sweaty rope in his hand while he caught his breath, then walked over to the high bar and started doing chin-ups, pulling his ninety-five Ks up by his biceps until the pain wrinkled the skin on his forehead and burned like a red-hot poker into his shoulder blades. How many movies had he seen where some American actor dangled from a clifftop by his arms for half an hour? Most citizens would be lucky to last three minutes. He glanced around for her on the floor and found her standing beneath him. For a crazy moment he thought she'd been trying to see up his shorts. Just thinking about it gave him a wood. He dropped to the floor with a thump, heard her say in a voice as cool as crushed ice, "I borrow your rope?"

"Huh?"

"Your skipping rope."

He rubbed his deltoids. "Go for it."

"You a boxer?"

Something in him wanted to lie, feed her some horseshit about his number five WBC rating, but he fought back the urge. "Used to be," he said. "While ago now."

"You keep in pretty good shape for an *older* man."

He wiped the sweat drops from his thick curly eyebrows. "You're only as old as you feel."

"Nice cliché," she said and threw him a smile that revealed a set of gleaming white teeth.

He stared at her mouth. "Been here before?"

"No," she said quickly and turned towards the instructor. "Hasn't Bert got a tremendous physique?"

Dedovic looked at the instructor's bull-neck. Yeah, he wanted to say. Apart from the shrunken testicles the guy had from the Centurabol he was on and his little roid dick. "Actually Bert's gay."

"I'm not surprised," she said, "the best bodies usually are." She brushed her hand against his arm.

It happened so quickly, but he was surprised to feel a sexual jolt in his loins, like some schoolkid. He looked into her pale green eyes. "Listen." He swallowed. "I gotta take a shower right now, but how about you and me stepping out for a drink . . . "

She stood there untangling a nasty knot in his rope.

"I know this nice little bar," he persevered. "Jus' up the street." He watched her frowning, convinced that she would say no.

"Why not?" she said, then turned and walked back to join her class.

Dedovic watched her go, eyes fixed on the muscles of her calves and her slender ankles. Then he hurried downstairs to the showers and peeled off his boxing gear. Whistling, he stepped in under the warm dribbling water and began to soap his hard muscled frame. It'd been a while since he'd made a move on a woman. Considering the circumstances he'd done pretty well, though there was one small thing niggling at the back of his mind. He lathered under his balls and up between the cheeks of his arse with the soap. The more he thought about it, the more uncertain he was of who'd picked up who.

# 2

Nickie Taroney braked on the corner of Wilson Street, headlights shining across the old railway yards. Lighted carriages flicked past behind the trees like film through a shutter. Beside her, Garth peered out at the grimy Reschs sign swinging from the hotel roof, the barred windows. "I don't like the look of this place," he said.

Wind rocked the car and an airbus droned low above the rooftops. Cars were jammed bumper to bumper up both sides of the street. "Come in with me, Nicola." He gripped the handle with his long fingers.

Nickie switched off the engine. God, she hoped it wasn't going to be one of those weekends with him. She watched Garth walk across to the bottle shop, tall, slim, his thinning hair streaked with grey. Distinguished looking, her friends said. Leaving her lights on park, she climbed out after him. The air smelled of burning industrial waste. Leaves and a flattened pizza carton swirled around her new suede mules. What the hell was he doing now? They were going to be late.

"Locked." He was shaking his long angular face at her.

She put a shoulder to the scuffed bottle shop door. Saw the sign blue-tacked to the inside of the fly-smeared glass. *Staff shortige tonite. Enter through main door.*

"Let's find somewhere else," he said.

"We haven't got time." Nickie checked her watch.

Garth pointed to a reddish-brown liquid trickling down the tiles. "That's not blood is it?"

"Engine oil," she said. C'mon, don't be a baby, she wanted to say. Grabbing his elbow, she dragged him around the corner. A guard dog barked in the yard opposite and drunken voices cheered from behind the dirty green doors of the public bar. She shoved the door open and stepped into a small packed bar. Men in blue singlets were staring up at three blaring TV screens where two bloodied boy boxers were slugging it out on the ropes. Cigarette smoke mixed with the sour cheesy smell of unwashed bodies.

"Excuse me." Nickie squeezed between solidly built men with broad freckled arms and thick creased necks, Garth following on her heels, trying not to get his Marcs suit soiled. She cut a path to the bar rail where an old woman with bald patches in her mauve hair made room around the service counter. Nickie reached a hand over and felt something rub at the base of her skirt. Hoped it was Garth. She tried to catch the attention of an overweight barmaid in a skimpy black dress.

"Whatcha want, luvvie?"

"Champagne," Nickie told her, but the barmaid brought back a cheap sparkling wine. Nickie wiped dust from the label with her finger. Porphyry Pearl. Probably sat on their shelf for twenty years. "Haven't you got anything better?" she yelled. "It's for a birthday."

The barmaid flounced through to the bottle shop, came back again, big jelly breasts flopping from side to side. As if it were Nickie's fault she was working here.

"Let's get out of this dump," Garth said.

"Say what, pal?" A man with a thick black moustache under a flattened nose leaned over.

"I was having a private conversation here, thank you." Garth opened his initialled pigskin wallet and detached a hundred. Nickie grabbed his change and the bottle of Yellowglen from the wet bar towel. To her left, three excited Korean men were watching Sky channel, slapping each other's arms. A mob of Anglos and a Koori woman closer to the door started yelling and cheering as a well-built man in a light blue shirt and navy blue trousers climbed precariously up onto a rickety bar table and unbuttoned his trousers.

"My God," Garth said. "He's not–"

Nickie blinked as the man turned around and slowly pulled his strides and then his underpants down to his ankles. The barmaid shook her head and several customers applauded. Inspired, the man bent over and parted his buttocks.

"See that!" Garth yelled in her ear. The man was holding the cheeks of his arse wide apart. Garth pointed again. "Look, Nicola."

"I see it, I see it," Nickie said. She wasn't blind. Wondering if that idiot up there would remember doing this tomorrow.

"No, his shirt," Garth said, as the man spun around.

But Nickie was staring instead at his face – a lick of curly blond hair dangling over his bloodshot eyes, thick lips. If he hadn't been so smashed she might've found him attractive in a coarse sort of a way. Pitied his wife if he had one. The other drinkers were whistling and cheering for more and the Koori woman holding onto a fun machine was laughing her head off. Someone yelled: "Go, Terry, go boy!" And the man grinned down sheepishly at them.

Then Nickie's eyes lowered to the insignia on the shoulder of his blue shirt, saw the lettering and the swooping eagle stitched there: New South Wales Police.

Mesmerised, she watched as the man produced a long black baton from around his ankles and begin to simulate the sexual act on top of the table.

Garth yanked on her arm. "Let's go."

They steered a path for the door. Drinkers were jammed so tightly into the narrow little bar that Nickie had to prod at soft quaggy stomachs to squeeze past. She felt the heat from a dozen cigarettes frizzle the ends of her hair, smelled sour beer on the breath of drinkers. The uniformed policeman had his baton poking out between his legs, hips gyrating like a stripper's, and then another man on all fours bounded around the bar floor barking and the policeman's boot slid off the wet edge of the table and down he came, crashing into the audience. Drinkers surged back. Nickie was pinned against the table of excited Koreans. Men started shoving each other. She dropped her champagne onto the tiled floor, heard it bounce. A voice yelled, "Don't push!" and Garth was slammed up against the doorway, then he tumbled under the legs of a group of workmen.

A bolt of panic ran through her. She rushed to Garth lying dazed on the dirty floor. "You alright?" She lifted his head onto her lap, ran her fingers quickly over his nose and cheekbones feeling for broken bones. The skin was starting to discolour around his right eye.

"Musta tripped," an old man in a blue singlet mumbled. He helped her hoist Garth to his feet, dusted him down. Other drinkers were muttering their concern and a Korean man with a Clutch Cargo jaw handed Nickie her unbroken bottle of Yellowglen.

"Air," Garth said.

The old man and the Korean helped him outside, propped him up against a concrete street lamp. "Sue the publican, mate. I would." They went back indoors.

"What happened?" Nickie asked.

"Some lout ran into me and I cracked my head." Garth stared at the knee of his trousers. "Oh God – a stain." He licked two fingers and rubbed at the fabric furiously.

"It'll come out."

"No, it's a grease spot. A fifteen hundred dollar linen suit. Why did you have to drag me into that shithole?"

"I'm sorry," Nickie said. She tucked his change into his pocket and helped him into the passenger's seat of the Corona.

"Just as long as you realise, you're to blame."

She let out the clutch. He was right. There was nothing she could say. She drove through the dimly lit backstreets of Newtown, swung right and then left into King. It wasn't until they got to Missenden Road, bogged in Thai-takeaway traffic, that Garth discovered his wallet was missing.

# 3

Terry Dedovic stepped out of the shower and examined his dripping body in the steamy mirror. He was in good shape, but not perfect. To have a figure like Bert's, the muscles as hard as raw pumpkins, he'd have to work out seven days a week, give up the drink altogether. He didn't want that. Not in this life. It was enough just to keep the flab at bay. He towelled down, drying carefully between his toes, heels resting on the slimy wet tiles. Water dripped noisily from a leaking showerhead. He dressed, sprinkled on a little sandalwood talc below the collar line and scooped up his Puma bag, then went out and stood beside the Coke dispenser in the foyer. The walls and carpet of the building smelled of sweat and Dencorub. When he'd first come to the gym the stink of liniment used to make him nauseous but now he sort of liked it. A bunch of boxers trailed down the stairs, one yelled, "Hey, Vic, where's the chick, man?" Laughing as they flowed out into the street. The idea raced through his mind that he'd been set up. It was too good to believe, pulling a woman in this dump. He watched the remainder of her class trail out through the double glass doors wearing pastel shorts and leather wristbands, gym bags slung across their sunlamped shoulders. It made you laugh the gear some of these clowns wore. He shifted his weight on his black Marlowes, glancing up at the clock. A feeling crept over him that she'd done a runner.

Footsteps tapped on the stairs and then she was standing on the bottom step wearing a pair of flat heels, a red pleated skirt, a clinging top and expensive jade earrings. She studied him with those cat-green eyes. "Ready?" she said.

He went over to her. Her raked-back hair was wet at the scalp and sweat beaded her top lip. "Good workout huh?"

She moved her head slightly. Her small breasts pushed against the satin fabric of her top.

Terry chewed his lip. The number of times attractive women had picked him up in broken-down gyms he could count on one finger. "It's not far. You want to walk it or drive?"

"Do you mind if we go via Crows Nest?" she said. "I need to drop a few things off."

"Crows Nest?" He rubbed at his jawbone. So what the hell was she doing over this side of town? She smiled fleetingly at him and he caught another glimpse of those teeth. They were big and sharp and made him wonder if she filed them. He picked up his bag and pushed at the heavy glass doors of the gym. A noisy wash of car horns and bus engines rolled over them. The air was hot and fumy. They walked down the side of the gym, stepping over steaming lumps of dog shit.

In the car park she said, "What's your name again?"

"Terry, but you can call me Vic."

"That a pseudonym?"

He shook his head. "Nickname."

Up close she looked older than he'd figured, twenty-eight, twenty-nine, a few faint lines like scratches around her pale green eyes. He stared at her reddened mouth, imagined those lips wrapped around his acorn. "I got this theory," he said suddenly, "that you can tell by looking at people what sort of cars they drive. Now you, I bet you drive something exotic, something northern European—"

"I've got a three-year-old Saab."

"What did I tell you?" he said. He didn't mention that her olive Saab stood out in the car park like a sore thumb. But she wasn't too impressed with his *theory* anyhow. "Want me to follow?" he asked.

She murmured something over her shoulder that he took to be a yes, as a silvery jet shrieked low over the Newtown rooftops. He squeezed between a pair of parked vans and opened the driver's door of his white Commodore, tossed his gym bag in and slipped behind the wheel. The tail-lights of her dark Saab 900 glowed as she pulled out into the traffic. He swung out after her fast, but the gap closed before he could get to it. He sat there pumping his accelerator, scowling at the grim-faced drivers shooting past. By the time a council truck let him in, the Saab was seven cars ahead. He clicked his indicator on, trying to muscle through on the inside lane. On Broadway she increased the gap to nine cars. A horn blasted behind him as he edged through the thick traffic, flashing his lights for the Daewoos and Subarus to get the hell out of his way. At Wattle Street, the Saab turned left speeding for the bridge. She wasn't making it easy on him. He stamped his foot down, trying to spot her three hundred metres away; changed lanes, shot up a concrete ramp and then he was driving between chunky glass towers, the studded steel spine of the bridge rising in front of him. He rolled his window down, doing seventy, seventy-five through peak hour traffic, concentrating so hard he didn't see the Ford draw alongside until its blue light flashed at the rim of his vision.

He glanced over at the uniformed cop waving him into the slow lane, pulled his badge out and held it up to the open window. "Task Force Jarrah," he yelled into the wind. "Suspect under surveillance!"

The young cop blinked. "Need any assistance, Detective?"

Dedovic shook his head firmly and slipped the badge into his shirt pocket as the patrol car dropped behind. He gunned the Commodore through the Pacific Highway exit, cursing those dumb uniforms. If he fucking lost her. The highway climbed through North Sydney. Office towers threw long shadows across his hood, speckled plane trees shimmered in the tinted windows. At the lights a man and a woman, both in black suits, stood back to back, their chins wagging into their mobiles. Dedovic accelerated past a Freedom Furniture store, scanning the traffic ahead for an olive-green Saab. He drove on past steak restaurants and sassy coffee shops. Why would she want to work out in Newtown if she lived over on the sharp side? It didn't make sense. She didn't smell like a junkie, but she was sure pale as one. He fingered the silver crucifix dangling off his rear-view mirror. Nor did he believe in any of that superstitious shit. She was either setting him up or this was his lucky day. He drove on, the traffic hemming him in on both sides. Up ahead, he spotted the Saab, its hazard lights blinking in the transit lane. He swung in behind her, braked sharply outside the Kookaburra laundry and watched as a blue Mercedes bus loomed in his side mirror. She came out of next door's liquor shop carrying two bottles in a paper bag, waved at him as she got into her car, flicked her headlights on and next moment she was edging that green Saab out into the river of traffic which parted effortlessly for her. Dedovic pursued her in his Commodore. He wasn't going to lose her this time. For a kilometre and a half he sat on her bumper bar while she wheeled right and then right again, around a palm tree roundabout and down a side street, past a computer store closing up in the dusky light. He wondered if he could find his way back. Two hundred yards on, the Saab slowed and braked outside a block of 1930s red-brick units with white wooden windows.

He stretched his neck against the headrest; he had a crick in it from following her tail-lights. She came up to his open window before he could even get his seat belt off, leaned one elbow against the door frame.

"Want to come in for a drink?"

"Sure." His eyes narrowed into slits. Suspicious as hell about this now. He jabbed with his thumb at the red button of his safety belt. Damn thing was stuck. He clawed at the clip for a few seconds until she reached a hand in over the top of his jerking arms and pressed the release button lightly with a finger. The belt slid open.

Dedovic blinked up at her. "Ta."

She walked off towards the units without a word, the bagged bottles clinking gently under her arm. A security light flickered on over the porch as she keyed open the ground-floor unit and then she was gone inside.

Dedovic ran a hand quickly under the front seat of the Commodore, his eyes fixed on the painted white door standing slightly ajar, a pinkish tinge glowing from inside her flat. Either someone had paid her to lure him here or else she'd taken a real shine to his torso. He intended checking between her toes at the first opportunity. Maybe he was paranoid, but he kept picturing a whacked-out junkie trying to shank him in the love handles when his shorts were down. His fingers fastened around the barrel lying underneath the seat. He slipped the Glock .40 calibre out between his ankles, checked that it was loaded and slid the pistol into his jacket pocket. He got out of the Commodore, locked it and walked towards the units. Congas were playing softly from somewhere inside as he eased the solid white door back with the toe of his shoe. He stood there for a moment, fingers pressing against the painted woodwork, until the gentle beguiling beat drew him all the way in.

# 4

Dedovic squinted down the long dim hallway, but he couldn't spot Mona anywhere. Cautiously he moved forward, his capped heels ringing on the polished pine boards. Closed doors ran off to the left. Three of them. He resisted the temptation to kick one open, see who was lurking behind. The sound of conga drums grew louder and some African guy was singing in Xhosa or whatever they sang in Africa. Dedovic liked the clicking beat. He passed through an archway, scanned a pair of speakers sitting in the dark, green vertical lines staircasing across the dial of the CD player. A guitar moaned softly. The electric light drew him through another doorway and into a big bright space with loads of windows. Standing at a long bench, Mona was working a corkscrew deep into the neck of a wine bottle.

Dedovic's eyes went from a set of German chefs' knives mounted on the wall down to the line of her long pale neck. She'd pinned her hair up, so that it spilled out on top of her head.

"Red?" she asked, her voice sounding a little huskier than before. Without waiting for a reply she filled two fluted glasses with a crimson drop and held one out to him.

Dedovic gripped it in his hand, pressing his back flat against the wall-stove so he could see the door he'd come through and the pair of glass ones overlooking a wild tangled garden at the far end of the kitchen. If anyone was coming for him he had both entrances covered.

"You seem a little tense, Vic," she said. "I'd offer you a joint, but I know you're a policeman."

"Na." He grinned. "I'm a security consultant."

She smiled and nodded her head.

"Don't believe me?"

"Men are not very good at lying."

"And women are, I suppose?"

She took a sip of wine, walked over to the back door and unfastened two bolts. When she turned to face him, her eyes held his gaze for a moment and then she said softly, "We're much more subtle."

She walked straight past him then, her pleated skirt brushing against his trouser leg. "Come through into the lounge." She picked up the wine bottle. "Its cooler in there."

Dedovic followed her. He was tempted to ask her straight out what she was playing at, but sensed that she liked things done indirectly. She switched on a lamp beside the bay window and threw open the thick heavy curtains. Dedovic caught sight of a couple eating dinner on the second floor of the three-storey block of flats opposite. A huge full moon was suspended above the flats like a cheap movie prop.

Mona moved away from the window, walked over to the chaise longue, kicked off her flat heels and curled up on one end of the shiny stretched leather.

Dedovic sat in an armchair opposite with his jacket folded in his lap, sipping his wine slowly. It had a nice fruity tang and made him relax his shoulders. The African voice was singing hypnotically and he decided that he liked her taste in music as well as her taste in men. He glanced over at one exposed foot, looking for scar tissue between the little pink toes. "You do this sort of thing often?"

"How do you mean?" She leaned over and refilled her glass.

"Picking strange guys up from a gym."

"You think I picked you up?" She held her glass up in the air and he could see faint lipstick traces on the rim.

"Don't get me wrong. I'm not complaining."

For some reason she kept touching her hair, playing with it like she couldn't get it into a shape that satisfied. Finally she removed the clip and tossed her head back and her long red hair spilled out onto her shoulders. She looked across at him then, the loose satin blouse showing an inch of pale, freckled breast, her greenish eyes flecked with yellow.

"So, Vic," she said, "are you comfortable?" She leaned back against the wall and opened her legs slightly.

Dedovic saw the strip of black underwear and a long keloid on her thigh like a cigar burn. He gulped down a mouthful of wine, feeling the 11.4 cm barrel of his automatic pistol press against his groin. "I've got a rubber with me," he said. Quickly he rose out of his chair and started fumbling with a square of foil, but Mona stopped him with her hand.

"I don't kiss on the mouth," she said. "And I prefer to be on top. That suit you?"

He moved his head.

"A woman has to be very careful these days."

Moonlight was streaming in through the coloured panes and a fly bumped against the window. He shuffled towards the chaise longue, knelt between her legs and touched her smooth white skin with his fingers. Tiny beads of sweat glistened on her upper lip and he wanted to lick the salt off. She dragged her red painted nails through his dark curly hair and pulled him onto the sofa. Mona wriggled out of her pleated skirt and folded it over the headrest behind her. He struggled to get his trousers off. "Do you want me to shut the curtains?"

Mona pressed a finger softly against his lips. Heat rose from her body like a twelve-bar radiator that had been left on. Her pupils were big and black and the swollen nipples stood out like dark thimbles on her breasts. From the far side of the room the phone started to ring. He looked up at her, trying to roll the greasy cap on, but she shook her head at him. "No," she said. "I like the real thing."

The phone kept ringing, loud and persistent, until the answerphone cut in and Dedovic could hear her velvety voice saying, "Mona can't come to the phone right now, but if you'd like to leave a message . . ." He listened for one but there was nothing at all and then the machine gave a little click and everything went quiet in the room.

Somehow he knew that she'd been waiting on that call. It seemed to bring her on. He lay underneath her while she rode him hard, clenching her teeth together as if she were biting on a stick, and then he forgot about the African singing on the CD player and her open back door and it passed through his mind that this was one of those special nights he'd remember always.

Afterwards, he lay on the chaise longue listening to the water pipes rattling behind the walls. It had surprised him how quickly she'd gotten up once she'd done with him. He pulled on his trousers, smelling her scent in the room. Something shiny glinted on the bare floor and he bent over, picked up a small green stone attached to a tiny hook. He put the earring in his pocket, checked his pistol and his wallet. Two flies were stuck together on the edge of the windowsill. Dedovic watched them pull apart and then the second fly flew off and rested on the lizard lampshade while the first fly began slowly and methodically to clean the long hairs on its rear legs. Dedovic squashed it flat with the heel of his shoe. He wiped the wings and gunk on the floorboards and looking up saw a young man standing at the third-floor window opposite. The man had blond hair, a pie-shaped face and was staring into Mona's flat. Dedovic got the impression he'd been there a good while.

Glaring, he racked the curtains together, slipped his other shoe on, grabbed his jacket and went down the hall. For a moment he stood there, listening to the shower, then clipped her front door shut behind him. He got into his white Commodore, switched the engine on and drove off. Five hundred metres further on he pulled over by the shoulder of the expressway, took the tiny jade earring out of his pocket and, leaning into the faint greenish light of the panel, rolled it thoughtfully back and forth between his fingers.

# 5

Twisting the wheel between his thick padded hands, Dedovic merged left. The road split in front of him. Tall city towers stacked together at the water's edge glowed through his windscreen. A lone ferry glided black and beetle-like across the harbour below. He felt good. She was the best sex he'd had in months; she was the only sex he'd had in months. In a few days he'd go back there, tell her how he'd discovered the earring in his trouser cuff. She'd appreciate the ruse. He dropped a coin into the toll box and his lane picked up speed. The mobile rang and flipping it up with his left hand, he steadied the wheel with his right and eased the antenna out with his teeth.

"Where are you, Terr?" a gravelled voice said. "I need to see you."

"Just coming over the Cahill." Dedovic stared at the small yellow lights strung out along the quay.

"Meet me at the Cross in fifteen. There's been a development on that other business."

"Yeah?"

"Something important's come up."

"What's the caper there?"

"Mate, a little fuckin birdie's dropped our names in

the shit. I can't give you the spread over the blower."

"Okay."

"Alright buddy. Catch you then, mate."

Dedovic bounced the Nokia onto the passenger's seat. The white line curved ahead and then he was tunnelling under the Gardens, climbing through the back door to the Cross; he always came this way. Parked outside the Pig and the Olive, double-checked that his alarm was on and walked up Macleay Street, thinking about the guy at the window tonight. He wondered if Mona'd known he was there the whole while. Guess she had to. Otherwise she would've drawn the curtains. Maybe she liked the idea of the next-door neighbour watching her fuck.

At the fountain he turned right along Darlo road past a red-eyed creature in leather pants lurking in a doorway. Rock music blared from a car window outside the Pink Panther; fat-gutted bikers stood around in greasy Levis feeding on steamy kebabs and drinking from beer cans. A Tongan waved at him from the booth of a strip club. "Evening, Mr D."

Terry nodded at the brown biceps bulging out of the spruiker's short white sleeves. Couldn't remember the cunt's name. A lot of the faces on the street were new; here and there some of the old joints padlocked up. One thing he never forgot about the strip was the smell of the place – a mixture of piss and petrol – and that ice-blue neon that burned through the night. He went into the Kings Cross Hotel, found Ray Doull sitting by the window peeling the skins off a handful of beer nuts. The older man's big dark moustache drooped over the corners of his downturned lips. His iron-grey hair was cut close to his scalp. Dedovic pulled a stool alongside, cleared a space amongst the empty glasses for his elbow.

"What's up?"

Ray Doull tossed a handful of skinned beer nuts back behind his denture plate, washed them down with a big swallow of beer. He waved two thick fingers at the bar-girl. The girl nodded. Dedovic stared across the road at the huge rippling Coke ad. The Real Thing. A pop clip on the TV wailed behind them and its mossy flicker played eerily in the window.

"Can you turn that shit down?" Doull said over his shoulder.

The bar-girl had a nose ring, a silver stud in her navel and was showing half a yard of midriff. Nervously she set two fresh schooners down on the tabletop and cleared away the empties.

Dedovic tasted the cold bitter beer on the tip of his tongue. "So what's the story?"

"Guess who's under investigation?"

"You're joking."

"No mate, I'm not."

"Not that old business?"

"They been out to the Bay, seen that fuckin Kratos."

"Mate, that's all shit under the waves, they're not going to catch anything there."

Ray Doull glared round the deserted bar. "They're going back nine, ten years, digging up every piece of dirt they can, talking to crims. It's full on."

"They got nothing on us."

"Today I get a message. From this fuckin barrister wantin' to know if I needed representation. Said he heard it through legal circles."

"Bullshit." Dedovic shook his head slowly. "Ring him back. It's bullshit. Barristers don't ring up coppers."

Doull wiped a line of sweat from his thick black eyebrows. "Got him on his mobile this afternoon. Said he never made the call, didn't know anything about it. But he recommended you and I come in for a chat anyway."

"Somebody's doing a job on us."

"I tell you one thing." Ray shifted on his stool. "I'll never squeal. I hate squealers." He drained his schooner in one hit, stuck two fingers in the air at the bar-girl. "Watch your arse, Terr. That's the message."

Dedovic stared at the liquid lights running round the border of the hoarding. Enjoy COKE. A police wagon flashed past, spilling blue shadows down the street. Dedovic nursed his cold beer under his chin, condensation settling on the side of the glass. The feeling he had earlier was gone, leaving him with a dirty sour taste in his mouth. What pissed him off most was that he had to hear this now – after everything going so well tonight. He glanced at his ex-partner burping away on his bar stool. The last thing he wanted to do was to get in a session with Raymond Xavier Doull tonight. Draining his glass, he stood up, stretched.

"I'm off, Dooley. Had a hard work-out today."

"So I heard. What was she like in the sack?"

"Mate, you know I don't divulge confidential information."

Ray Doull gave a great snort of a laugh and started to cough. His coughing grew in intensity until tears came into his eyes. Dedovic clapped him across the back. The older man grabbed a schooner from the approaching bar-girl, rushed it to his lips and smothered the cough. When he'd recovered, he blew his nose loudly.

"You alright, Sarge?"

Dedovic turned, saw Steve Bia standing by the staircase. Figured he must've been dining upstairs. His greasy black ponytail fell over his collar and he was wiping his mouth on a red paper serviette.

Bia moved towards their table, but Ray Doull, eyes swimming, waved him off. "Stay over there, you prick. Can't you see we're drinking."

"Got a sec, Mr Dedovic." Bia indicated the door behind him.

Dedovic stiffened, looked to Doull then back to Steve Bia, Charlie Kratos's right-hand muscle.

"Watch the bastard, Terry. He's probably got a wire sticking out his arse right now."

"Hey, Mr Doull, what do you think I am?"

"I know what you are, Bia." Doull gripped his schooner of Reschs, sweat lining his forehead.

Dedovic followed Steve Bia through the swinging door, stood at the washbasin while Bia checked the urinal and then each cubicle. Empty.

Bia yanked his silk shirt out from his belt, hoisted it up. "See, Mr Dedovic. I'm clean."

Dedovic saw the man's quilted abdominals, a blurry figure of a kickboxer tattooed across his chest. When Bia made to unzip his chinos, Dedovic raised a hand. "Okay, Steve," he said. "Skip the tease."

"I wouldn't wear a wire on you, Mr Dedovic. I'm no fuckin dog." Steve Bia tucked his purple shirt back under the brass buckle on his belt.

"How's Charlie?"

"I'm not working for Mr Kratos no more. Got my own place now, but everything is fuckin bad up here. We cop a lotta pinches. That's what I wanna talk about."

"Can't help you, Stevie."

"See, I got a big problem."

"You're not hearing me." Dedovic could smell shit from one of the pans. "First I don't work the Cross any longer. Second I never do business in a public toilet."

Steve Bia nodded slowly, as if he were digesting fresh information. He slipped a hand into his right trouser pocket. "How's your daughters, Mr Dedovic?"

"Growing up fast."

"Here. Look after your kids." He extended his hand and Dedovic saw the grey bills tucked flat between thumb and forefinger. Four or five hundred. The thought of what he could do with that extra dough brought his own hand up in a reflex action. At the last moment he caught a glint in Steve Bia's crazy blue eyes that warned him off. He smiled and dropped his hand like it was burnt.

"You take good care of yourself, Stevie."

Bia stood there, hand extended, the veins corded on the sides of his muscled neck.

Terry Dedovic turned and walked out of the toilet. In the bar Detective Sergeant Doull had a fresh schooner in front of him and the scar across the bridge of his broad nose looked raw. "Watch that cunt," he said. His eyes were sick.

"Drive you home, Dooley?"

"No, mate, I'm on night shift."

"Look. I'll ring you." Dedovic stepped past the older man's stool and walked out into the night. The red lights on the giant Coke sign pulsed like a double heartbeat. A gang of bleary-eyed youths shoved past, heading for the strip clubs. Dedovic IDed the faces along Darlo road, just to keep his mind occupied. Doull's drinking was out of control, but he had to trust him. Raymond X was old school. He wouldn't give another copper up if they cut his toes off. Keep away from the Cross and watch his back – that's what he had to do. They were under investigation, but he'd been expecting it for a long time. When Steve Bia'd offered him that handshake he had refused not so much out of a fear of being set up, but because of the look he'd seen in Bia's eyes, the certainty that a copper would never say no. Well he had, and now he was walking away. He stopped close to his car, saw an identical white VT Commodore parked behind his. For a moment he couldn't decide which set of wheels were his. He circled the first vehicle until he saw the blue and white checked sticker attached to the back window – *COPS are TOPS*. Then he opened the driver's door and got in behind the wheel.

# 6

"C'mon, c'mon," Nickie said, locking the language lab door after the last little one. She hurried down the corridor, clutching pronunciation tapes to her breast. Students spilled out in front of her, black shiny hair, nut-brown skin, fine gold bracelets. The air filled with yelling tongues – Japanese, Mandarin, Bahasa, Cantonese, Korean. She pushed through the staffroom door, swept past three sad-faced teachers queued at the copiers. In the kitchenette she hunted out coffee, cup and spoon. Clattered metal on the sink top and stirred manically while she stared at a plate of yellow tofu glowing in the microwave. She weaved between the desks balancing her coffee in one hand. Teachers rushed down the aisles like giraffes on fire. Racks of tapes and shelves of books crowded the cheap partitioning; open filing cabinets bulged with folders and plastic lesson kits. Men and women crammed into a tight little space like Inghams chickens. Nickie slumped into her chair, took a long deep whiff of instant. The smell yards better than the taste.

"I'm as nervous as hell."

Nickie glanced over at the red-haired teacher at the adjoining desk. "You'll be fine," she said. "Just remember. Don't be intimidated."

29

The younger woman scribbled something on her pad and shut her eyes, whispering: "I believe I can bring a mixture of experience and enthusiasm . . ."

A voice called from the front desk: "Nickie T – telephone!" Nickie got up and went down the aisle, dodging the dishevelled teachers hurrying back from the overheated copiers with wads of paper. She scooped up the receiver. Garth, she'd bet anything it was Garth.

"Nicola Taroney?" a male voice asked.

"Speaking."

"Drop it, sister."

The engaged tone beeped in her ear. She stood there with her fingers wrapped around the shiny light receiver of the Touchfone, staring at a row of Advanced Learner's Dictionaries. For the life of her she couldn't think who it could be. Had to be some kind of dumb male joke. She buzzed reception. "That call just now. He say who he was?"

"Same man ring twice when you in class," Ngoc said. "Wouldn't lee his name."

"Wouldn't or didn't?" Nickie asked. She went back to her desk, sat there puzzled. "Some creep on the phone just then. Told me to drop it."

The younger woman looked up. "Drop what?"

"I don't know, but it was an imperative." Nickie picked up a biro and started marking off the class roll automatically: Selvi, Sittiporn, Bambang. She tried to replay the voice in her head. Broad Australian accent, rapid delivery. *Drop it.*

"There's a lot of creeps around. Laurie still rings me up. I have to screen my calls."

"I'm never getting married to a man," Nickie said. "I'll sleep with them and I'll talk to them, but that's as far as I'll go."

30

The younger woman laughed. She retracted her lipstick and fiddled with her top button. "How do I look?"

Nickie caught sight of a black bra strap under the loose satin blouse. "You'll kill them, kiddo."

"If I get this, Nicola, I'll owe you a big lunch." The younger woman glanced at the clock. She stood up, patting her red hair with her fingertips, took a deep breath and walked down the corridor.

Nickie stared at the photos above the neighbouring desk. A line of cute male buns bending over a ballet rail in coloured tights. She spooned her coffee. They'd give that position to a man; she'd bet the house on that. She slid the cup away and turned back to her class roll: Nobuko, Mimi, Shu Lan. Strangely, she didn't feel at all frightened by the phone call. She wanted to find out who it was and confront the coward.

Afternoon teachers were filing back for the second half, grabbing tapes and Scrabble sets from the shelves. Nickie put an X next to Ling Ling's name. It was so unlike her best student to miss a class. All week Ling Ling had badgered her for references on AIDS in South-East Asia; now she hadn't even turned up to give her seminar. Nickie went down to her classroom, poked her head in around the door. Fourteen black-haired students, eleven of them wearing glasses, stopped filling their faces with sticky buns. "Ling Ling not here yet?"

"No, Nickie." A chorus of voices broke into cryptic giggles.

She passed the Managing Director's office on the way to reception, caught a glimpse of Mr Lipmann leaning back in his chair. Thank God it wasn't her in there. The air-conditioning whirred and strips of fluorescent lights glowed in the rectangular glass

31

panels. At the front desk the Vietnamese receptionist was sorting through boxes of coloured pens.

"Ngoc, do me a favour? Ring Kua Ling Ling's homestay and see if there's any message. I can't understand what's happened to her."

"How you spell?" Ngoc's nails scratched at her keyboard.

"Ling Ling – like the telephone," Nickie said.

Ngoc's mouth formed an O.

"And if you get another call for me, make sure you get his name."

"Sure, Nickie," Ngoc said, but Nickie wondered if she'd understood her properly. The college had a firm policy of employing people from non-English-speaking backgrounds and Ngoc spoke three languages fluently; English wasn't one of them.

With a screech from her semi-bald tyres, she reversed out of her thirty-five dollars a week rented parking space and into the Chinatown traffic. Her head reeled with prepositions and cracked sentences. An FM announcer said, "You're listening to the best songs of all time." Really? Did that include the Sumerians, the Mycenaeans and the Hittites? Local radio was such a joke, junk mail for the ears. She turned left into Harris Street, engine vibrating noisily, the steering wheel playing loose in her hands. The unijoints were gone and the front and rear panels were blistered with rust. Cancer, is what the mechanic said. *Gotta cut it out, love.* She needed a new car, something with a bit of body behind it so if you banged into a bus on Parramatta Road you could walk away in one piece. She rubbed at the grimy windscreen with the heel of her small fist. The sky was pink and streaky; the city a giant bloated hibiscus closing its petals. A jet rumbled low over City Road, drowning out one of Kylie's best songs of all time.

The more Nickie thought about that call, the more she realised it had to be the cop from the pub. The only people she'd given her work number to were the two uniformed police who'd interviewed them at Redfern station afterwards. Cops always wanted you to fill out forms. If a girl'd been raped and stabbed, they'd probably try to shove some ten-page document under her nose: *Just sign this, miss*. And Garth hadn't made it any easier. There was no better way to antagonise police than to remind them that your taxes were paying their salary. Wasn't even true now – probably only half their salary. Maybe that's why they'd been shunted from Newtown to Redfern, Garth repeating his story over and over like the ancient mariner. Well, she wasn't going to be intimidated. If she could handle a classroom full of short-haired Koreans fresh out of Yuk Gun then she could handle one dirty New South Wales cop. He'd probably set the whole thing up. Had some shady accomplice lift Garth's wallet, then rang to frighten her off. But she didn't frighten that easily.

She swung left off King and then right into Wilson, pulled up in a cloud of grimy black exhaust smoke behind the bull-bar of a parked Mack truck. She stared across at the barred windows of the dirty green hotel, her small sandalled foot pumping the accelerator nervously. It was probably a really dumb idea to go in there alone, but what the hell. She climbed out of her Corona, slammed the rusted door twice before it caught, crossed the road and went into the public bar.

# 7

Nickie carried her small beer over to an empty table, inspected a grease mark on the glass and turned it round. A couple of men in Tooheys Blue T-shirts glanced over at her and she could see them contemplating the idea of actually physically getting up off their stools and approaching her, then their eyes glazed over with the effort. She pushed a slimy ashtray away from her cork mat. A few grey faces huddled around their flat drinks. Hotels like this reminded her of old people's homes. Cricket blared from the TVs and a large Koori woman with a face like a chocolate pudding smiled at her from the next table.

Nickie lifted her glass. The woman took that as a signal, bundled smokes, matches and an empty port glass together and bustled over.

She slumped down in a stool opposite and stared at Nickie as if she was trespassing. "Whaddya doin here, eh?" she said.

"Looking for a man."

"You itchy, girl, eh? Well, you won't find any scratch here. Taking a piss is the best this lot can do with it." The woman's black hair was threaded with coarse white filaments like strips of magnesium. She could've been anywhere between forty and sixty-five.

"Not that kind of man," Nickie said. "A policeman. He was in here last Friday. Very drunk."

The woman's eyes gleamed. "Not his wife are yer, unna?"

"No, but it's important that I find him."

"Terry the bull. Thas what they call him. Was here last Friday, yeah."

Nickie opened her purse. All she had in it was a five and a twenty. She placed the bills side by side on the sticky tabletop. "Want a fresh one?"

"Thanks, love." The woman took the five, went over to the bar and came back with a schooner and a packet of Smiths plain chips. She handed Nickie five cents change, ripped open the pack and started feeding as if she hadn't eaten for days. "Yeah, big strong copper. Flashing his breakfast in here. If I wanna see a pig's arsehole I can go up the butcher's in King Street."

"You don't know his surname?"

"Know he plays for the Police Rugby League team. Know he's a cunstable. That enough for yer?" The woman grinned and licked the last granules of salt from her palm. "You don't look real happy girl, you got yourself a house somewhere?"

Nickie nodded. "Why?"

"Aboriginal people they put a curse on property in this country, you know."

"Yeah." Nickie downed her Light and climbed off the stool. "It's called mortgage."

"Hey," the woman called, "you left this red feller." She held up the plastic twenty dollar bill and wiggled it like a fish.

"Keep it," Nickie said. She went out the door and got into her car, started the motor up and drove off.

35

When she got to the end of the street, she swung right and then turned left into King Street. Clouds of diesel smoke spurted from a semitrailer laden with steel mesh. She wound her window up against the fumes as the road curved past the giant brick stacks. What had she expected – to find the cop there with his pants down, holding Garth's gold Mastercard over the bar?

That old Koori was right. It wasn't just the phone call or this business with Garth's wallet. For years she'd had a recurring nightmare of living in a rat-infested boarding house in Surry Hills, shuffling up Oxford Street at dusk, picking empty Coke cans out of bins and stuffing them into canvas sacks tied to the sides of a baby's pusher. So one Saturday, she bought the *Herald* and drove out and looked at semis and terraces and deceased estates. Shadowed by neat men with clipboards, she poked under stairwells and went into the musty bedrooms of pensioners until she found a place that she could imagine herself living in, a two-bedroom semi-renovated terrace in Silver Street.

On the Monday she visited three different banks in Newtown before she found one willing to lend a single working woman eighty per cent of the purchase price and later that week she sold her grandmother's piano and several pieces of art deco furniture to a male teacher who had always coveted them. Armed with her letter from the Commonwealth Bank she attended the auction on the second Saturday in March. The *ren* terrace *with RLA, suit 1st h/b* was too small to accommodate the large number of bidders expected so the auctioneer stood outside on the pavement in his shirtsleeves, surrounded by half a dozen bidders in shorts and thongs, and half a dozen agents in suits. The bidding was strong and Nickie kept lifting her hand in a guilty sort of way until only one other buyer remained, a man wearing wire-framed glasses, and at $194,000 he too dropped out and the auctioneer went inside to confer with the vendor, a skinny stooped plumber who stayed in the lounge room during proceedings. When the auctioneer came out, the vendor's agent and her agent huddled together because the terrace hadn't yet reached its reserve and finally, after much consultation and with agents going back and forth to check with the plumber, she got it for a hundred and ninety-five, five more than she'd intended paying. Six weeks later when she picked up the keys she saw the man with the wire-framed glasses, sitting in the plumber's van outside the estate agent's. So she had a mortgage for $150,000 at variable interest over twenty-five years and she calculated that as long as she didn't go out for the remainder of the decade and lived as frugally as a fruit bat she could just pay the monthly sum owed to the bank, insurance included, and get to work. She now began to have new dreams of crawling about in the sub-floor with the weight of the house pressing down on her spine. But not one of her friends sympathised with her plight. To those who rented it was simply greed; and to those who owned it was incompetence. Either way it was all her own fault.

She turned into Silver Street and stopped outside a small terraced house with grimy iron lace out front. The roar of a jet's engines grew so loud that it drowned out every other sound. She climbed out of the Corona and looked up at the shimmering belly of a wide-bodied Boeing 747, the dusky light glinting on its aluminium skin, its dull black wheels extended, and then its shadow darkened one side of the street. Nickie ground her back teeth together as the jumbo thundered low above the rooftops. The air smelled of kerosene, the sky shimmered brown with sulphur dioxide, tetraethyl lead and hydrocarbons. She watched the jet descend towards the new runway and then pushed open the front gate to her home.

# 8

The smell of yakisoba drifted down the hall. "Of all the meals I have each day breakfast is the one I like best," a perfectly articulated voice said. Silence. Then the voice was repeated slowly as the front door caught the wind and slammed shut behind her.

Crosslegged on a woven Turkish kilim in the front room, Hiroshi Yamaguchi looked up from his Sony tape-recorder, two fingers poised in the air. "Of all the meals I have each day–"

"Hiro." She raised an eyebrow at him. "Please?"

Hiroshi Yamaguchi hit the stop button on the recorder, unlocked his legs and stood up. "Welcome home Nickie san." He gave her a mock salute. Tossing her Italian shoulder-bag onto the phone table, she checked the unblinking red eye on the machine. Now that all the hard mail she got was bills, she looked forward to her phone messages. "No calls?"

Hiroshi said, "Garth ring."

"What did he want?"

"Doesn't say. I make your favourite soup," he said. "Two seaweeds."

"Hiroshi, you're an angel." Up close she smelled the

spice he'd splashed on. Hiroshi was the cleanest man she knew. Sometimes he took three showers in one day.

"We eat now, then I go to airport," he said.

In the kitchen he checked the blue flames dancing on the stove. Nickie breathed in the combination of hot kelpy soup, steaming noodles and parboiled vegetables. In the last few months she had come to love the taste of speckled konbu. She poured herself a wine from the bottle in the fridge, watched Hiroshi working deftly, the sharp crease of his trousers discernible below the line of her vinyl apron. When he served up, he waited quiet as a butler for her approval.

"Mmnn, this is delicious."

Only then did he allow himself a nod of satisfaction. He sank into a seat directly across the pine table from her. The soup was hot and steamy and made her blow her nose. Hiroshi frowned to himself, looked away unhappily. She tucked the tissue back down her sleeve and glanced around the kitchen at all the improvements she'd paid for, the laminated benches from Mr Benchtop, the newly installed aluminium skylight. Maybe it was all worth it. "Wonderful soup, Hiro."

Hiroshi nodded and began to noisily slurp noodles up from his bowl, sucking them quickly and efficiently through his lips with the rapid assistance of a pair of ceramic chopsticks.

Nickie tried not to listen. Hiroshi was addicted to buckwheat noodles. She poured another wine and tried to tell him about her shitty day, then got frustrated with having to repeat herself.

"Uh," he kept saying, "uh?"

A batch of planes flew low over the house, whining like huge mosquitoes. Out of politeness Hiroshi never mentioned the planes, yet strangely that made her feel even more responsible for the noise. When she began to stack the plates in the sink and squirt them with Kwit, Hiroshi tried to wrench the dish-brush from her. "No, no, I wash."

"Hiro, trust me. I can do it."

For several minutes he stood behind her watching her like a hawk until he was convinced that she was rinsing each plate separately in hot water. The phone rang and removing her apron, he went to answer it. Two nights after he'd moved in he'd knocked on her bedroom door in his pyjamas. Handed her an article clipped from a Japanese magazine about the high incidence of stomach cancer in Australian families. "Detergent," he said, clutching at his stomach. "No good."

Now she could hear him saying, "Say again please."

"Hiro, is that for me?"

"Can you repeat information?"

She peeled off her pink rubber gloves with a squelchy sound and went into the lounge room. Hiroshi was frowning into the phone. "I think is for you, Nickie."

She took the receiver and even before the voice at the other end had spoken a word she knew it was the creep. "Yeah," she said. Silence weighed heavily in her ear and then the broad Australian accent snarled,

"Lay off you bitch."

She switched on the speaker button, reached across the table quickly and fastened her fingers around Hiroshi's tape-recorder. With her thumb she pressed in the REC button. "What do you want from me?"

"If you don't back off, something bad's going to happen to ya."

"I know who you are," she said. "You're that cop from the pub."

"Fucking bitch dyke. Think you're so smart, eh?"

"Want to know something?" she said. "I'm taping your voice right now, and you're going to go to jail."

She hung up the phone, rewound the tape until right at the end of Unit 4, she heard the cop's voice as clear as if he was in the room: *If you don't back off, something bad's going to happen to ya*. Her face broke into a grin. She had the bastard by the balls.

Hiroshi appeared in the doorway, dressed in his piped Thomas Cook uniform. Nickie eyed the neatly pressed jacket and shiny black shoes. "You look very handsome," she said. "Like Mr Toyota."

"No no." Hiroshi shook his head. "Mr Toyota very old man."

When Hiroshi had gone, she lit one of her two evening cigarettes, hid *Asking People to Do Things* in the tall wooden cassette rack in the front room and curled up on the couch ready to dial. Her teeth tingled with anticipation of taking that tape to Internal Affairs or the Professional Integrity Branch. They'd have to charge the bastard. At the very least he'd be sacked. They couldn't fudge hard evidence. She leaned back blowing smoke at the eleven-foot-high ceiling as another plane roared overhead, rattling the windows and the front door. Some nights they came over so low she felt like asking the hostess if she could see the in-flight entertainment. She stared up at a wide jagged crack in the floral centrepiece, convinced it wasn't there a week ago.

She tried Garth with the ashtray balanced on one knee, but the line was engaged. Maybe now that she'd found the thief he'd forgive her for dragging him into that pub. She didn't know anyone who sulked as much as Garth did. She pictured him upstairs in his big Paddington terrace and knew that he was either talking to his neurotic mother or his neurotic Sri Lankan therapist. On the third attempt he answered immediately.

"Got him," she said.

"Who?" Garth sounded weird, like he was speaking from the bottom of a well.

"That policeman from the pub. I've got his voice down on tape. What are you doing?"

"Meditating."

"I've just been threatened. He wants me to withdraw our complaint."

"Okay."

"What do you mean, *Okay*?"

"I just want to forget the whole evening."

"Listen. Not only did this bastard steal your wallet. But now he thinks he can threaten me."

"Leave me out of it."

She jerked her knee, spilling the ashtray onto the floor. "I can't understand you," she said.

"You made me go in that filthy bar."

"Garth, you are such a fucking jellyfish."

He hung up in her ear and she sat there with the phone in her sweaty palm, toes digging angrily into the springs of her couch. Couldn't believe the man. She'd bet anything that cop had rung him. Bet that's who he'd been talking to. He frightened so easily. She stood up, fetched a broom and swept up ash and butts. Dumped them in a bin. She couldn't believe that a man of forty-three could act like such a baby. How he ran a contemporary artspace was beyond comprehension.

Standing barefoot on her rug, Nickie massaged two fingers into her cervical vertebrae. She tried to unstress, closing her eyes and controlling her breathing. A siren wailed in the distance and grew louder and louder until it seemed to be coming from outside. The fourteen-year-old girl two doors down suffered from leukaemia; she hoped it wasn't for her. She hurried down the hall, threw open the latch expecting to see the stretcher going into number forty-four. Instead, two paramedics were pushing open her front gate, striding up her steps. The older one, with a blurred blue tattoo on his forearm, approached her cautiously.

"Nicola Taroney?"

She blinked at him. "Yes?"

"You okay?" His red-haired partner was staring at her wrists. He came up on her other side, like she was dangerous.

A feeling came over her that if she made any sudden move they meant to restrain her. She kept very still. Several of the neighbours had come out onto their little front porches, watching the ambulance lights paint their terraces red.

"We got a call." The older paramedic peered down her hall. "Your husband–"

"I haven't got a husband."

Both men regarded her oddly, as if she were lying. "You haven't been doing anything silly tonight?"

"No more than usual."

The older one leaned forward, looked right into her pupils, then exchanged a glance with his partner. Like two big cats on either side of her. "You realise that prank calls can jeopardise lives," he said.

"None of my friends would do this."

"Miss, what some people do would astound you."

The two paramedics turned and went down the steps, out the gate and sat in the meat wagon talking audibly into their radio. Slowly they drove off, cherry-top whirring. Her neighbours were still standing at their spiked fences. "Wrong house." She waved her arms weakly at them.

She deadlocked the front door. Went into every room locking windows. She grabbed the phone, held onto it tightly. Considered ringing her parents first. But they were too old for this kind of harassment. Besides, she'd have to explain everything five times to her father. Imagined him driving two hundred kilometres up the Princes Highway in the dead of night, rubbing his worry beads, asking her why did she keep a Japanese boy in the house? Hiro's not a pet, dad, he's a flatmate.

She stroked the white phone in her lap, thinking of all the friends she could call.

Then it rang. So suddenly she jumped with fright. She could feel the vibrations through her fingertips. It had to be the cop. After thirty-four years of watching American TV dramas she knew that stalkers, creeps and wackos always rang back, laughing maniacally down the line. She scooped up the receiver, said with a rush into the mouthholes, "You don't scare me."

"Hello, Nickie?" An older man – the voice vaguely familiar.

"Mr Lipmann?" she said. "Gee, I'm sorry." She listened. "No, just a nuisance caller. Is anything wrong?"

Closing her eyes, she tried to concentrate on what the Managing Director was saying, as a loud, curfew-breaking jet roared overhead, its landing lights illuminating her hall. She waited until the shuddering had passed and the furniture had settled.

"Are they certain?" she asked. "Yes I will, first thing tomorrow, yes." She replaced the phone. Her own problems were swept away in an instant. Softly she uttered the missing girl's name to herself.

"Ling Ling."

# 9

Wednesday 7.25 a.m., Dedovic pushed through the glass doors of the City of Sydney police station and rode the lift up alone, tugging at his wide tie. Either he'd bulked up around the splenius neck muscle or else that drycleaner had shrunk his shirt, for his collar was choking him.

A large whiteboard, a dozen desks and rows of metal filing cabinets filled the fifth floor of the City of Sydney station with a narrow pathway winding through the maze to the glassed-in offices of the TFU Commander and his 2IC. On every desk sat a large beige computer terminal hooked up to the COPS data base; half a dozen detectives in white nylon shirts and leather shoulder holsters were staring into their screens. Dedovic strode past them, eliciting an occasional raised eyebrow from those older coppers less preoccupied with their mouse pads. Forget the Mafia, the computer had already taken over the world. More and more a detective's role had been reduced to collating intelligence. Dedovic could remember in Darlinghurst when he had to *ask* to use the telephone.

He stopped at the wide aluminium window outside the OIC's office, looked down across the gummed traffic to the cat's cradle of wires suspended over Darling Harbour. Rubbed his nail at a smear on the safety glass before he realised it was pigeon shit on the other side. Cars were crawling towards the bridge and a few simple casino tourists were licking cones down on the pavement, but all Dedovic could hear was the slow tap of fingers on keyboards, all he could smell was an ammoniac disinfectant the Korean cleaners used. Sunlight sprayed across the concrete towers, the sky shining like a fresh coat of duco on a new car. Half the reason he'd joined the force was the wish to be out there on the streets, not stuck inside some air-conditioned office, going grey under the fluoro strips. He remembered the Black Knight at Darlinghurst. Used to come storming out of his office whenever he spotted a copper hanging around the station, wave his big hambone hands in that man's face, yelling: "Get out there and arrest some cunt!" From day one until Senior Inspector Barney Knight retired and drank himself to death in Clovelly Bowling Club, he referred to Dedovic as Constable Wogavic. It had taken Dedovic longer than most to figure out how the Black Knight could afford a four-bedroom Spanish-styled villa with a kidney-shaped swimming pool and hundred-and-eighty-degree ocean views in Bronte, but he was as green as tinned peas in those days, spent half his time picking drunks out of the gutters in Stanley Street, charging them with the trifecta: offensive language, assault and resisting police. The good old days. Now the force was the service and Dedovic wasn't a man that hankered for the past anyway. All he knew was that the city kept changing, moving ahead, buildings went up and buildings came down, and a Detective Senior Constable had to be very very careful not to get left behind.

The Task Force Commander was gesturing at him through the glass partition. He went into his boss's office, clicked the door shut behind him.

"Sit down, sit down, Dedovic."

He parked his arse on a bent blond chair, directly across the table from Task Force Commander Bob Winch. Forty-eight years of age with the jowls of a bloodhound and a long pointed nose you could hang a hat on. The Chief Inspector's fingers were bunched in front of him like a tray of thick pork sausages. "Received your summons yet?"

"No sir." Dedovic yanked at his shirt collar.

"Well, no doubt they'll be talking to you soon enough." Chief Inspector Winch brought one of his big spotted fingers up and scratched at his nostril. "I'm splitting you and Rainey up."

"Shit." Dedovic shook his head.

"Teaming you with a new addition to the squad."

"With the greatest respect, sir–"

"This is not negotiable, senior constable. I want you to show your new partner the ropes."

Dedovic clawed at his collar. The idea of being handcuffed to some kid detective, it just wasn't on. The top button popped off his shirt and bounced under the Inspector's desk. He got down on his hands and knees and recovered it between Winch's polished shoes. Stood up and dusted his trousers off.

Winch was staring at him oddly. "You alright, Dedovic?"

"Fine, sir." He dropped the grey button into his shirt pocket.

"Nothing you want to unload?"

Dedovic shook his head.

"Everyone in this squad is right behind you, I want you to know that."

"Thank you, sir." Dedovic walked over to the door. That meant he was fucked. "There is one thing." He touched the metal handle with the knuckle of his fist. "Maybe you could pass it on to Internal Investigations. Tell them . . . "

The Task Force Commander's eyes flickered keenly.

"Tell them whoever's making these allegations is lying through their teeth."

Dedovic shut the door behind him and walked out into the squad room. Half a dozen detectives were peering over the tops of their screens and when they caught sight of him they pulled their heads down. Dick Rainey, his partner for the last nine months, looked away guiltily and Dedovic understood who'd requested the split. He walked through the intelligence collating room, sensing the wall separating him from his workmates. They could smell it on him – Under Investigation. Same thing had happened back in '87 when he was facing departmental charges for associating improperly with informers and not writing up his charge book. Papers had been served on him then and he'd appeared before the Police Tribunal. But the charges were not sustained. Nowadays things were different. Winch would try and have him transferred from his squad as soon as possible. This whole business would drag on for months and Winch wouldn't want any bad apples tainting his Task Force. Not even apples rumoured to be bad.

Dedovic stopped at the whiteboard and studied the flow of names, dates and places arrowed underneath the blown-up photographs of two Asian girls. Lin Lu Pei and Mo Ching Wan. Nineteen and twenty years of age. Shiny blue-black hair, soft doe eyes and delicate faces. Dedovic tried to concentrate on the similarities, but his thoughts kept wandering back to the internal investigation. They had to be doing a number on him. The way the system worked, somebody minor took a fall every now and then so those further up the chain could lean back and point to the ruthless extirpation of corruption. The smell of the whiteboard markers gave him a headache. He went into the toilet, splashed water on his mug and stood at the urinal, aiming his spray at the yellow pucks of disinfectant. Wondering who he could get to sew his shirt button back on. Couldn't think of anyone off-hand. He zipped his trousers up, swung the toilet door shut behind him and collided in the corridor with a tiny Asian woman.

"Senior Constable Dedovic?" she said in a thin reedy voice.

"Yeah."

"Special Constable Wai Yi Chen, attached to Task Force Jarrah."

He looked at her little moon face, the finely pencilled eyebrows. She was so small he could've scooped her up and dropped her in his coat pocket. "Don't tell me–?" he said.

The woman smiled eagerly. "I'm your new partner."

"Wait here." Dedovic strode down the corridor through the squad room and burst into Winch's office. The Task Force Commander was drawing up the duty rosters.

"A word, sir."

Winch scowled at the intrusion. "What is it, man?"

"This Asian girl, sir. It's not on. I need a partner who can back me up if we have to go through doors together. I need someone with a bit of muscle on them. You seen the size of her?"

Winch slapped the duty book shut. "Listen Dedovic, Constable Chen has been designated a detective in record time. She was highly commended for her arrest rate in Cabramatta and she speaks three Asian languages. I'm teaming you two together and that's final."

Dedovic stared at the framed Diploma of Criminology hanging on the wall behind Chief Inspector Winch's head. "With the greatest respect, sir, this is a fucking joke–"

"Just get out there, senior constable, and do your job. I want a result on those follow-ups."

Dedovic nodded at the Commander. There weren't many rules in this game, but one thing he knew for certain. Never trust a man or woman who mounts their glassed diploma on the office wall. He left the Chief's office, shaking his head in disgust. His new partner was standing straight-backed outside the Gents, as if she was guarding a bank vault. He looked her up and down, thinking she would've been lucky to make a hundred and fifty centimetres in high heels. "What's your name?" he said.

"Wai Yi Chen." She nodded, keenly. "But you can call me Ida."

"Ida?"

"That is my English name."

"Well, you can call me Terry. Or Vic, that's my Chinese name." He didn't smile. "Go get your things, Constable Ida. Looks like we'll be doing time together."

He watched her scurry down the corridor. How many years was it since the New South Wales Police had abolished minimum height restrictions? Least she would've passed her body fat test. He'd bet his service pistol she didn't weigh fifty kilograms.

In the squad room he caught Rainey clearing out half of the desk they'd shared together. Rainey had an armful of briefs and manila folders tied with solicitors' bright pink ribbon and his face took on a similar shading when he saw Dedovic. "Hey, Vic."

"Don't Vic me, you sleazy prick."

"I didn't ask to be moved."

"Wouldn't want any dirt to rub off?"

Rainey rolled his bulky shoulders. He was shaved, oiled, and smelled as clean as a rose. "Just following orders, Terence."

"What you got there?" Dedovic reached over. "That's my liquid paper." He snatched up the bottle. "Get outta here, you grub."

"No hard feelings, buddy boy." And carrying his files under his chin, Rainey walked across to the other side of the squad room.

Dedovic slumped in his swivel chair and thumbed through the thick pile of follow-ups forwarded in from other city patrols. For eleven months now, twelve detectives had been working full-time on operation Jarrah. Chasing leads all over Sodomtown. Interviewing perverts and shopkeepers. Running up thousands and thousands of man-hours and what had they come up with? Zilch. Even if they got nowhere in this case, what mattered most was they had to be seen to be trying. That was the politics of the town. Dedovic fingered the loose button in his pocket, wondering who on earth he could get to sew it back on. It was weird. He knew where to buy rock, he could buy a shooter day or night, he knew the best places in Darlinghurst and Potts Point to get all kinds of sex, but he didn't know one person in this town who would sew a button on his shirt. He watched Constable Ida shuffling between the rows of desks carrying a shiny black briefcase and a large sealed cardboard box that would've weighed more than she did. Her little bow legs sheathed in black stockings made her look like she'd just got off a Shetland pony. He wondered if she sewed on buttons.

The phone rang on his desk. He scooped it up. "Task Force Jarrah," he said. "Dedovoic speaking."

The man on the other end was a cop. Dedovic could pick a cop's voice in a crowded bar. This one, a Detective Jim Bonney from Homicide Squad, South Region, had some important information he wanted to relay to the Task Force Commander. "Let's have it," Dedovic said.

He listened to Bonney, staring at Constable Wai Yi Chen who was unpacking her cardboard box next to him, bringing out an orange English-Mandarin dictionary and a framed photograph of several elderly Asian persons wearing ceremonial red dragon costumes.

"Okay," he said. "We'll be there rightaway." He slapped the phone down, stood up and grabbed his keys. His new partner was holding a minature ivory statue of the Buddha in one hand, a pair of regulation steel handcuffs in the other.

"Get your skates on, Chen. We got ourselves a body."

# 10

Dedovic turned off the Princes Highway and sped east along a narrow winding road bordered by eucalypts and blackened banksias until a small brown tollbooth came into view. He braked and rolled his window down. "City of Sydney detectives," he said to the Ranger. "Believe you fellas've found a deceased."

The Park Ranger was a big sunburnt man with a loose fleshy mouth that he kept half open as if he had trouble breathing in the unventilated booth. "Call came in an hour ago," he wheezed. "Some German campers stumbled on it." He inked a cross on a park map and wiped his sweating forehead with a grubby grey rag. "Go fifteen Ks 'long this road. You'll come to Curra Moors Track. There's a heap of coppers down there already."

Dedovic took the map and handed it to Constable Chen, then planted his foot down on the accelerator. The road dipped and snaked down to a concrete weir and a flock of noisy white birds took off from the water's edge. "Cockies," Dedovic said, but Chen didn't answer. She was scribbling madly into her police notebook filled with Chinese characters that looked like little shithouses. "What are you doing?"

"Taking notes, sir."

"But we haven't found nothing yet."

Constable Chen glanced up at the treetops as if she was looking for evidence. "What time does the National Park shut, sir?"

"Dusk, but this road stays open permanently because of the townships." Dedovic concentrated on the broken white line. Insects thrummed in the bushes and heat shimmered on the hood of the car like a thin film of oil. He switched the air-conditioning on, wound his window up as the blacktop climbed past rugged sandstone walls. Now and then he could see a patch of blue sky shining between the overhanging scribbly gums. The charcoaled trunks of the banksias were strong evidence of the bushfires that had swept through here last year. He lit his first cigarette of the day and blew smoke out between his bottom teeth.

"Do you mind not smoking, sir?"

Dedovic jerked his head at Detective Chen who was fanning the tip of her nose with her hand. "Say what?"

"Sir, it's against Service regulations to smoke in a police vehicle."

Dedovic stubbed the smoke out in the ashtray. "Just who I want for a partner," he said. "Smokey the Bear." He caught a glint of metal in a clearing off to the left just as Chen tapped on the window with her nails. He slammed on the anti-skid brakes and reversed a hundred metres back to a dirt parking area carved into the bush. Three police vehicles were nosed in under the trees and a Parks and Wildlife sign erected between two angophoras said, *Curra Moors Track*.

Stretching his legs, Dedovic got out of the car, then headed off down the track on his own, trying to shake Little Miss Shanghai. The moment he entered the bush he felt the shade of the trees on his skin like a cool drink of water. He breathed the early morning air in; it smelled fresh and woody. Stepped over an uprooted tree trunk and something above his head screeched at him. A pair of fat ravens hopped along the forked branch of an old ironbark. One of the birds stopped, ruffled its black feathers and watched him out of one yellow eye. Dedovic strode on. Several kilometres in he heard voices and saw blue uniforms moving through the trees off to his left. He cut through the grass and the bush opened up into a wide clearing consisting mainly of bare rock. Four uniformed police, two plain-clothes detectives and a National Park Ranger were standing in a circle, smoking, and staring down at something that they couldn't take their eyes off.

One of the detectives detached himself from the scene and came over. He had a trimmed dark beard, flat pointed ears and an enlarged thyroid. "I'm Bonney," he said and lit a cigarette, but didn't offer his hand. "You from Jarrah?"

Dedovic said he was.

"Guess you'd better take an eyeful at this."

Dedovic followed him over to the spot where the Ranger and uniformed police were standing. The whiteness of the body is what he noticed first. She was lying on a slab of sandstone, hands tied behind her neck and her thin legs secured to the rock with tent pegs. What little blood there was left in her body had drained to the underside. Dedovic chewed on the edge of his bottom lip. He looked away from the dead girl and spat into the bushes. Transfixed, the other police kept staring down at her as if they were staring into a fire. Already the loose flap of skin on her left breast had attracted a horde of small hungry bush flies.

"Cover her up," Dedovic said. "Christ."

"Forensic Services don't want us touching a thing before they get here." Bonney shook his head. "My orders are to secure the crime scene and wait. Seems there's a bit of a blue on between South Region Homicide and your TF Commander over who's in charge of this one. She looks a Chink to me, so I reckon she must be one of yours."

The girl was about nineteen, Dedovic figured. A couple of years older than his eldest daughter. It was too early to tell if she was a foreign student. He'd seen enough dead people in his time to pack the Hilton Marble Bar, but he never got used to seeing dead teenagers. They bothered him more than kids, as if the waste of their potential was even more evident.

"Some sick fucker's done this one alright." Bonney crushed a cigarette under his shoe, picked it up carefully and placed the dead butt in the right-hand pocket of his suit jacket.

"What are those marks on her?" the Ranger asked.

Dedovic squatted on his haunches in front of the girl's body. The flesh had been excised on her chest and there were puncture marks along the length of her throat.

"Looks like something's been chewing on her," Bonney said.

In death her limbs were stiff and shrunken, her teeth were locked together, but it was the pair of thick-lensed glasses she wore that moved Dedovic. The glasses seemed so incongruous, so pathetically human. In the corners of her flattened eyes were a few granules of sleep. Dedovic stood up and the bones in his knees cracked loudly. The other cops were still staring at the pegged-out corpse. Dedovic took a big breath of air and let it out through his teeth. Between a clump of blackened grasstrees Chen appeared; Bonney saw her at the same moment and thrust up his hand like a traffic cop.

"Stay back there!"

"It's alright," Dedovic said in a low voice. "She's with me."

The Ranger and the five other police swung around and stared at Chen instead of the murdered girl. For an instant Dedovic saw her through their eyes: the bow legs sheathed in thick woollen stockings, the straight black hair pulled back off her moon face. She smiled. "Good morning everybody," she said pleasantly, as if she were about to give a seminar. "I'm Detective Constable Chen."

Two of the uniformed police responded, but Detective Bonney rolled his eyes and muttered into his beard. From her shoulder-bag Chen produced a bulky notebook and started jotting details down in it while she crouched close to the mutilated body. Bonney clicked his fingers and barked directions at the uniformed officers, "Zagorski, go and see what's happened to the scientific unit. Kiker, McBroom, spread out. I want every blade of grass between here and the track searched thoroughly."

"What we looking for, sarge?"

"Anything with murder weapon written on a tag attached to it," Bonney answered flatly.

Dedovic couldn't figure whether it was because Chen was a female or whether she was Chinese, but the five police immediately sprang into action. "Might be a good idea too," Dedovic suggested, "if you stationed a man back at the roadside. Keep the public away."

"That's all I need." Bonney's lip curled. "Task Force Crab-apple teaching me how to suck eggs."

"It's Jarrah," Dedovic told him.

"Well down here, sunshine, we're real cops not computer jocks."

"It's a shame to let your mouth do all your thinking," Dedovic said quietly.

"Sir," Chen called. "Take a look at this." She beckoned him with one hand. Dedovic went over and squatted on his haunches beside her. With the tip of her blue felt pen she reached out and touched the dead girl's pubis. Protruding three millimetres from her labia majora were two narrow stick-like shapes, ivory in colour and tapered at the ends.

"What the hell is that?" Dedovic said.

"I think it's bone, sir." Chen probed gently with her pen as Bonney's shadow fell across the corpse.

"Don't touch nothing," he said. "Wait 'till the dusters get here."

"I think this might be significant too." Chen traced several prominent markings in the sandstone slab with the ball of her finger. At first Dedovic didn't understand what she was referring to. He wiped sweat from the corners of his eyelids and suddenly the disparate patterns in the stone converged into a single stark image. Carved deep into the rock was a figure with human hands and feet, an emu-like head and crocodile teeth. "Christ," Dedovic said, "how long's that been there?"

"Several thousand years, sir. It's an Aboriginal engraving."

"I never spotted it neither," Bonney admitted. "It's like one of them ink blots. Now you see it, now you don't, if you get my drift."

Dedovic ran his hand over the weathered grooves cut into the sandstone. The figure was decorated with striped markings and the dead girl's body had been deliberately positioned over a spear the figure was holding. "Hunting magic," he said.

"Say what?" Bonney said.

"The Aboriginals made these carvings in the rock to ensure a plentiful supply of birds and fish," Dedovic explained. "Maybe if you introduced Detective Chen to the Ranger over there, we might be able to learn something useful."

Bonney eyed Dedovic distrustfully, his Adam's apple shifting in the pouch of his throat, then he gestured at Chen to follow him. When they were gone, Dedovic bent down and prodded the dead girl's skin with his fingers; she felt cool to the touch. A small horned beetle was crawling around under her glasses, a line of black ants trailed across her rib cage and several small green flesh flies were feeding in the wounds. Already she gave off the unmistakable odour of death. The sound of whistling distracted him and he turned to see the police photographer, a beetroot-faced man with a huge gut that hung over his trouser belt. "Took two wrong turns getting here," the man said, brushing flecks of dandruff from his bomber jacket.

"I need a snap to go," Dedovic told him quietly.

"Can do you a pol'roid." The photographer knelt on the stone between the girl's legs whistling Neil Young's "Harvest".

"No, no. Just her face."

"Right." The photographer nodded as if he'd misunderstood. Seconds later Dedovic was blowing gently onto a shiny wet polaroid. When it was dry, he slipped it in his pocket and went over to Chen. "Learn anything?" he asked.

Detective Chen consulted her notes. "It's a sky-world figure, sir, used by Aborigines in their initiation ceremony. The Rangers refer to it as Crocodile Man. Carbon-dating indicates it's three thousand year old, though someone more recently has regrooved the outline."

"Like who?"

"They don't know, sir. The Ranger suspect it was the local vandals."

Detective Sergeant Bonney sidled up alongside Dedovic. "I hear you're a mate of Ray Doull's?" he said softly.

The man's breath warmed the hollow of his ear. Dedovic looked at him straight.

"Any truth to these rumours about Ray?"

"None whatsoever."

"Na, I didn't buy that corrupt shit neither," Bonney pulled back. "I worked with Doully back in Petersham. He was a good fucking detective and straight as a die. You shoulda told me you were a mate of Ray's. Thought you was just another screen jockey." He proffered a long bony hand that was two fingers short. "No hard feelings, Dedovic, okay."

Dedovic returned the grip, met his gaze firmly. "Right," he said to Chen. "We're out of here."

The forensic services unit and a government medical officer had arrived on the scene and had started bagging the dead girl's hands and taking her rectal temperature. Most of her blood had soaked into the porous sandstone. It wasn't until Dedovic had seen his first stabbing victim, a forty-two-year-old transsexual in Bourke Street, Darlinghurst, that he'd realised how much blood the human body contains and how easily a few slices of a sharp blade, particularly an eighteen-inch boning knife, can empty it out. He walked back to the police vehicle, rubbing his jaw. Chen hurried alongside him, trying to keep up with his long legs. A velvet gecko darted across the track and disappeared into the spiked leaves of a giant flame lily. Deep pink clouds drifted across the sky and he could smell the briny sea in the distance, hear it rolling on the shore. The track entrance was filled with local police standing around like bowling pins. Dedovic backed the car out, careful not to hit any of them, and sped off through the hundred-year-old park, Chen in the seat beside him searching excitedly through her notebook as if she'd mislaid some crucial detail. "How long you think that girl's been dead?" he asked.

"Six to eight hours going by the dorsal lividity, sir."

"The what?" Dedovic said.

"Fixed lividity in the back and lower side, sir. Rigor mortis was also fairly advanced in the neck, jaws and limbs." She read from her extensive notes. Her skin was paler than his and stretched tightly over her high Chinese cheekbones. There was no sweat on her face while he could smell his own sour dusty odour, feel the drops oozing out of his forehead and down between his legs. He half-listened to her read, watching the road, the swirling sky, the red-eyed guide posts wink past his window. He pictured the girl on the rock, her white teeth clamped together in that final embrace of death and said suddenly, "So why'd you join the service?"

Chen jerked in her seat as if he'd asked her the most intimate question.

"Being a cop is a very un-Chinese thing to do."

"I'm Australian-Chinese," Chen said, emphasising her syllables. "There are many different kind of Chinese."

"She one of yours?" He tilted his head backwards as if the girl was laid out in the seat there behind them.

"I'm unable to be certain about the victim's precise ethnic background, sir."

"Makes it hard with no clothes on, right?"

"Yes it does, sir."

"You can drop the sir, incidentally. I only like people calling me that when I'm trying on a new suit."

Chen looked at him blankly, but said nothing.

He pulled off the highway at the first town they came to, cruised through the quiet suburban streets and parked outside a flat-roofed hotel. "Wait here," he said to her, got out and walked into the shaded front bar, ordered a double straight Dewars and downed it one hit, staring at the long-necked liquor bottles while the man poured him another. He drank that much slower, wiped his lips on the back of his hand and dropped a small note on the wet bar towel. He went outside, got into the unmarked police vehicle and stuck his key in the ignition. Detective Chen looked up from the Olympic street directory she was consulting. "Something wrong..." she hesitated, sniffing the air. "Terry?"

His name sounded foreign on her lips. He stared at a small blue vein pulsing beneath the hair on her temple, ran his tongue around his molars, trying to remove a foul taste from his mouth. "No," he said to her, "nothing wrong."

# 11

Tailgating the cars in front, he sped out along Parramatta Road, his shoulder holster chafing at his armpit and the white lights of the traffic swimming towards him like big schools of fish. He turned into Meadowland Avenue and parked outside a well-kept red-brick house with white trimmed windows, an umbrella tree out front behind a line of rose bushes that had long shed their petals. He sat there for a moment with the engine ticking softly and the vee of his elbow poking into the cool night air, staring with familiarity at the only house he'd ever owned. A yellow light burned in the front window and he could smell fresh grass clippings on the council strip. Black recycling bins lay turtle-up on the lawn. He checked out the cars parked along the avenue, got out of the Commodore quietly and padded up the driveway. He took a key from his pocket, unlocked a brown door at the side of the garage and clicked it shut behind him.

Listening in the darkness to the sound of footsteps vibrate on the boards overhead. He squeezed past her Renault Alize, the hood still warm, and crouching, went up under the back of the house, brushing cobwebs from his hair. At the far wall he moved aside two slabs of broken concrete, pulled out an old tobacco tin and wiped dust from its lid until he could make out the faint lettering in the dark: Craven A Filter Tips. With his car keys he levered the tin open and felt the thick bundles of notes with his fingertips. There were five of them, each wrapped with a red rubber band and identical in weight. He trousered one bundle, pressed the lid back on the rest and buried the tobacco tin under the concrete. Half-squatting in the tightly confined space, he shuffled back along the path he'd come, the muffled rhythm of a Coca-Cola jingle penetrating through the gaps in the floorboards.

Outside he dusted his jacket down, removed the rubber band from the wad of notes and flicked it into a clump of ferns. He went up the concrete steps that he'd boxed and poured fourteen years ago, strode across the pebbled porch and pressed the bell.

His wife's shape materialised in the rippled glass. She opened the door and brushed her lips faintly against his cheeks. "Ray just rang," she said with her faint accent. "Left a message."

Dedovic walked into the living room and stared at the powder-blue walls he'd painted. Wherever his eyes turned he could see beading he'd installed or a pelmet he'd put up. His prints were all over the place. The house looked much better since he'd left. He waited until she'd turned down the Depardieu movie she was watching. "Do us a favour, Gab," he said. "Sew this on for me." He held up the button that had been bugging him for hours.

"You've got to be kidding." His wife laughed and shoved his arm away. "When are you going to get it through your head that I don't cook for you anymore, I don't screw for you and I certainly don't sew for you."

He stared at her boyish fringe. She had hair the colour of butter, cornflower blue eyes, and a chin that had started to run into her neck. "So what's the good of you then?"

"The good of me, Terry, is that legally I'm still your wife, so I can't be called to give evidence against you in a court of law."

"What are you on about?"

"You're being investigated again, aren't you?"

"Doull told you that?"

"Raymond told me nothing. He didn't need to. I'm not stupid, Terry. I've lived through this once already, remember."

"They got nothing that'll float. They're just fly-fishing."

"It's the girls I'm worried about. They're the ones who'll suffer —"

"Some drug-dealer shoots his mouth off in Special Purpose, so they jump up and down all over the Avery Building. It's just a bunch of crap."

"Listen to me." His wife waved a small plump hand in his face. "These investigators aren't fools. You had better take them very very seriously."

"Yeah," he said. It was no use arguing with her. She was right. She was always right. Before he looked in on his daughters he washed his hands thoroughly in the bathroom. On the way down the hall he poked his head into his former bedroom. The wardrobe had been switched around. He flicked on a lamp and rifled in her bedside table, checking for evidence that the psychiatrist had stayed overnight. Only thing new he could find was a small brown bottle of massage oil.

"Need any help?" Gabby was standing behind him, arms crossed.

He smiled back at her. "Just looking for my old nail clippers, hon." He dropped her oil back in her drawer and squeezed past her bosom in the doorway. She'd put on five kilos since they'd split. Happy fat, is what she called it.

He knocked lightly on Giselle's door, waited until he heard his daughter say "*Entrez*". She was sitting at her desk, scratching away at the keyboard. "Hello, Dad," she said, but didn't look up from the screen. He went over and kissed her on the top of her soft flaxen hair. Little yellow lights flickered across the faxmodem. "What are you doing, sweetheart?" She told him about her school project she was working on, moving her mouse, while an image of a black bird materialised slowly on her screen. "This doesn't have enough memory, Dad," she complained. "You can't do anything with only eight megabytes." She took a sip of Diet Coke from the two-litre bottle on her desk and stared up at him through her thick-lensed glasses. Except for his nose, she had inherited most of her mother's features. He listened to her pinpoint the deficiencies of the computer system they had bought her last birthday and felt sorry for his daughter inheriting his beak. "I can get a RAM upgrade for just two hundred and seventy-nine dollars, Dad, and I've already saved up thirty. If you lend me the rest, I'll pay you back, I promise."

"Mum had any visitors this week?"

Giselle shook her head at him.

"I thought you promised me to give up smoking," he said. "I can smell it in your hair." He took out his roll, peeled off five fifties and tucked them under her Coke bottle.

"Dad, you're the greatest," Giselle said. "No, I mean it. You're the best." She kissed him on the cheek. "I wish you could stay here with us." He watched as the sharp head crest and finally the bright red face patch of a magnificent palm cockatoo filled the screen.

"Endangered species, huh?" he said.

"*Bonne nuit*, Dad," she called out as he closed the door gently behind him. He went into the smaller room down the hall. A soft light rain was falling and he could hear the sound of big fat drops slapping the bushes outside the window. He parted the poplin curtains with the edge of his hand, saw a ragged black cat slinking along the top of the brick fence. The air smelled of damp earth that had been opened up. He locked the window securely and slipped the steel bolt into the deadlock, then lowered himself into a chair. He watched Lucy's chest rising and falling under the pale-blue cotton covers, her long black hair sprawled out across the pillow, the soft downy skin of her throat. He sat there, wedged in her tiny tub chair, eyes adjusting to the moonlight, listening to the rain brush against the glass, thinking of the randomness of two sets of genes being shuffled together. If he'd done anything right in his life it was his dusky-haired daughter. He loved her with all his soul. Just being in the room with the child filled him with positive ions. Made him feel clean. He took a fifty dollar note from his pocket and, careful not to wake her, slipped it under a tiny statue of a female hedgehog holding an iron on her dresser. Quietly he got up and tiptoed out of the room. In the hallway he checked his watch; found that he'd lost track of the time. 12.05. Gabby was lying on her black and yellow sofa, watching Gerard Depardieu being carted off to the guillotine.

"We gotta get security bars on the kids' windows," he said quietly.

Gabby sat up. Kept her eyes fixed to the screen.

"Just to be on the safe side." He went over to the front window and peered out through a chink in the blinds. The suburb was fast asleep; all the shiny neighbours' cars garaged except for his own white Commodore and one other vehicle, a Magna or a

Camry, parked further up Meadowland Avenue. He stared at a small red light glowing faintly in the front seat.

"Bars are so ugly," Gabby was saying. "It's like living in a prison. Anyway you'll have to pay for it. I had to buy Lucy a new pair of ballet shoes this week. Every cent I get goes on house bills."

Dedovic replaced the slat carefully and studied his wife for a moment. She was wiping tears from her eyes and telling him about some monster Optus phone account they got yesterday. The credits rolled on the TV screen accompanied by sad chamber music. "Two hundred and six dollars." She sniffed. "Can you believe that? Just for talking."

Instinctively, he pulled out his roll, counted off four fifties and poked them down between the cushions of the sofa. She took the notes without saying a word and transferred them to the pocket of her blue CR shorts. "You look tired, Terry," she said. "Why don't you get out of there for Christ's sake?"

"And do what?"

"Anything. You could do anything." She blew her nose loudly, reached over and switched off the set. Silence filled the room between them like gas.

"Where's that message for me?"

She pointed to the table by the phone.

He went over and snatched up the receiver, listened for a clicking sound down the line, but could only hear the dial tone. He tore off the top leaf from a small lined notepad and crumpled it up in his coat pocket. For some reason he didn't want to read the message here. He said, "I guess you're still seeing that therapist?"

"Bernard's got a name."

"Yeh, but it's not the one I call him."

Gabby waved him down the hall like some bad actress feigning displeasure. It was strange how many of the qualities he'd once found delightful in her – her faint French accent, her extravagance – now irritated him. He still loved her, but in a different way; there was too much history between them not to remain close. Nobody understood better than she did how hard it was to raise a family on a cop's wage.

"Think about it." She held the front door open. "For the girls' sake."

He went down the steps, got into his Commodore and pulled away from the kerb. The road was slippery and black as ink. He checked in his rear-view mirror. Nothing behind him. He brought out the note from his coat pocket, uncrumpled it with one hand while he steered between a narrow row of bricked-up industrial estates. Trying to decipher her handwriting under the rain-streaked yellow lights.

*Tell Terry. The Dogs are Barking.*

# 12

Nickie pressed her button nose against the glass. She rattled at the door with both hands. On a corner of the reception desk she could see a big bunch of keys. She banged again with her fist. "Ngoc," she called, "you there?"

Why the Director didn't allow the teachers to have individual keys to the building, she couldn't understand. It was ridiculous. Frustrated, she paced up and down outside the lift. She needed to use the photocopier, she needed to use the toilet. She kicked at the heavy doors with her Italian sandals. C'mon. In the whole three years she'd worked at SPICE, the college had always opened punctually at 7.30 a.m. She checked her watch: 8.10, Thur, Jan 30. Classes began in twenty minutes. There was a noise from inside and a light flickered on at the rear of the offices. Nickie pressed against the thick glass again, cupping a hand to her forehead. A woman dressed in red and black came out of the Director's office, picked up the bunch of keys from the reception desk and walked briskly towards the double doors.

Mona.

Nickie waited while the younger woman fumbled with the deadlock. The door opened and Nickie barged in past her, glanced around the college foyer. "Where is everybody?" Her eyes came to rest on Mona standing in front of her, wearing an expensive woollen jacket, red skirt and black stockings. "What's going on here?"

"Mr Lipmann asked me to open up," Mona said. "He's with the homestay family now."

"Any news?"

Mona shook her head.

"Poor Ling Ling. I hope she's alright." Nickie stared at the younger woman's black tailored jacket. "Is that a David Lawrence?"

Mona nodded solemnly.

"It suits you," Nickie said. She wished *she* could buy designer clothes, but with her mortgage she was lucky to afford a bottle of Tyrrell's Long Flat Red once a fortnight. The phone rang on the receptionist's desk. Mona answered it, said in an efficient tone: "South Pacific International College. Mona speaking."

Nickie dumped her bag on a chair, thinking of wild scenarios that might explain Ling Ling's disappearance. She'd gone to a Darlinghurst rave party or spent the night with some boy she'd met at McDonalds. But good Indonesian girls didn't do that, and above all Ling Ling was a dutiful daughter. Deep down Nickie feared that something terrible had happened to her. She could hear Mona's tone wearing paper-thin: "I assure you, Mrs Wong, everything is fine." Mona hung up, turned to Nickie and said, "Concerned parent. The news is out."

"Already?"

"Mr Lipmann left strict instructions that we're not to mention this to any of the students. He doesn't want them worrying."

"I can imagine," Nickie said.

Mona picked up her big bunch of keys. "I'm relying on you, Nick."

Nickie squinted at the younger woman. Suddenly the designer clothes, the boss's monogrammed keys – it all made sense. "You got it!" she yelled.

Mona's green eyes sparkled.

"Congratulations," Nickie said. She went over to the younger woman and gave her a big warm hug, squeezing Mona's rib cage beneath her fingers. "Finally we've got a woman in a senior management position."

"I still find it hard to believe myself."

"It's incredible." She gave her head a decisive shake.

"I'm so glad that you're not envious. You've had a lot more experience than me, and you're older and everything. I mean that in the nicest possible way of course."

"Of course." Nickie hugged her again, though not so tightly. The lift doors juddered open behind them and students swarmed through the glass doors, swinging their bags and pastel-coloured back packs. Half a dozen of them raced up to Nickie and tugged at her arms. "Nickie, Nickie," they chorused. "What happen to Ling Ling? Is something bad?"

"No," Nickie shook her head firmly. "Ling Ling's alright."

Shu and Po Yik were staring at her with wide brown eyes. The two Indonesian girls, Mimy and Selvi, clutched hands. Trang, Ma and Duc all started yelling excitably in broken English: "We hear Ling Ling dead?"

"That's not true."

"Japanese boy say that she rupt." Mimy and Selvi started sobbing and the silent towering Korean, Yong Wook, pulled at the sleeve of her cardigan.

"Listen to me," Nickie said. "Ling Ling stayed out overnight, that's all. Lots of Australian girls do that. It's perfectly normal in this country." She glanced over at Mona for assistance but Mona was besieged by dozens of agitated students. Unattended, the phone was ringing on the receptionist's desk. Po Yik stuck a clock face in front of Nickie's. Her breath reeked of garlic. "You promise us she be alright?"

"Don't do that," Nickie said to Yong Wook still tugging at her sleeve. Even though they were all over eighteen, they often behaved like schoolchildren. She wrapped an arm around sweet-faced Mimy who was snuffling into her lunch box. "I want to go home," Mimy said. "Me too, Nickie," Selvi joined in. "I want to ring my mudder in Taipei," Shu said, then switched to Mandarin. Suddenly, as if on signal, all the students dropped their English and launched into a hailstorm of Thai, Vietnamese, Korean and Bahasa. Yong Wook gripped the crook of her arm.

"What is it, Yong Wook?"

"Downstair." He nodded methodically. "Downstair . . ."

"What's downstairs?" Yong Wook rarely spoke in class, so Nickie waited for him to effect the slow translation. He held up two fingers. "Two people?" she asked. Yong Wook nodded, lips moving silently. She tried to prise the language from him. "They want to speak to me or the Director?"

"Yes," Yong Wook said, eyes shining eagerly. "Yes."

Nickie took a deep breath. It was like playing charades. "Who are these people, Yong Wook?"

He stood to attention, saluted crisply.

"Soldiers?

Shaking his head, Yong Wook mimed handcuffing her to the water cooler.

"Right." She forced a path through a bevy of timid Thai girls who were listening, wide-eyed, to Mona reassure them. "No, Sittiporn," she was saying, "Sydney is not like Miami." The phone was still ringing, but Nickie let it go. She was busting to get to the toilet. She tapped Mona twice on the shoulder before she swung round. "What's the matter?" Mona snapped.

"There's two police officers downstairs."

"Fuck it," the new Director of Studies said. "That's all we need."

# 13

Nickie stepped into the spongy lift, pressed G and felt a pain shoot through her shoulderblade. She rubbed two fingers into the socket, rolling her scapula forward while the lift slowly descended. Ever since she'd bought her house she'd experienced recurring pains in her shoulders. Her masseuse said she was carrying too much load in her life. She hoped it wasn't arthritis. She needed a massage, she needed a long lazy holiday. The lift doors sprang open and a wave of SPICE students surged towards her. She stopped them with one hand while she peered up and down the foyer looking for the two police officers Yong Wook had described. Nobody there except for three Taiwanese students, two Thais, one dour Swiss and five Koreans who jammed in beside her. Lead weights clanked overhead, the lift gave a little gasp and then started to rise. Two of the Korean girls pressed against her, smelling strongly of garlic and duty-free perfume. Nickie let them out first, holding the O button in with her finger. A big man wearing a crumpled grey suit was standing inside the college doors gazing at a Warrumbungles poster. Beside him stood a tiny, slightly built Chinese woman. Nickie's heart sank in her chest.

Right away she knew he was a cop and that he'd come about Ling Ling. She walked straight up to them and said, "Can I help you two?"

The cop swung around. He had a big busted nose, like a bent prow on a ship, a tanned lined face and deep river-blue eyes that looked inviting and dangerous to her at the same time. She guessed he was of Polish or Jewish background. He brought out his ID and passed it quickly under her eyes. She saw the name was something foreign, Slavic sounding, her thoughts careening off ahead while he explained to her that they were calling into all the English colleges in Chinatown. The tiny, fine-boned woman accompanying him was obviously an interpreter. They looked so incongruous together, the top of her jet-black hair barely coming up to his armpit. "I'm sorry," Nickie said, "what was your name again?"

He told her, but her thoughts were wandering from the cop who had threatened her on the phone and back to Ling Ling. She heard him say with a broad Australian accent: "And this is Detective Chen."

Nickie tried not to register her astonishment. This sparrow of a woman was a *real* detective? She led them into the MD's office where they declined her offer to be seated. "Now," she said, "has this anything to do with a missing student?"

"We'd like to speak to the person in charge if that's possible, miss. It is a very sensitive matter."

"I *do* work here," Nickie said. "I've taught at this college for three years–"

"Can I be of any assistance?"

The two detectives turned their heads. Mona was standing in the doorway dressed in her tailored jacket and scarlet skirt and suddenly her jaw dropped open like it was hinged.

The male cop said with a rush of air, "You".

Mona's face reddened to her hairline, and gathering her composure, she said quickly: "I don't think we've been introduced, have we?" The Chinese detective didn't understand what was going on, but Nickie did. She hadn't sat in the desk next to Mona for twelve months for nothing. She watched the cop suppress a smile, his eyes glistening. "This is Mona Limacher," Nickie said, "our new Director of Studies. And Detective ah . . . "

"Dedovic," he replied, staring fixedly at Mona. "Terry Dedovic."

Nickie wondered why all the male cops she ran into lately were called Terry. She turned to the Chinese detective who hadn't said boo so far and began to introduce her when Mona cut her short. "Thank you Nickie. I'll handle this."

"Pardon?"

Mona indicated the corridor with a sweep of her fingers. "You can go back to your classroom now."

Nickie couldn't believe her ears. Mona was giving her the brush-off. She'd probably picked this cop up in one of those little mirrored cocktail bars she habituated in Neutral Bay. "I think it's important that I stay," she said. "Especially if this has to do with Ling Ling's disappearance."

The two detectives exchanged glances and Mona worked a thumb under her bra strap, trying to force a conciliatory smile. "Alright," she said. "Suit yourself."

Detective Dedovic dug around inside his coat pocket and brought out a photograph. "You mentioned a student was missing." He spoke out of the side of his mouth.

"That's right," Nickie said. "Kua Ling Ling."

"Anybody reported the disappearance?"

"Our Managing Director." Mona fiddled with a button on her jacket. "He's with the host family now."

"Would you mind taking a look at this photograph, Ms Limacher." Detective Dedovic held it up in front of her. The knuckles on his hand were red and skinned as if he'd been beating up on suspects. "Tell me if you recognise this individual."

"I can't be certain." Mona shook her head. "We have so many Asian students—"

Nickie snatched the polaroid from the cop's fingers and examined the soft adolescent face, the thick-lensed glasses slightly askew on her nose. The girl's buck teeth had bitten clean through her bottom lip. Nickie handed the polaroid back, walked over to a china blue filing cabinet in a corner of the room and rested her elbow on its smooth metal surface. She felt the bile rising in the back of her throat and forced it down. She took a deep breath and swallowed again, nodding her head slowly as the cop fired questions at her, but it was like she was swimming underwater. Every time she went to open her mouth she had to close it fast. The detective probing her with questions: Who were the girl's friends at the college? Was she happy? Of course she was. Nineteen years of age, at the crossroads of life where even catching a ferry to Manly was a thrill. Despite her family's apprehension, Ling Ling had come to Sydney to learn English on her own, and enrolled in the MBA for next year. When she returned to Jakarta she planned to manage one of her father's hotels. She'd seen the future as a series of exhilarating opportunities and now she was lying with her little teeth clenched together on some sandstone rock. Nickie sat down in the Managing Director's swivel chair and breathed out a lungful of air.

"Can you give me her full name please?"

"Kua Ling Ling," Nickie pronounced the words slowly.

Detective Dedovic wrote in his black notebook. "We'll need to contact the relatives in Indonesia as soon as possible."

"Was she murdered?"

"We believe so."

"And was she . . ." Nickie's voice trailed off.

"We haven't received the full autopsy report yet, Miss . . . "

"Taroney," Mona put in. "Nickie is our most senior teacher in General English."

Nickie nodded her head zombie-like. The way Mona said it made her sound like some ancient, apple-eating spinster. Maybe thirty-four was old, but she didn't eat apples. She couldn't work out whether Mona had always been so condescending or if she'd just never noticed it before today. The phone was ringing persistently on the receptionist's desk and the frightened faces of Yumiko, Sittiporn and Bambang peered for a moment through the perspex walls of the manager's office.

Detective Dedovic turned to his partner, said in a loud whisper, "Take this one outside. Get her to provide you with the names of any students who knew Ms Ling personally."

"Kua," Nickie corrected him. "Ms Kua."

Dedovic stared at her with his hard blue eyes.

"Chinese people put the family name first," Nickie said, following Detective Chen out to the corridor. Behind her she heard Dedovic say, "If I could have a word in private, Ms Limacher."

"Certainly," Mona replied and shut the door on them.

Nickie picked up the ringing phone on Ngoc's desk and slammed the receiver down. Students were hollering in a mix of Khmer, Thai and Lao at the far

80

end of the corridor. "Go back to your classrooms," she waved to a group of timid Indonesian girls huddled uneasily near the Coke machines. The girls crept back inside.

"It's chaos in here today," Nickie said to Chen. The phone started ringing again. She bent over and ripped the plug clean out of its socket. She heard Mona's voice through the thin ply-door saying, "They're my favourite earrings!"

Then Dedovic laughing. Nickie wondered how Mona could carry on like this after one of their own students had been murdered. It was no secret in the GE staffroom that Mona preferred younger men, but this blue-eyed cop was a lot older than her usual scalps.

Detective Chen took out a police notebook. "I know you feeling upset right now, but if you could answer some question for me?"

Nickie nodded, listening carefully to Chen's pronunciation. Her vowels were good though she tended to overstress her pronouns. She had no trouble with her /r/, but it was more like the retroflexed American /r/ than the Australian. Her main problem was with her final consonants.

"Did Kua Ling Ling have any boyfrien'?"

No. Nickie shook her head. No, Ling Ling didn't drink, she didn't smoke, she didn't do drugs. She was a diligent, hard-working student with a bright personality.

Chen scribbled this down. "What about frien'?"

"She didn't mix with the other Indonesians," Nickie said.

"Because she is ethnic Chinese?"

"Not really. Ling Ling was preparing for her IELTS test, so she spent most of her spare time perfecting her English. Her father wanted her to enter the university."

"Chinese people push their children very hard," Chen said matter-of-factly.

Nickie said, "You're from Bejing?"

Detective Chen blinked.

"You came here when you were what – thirteen, fourteen?"

"How do you know?"

"I'm a language teacher," Nickie said. "It's my job." She didn't mention that she had lived in Shanghai for two years. The door opened and Nickie half-expected to see Mona sidle out of the Manager's office, re-hooking her bra strap, but she came out briskly, biting on the edge of her lip, concern lines scored across her forehead. "They want to talk to your class, Nickie," she said.

Dedovic stood behind her, watching with that big steely face, rubbing at the bridge of his nose. His suit was a size too small.

"I'd like to break the news to them myself first," Nickie told him. "If you don't mind . . . "

Dedovic shrugged and came over to where she was standing. Her heart started beating faster. She smelled the woody cologne on his tanned neck, sensed the solidness of his arms and chest. She could feel her body betraying her at the knees. Why was she always physically attracted to the wrong sort? Why beefcakes? He touched her wrist with his hand and her eyes focused on the plain grey card he was holding out to her. She took it, turned it over as if she was looking for the lucky door prize. There were two phone numbers and the name: Detective T. Dedovic.

"You remember anything. Ring me. Okay."

She tried to concentrate on Ling Ling, not this blue-eyed, wide-shouldered cop. Her mother always told her that she had terrible taste in men. She slipped the card into the elastic of her skirt, turned her back on the three of them and strode down the corridor, pushed open the door to her own classroom and a babel of sounds assailed her ears. Students were running wildly around the room, waving their fists, yelling in a medley of languages. Shoes clattered on skirting boards; a mobile phone was going off in somebody's satchel; and in the middle of it all Yuko, a quiet Japanese girl, was carefully applying her make-up in a little seashell mirror. Nickie stood in the doorway, nobody taking the slightest notice of her. For a moment she thought she was going quite mad and then she walked over to her desk, picked up a fat green Macquarie dictionary and slammed it on the floor.

Wide-eyed, the whole class turned to look at her – Mimi, Selvi, Duc, Po Yik, Dedy, Adio, Yuko. All of them.

"Listen to me," she spoke slowly. "I've got something very important to tell you."

The room went deathly quiet.

# 14

Nickie spun the rattling Corona through narrow street corners, her thighs clamped together. Racing to get home. Tyres bumped over a traffic hazard and the tail pipe scraped on bitumen. She drove down Silver Street looking for a park, trying to ignore the burning pain between her legs. A red-tailed jet skimmed over the flat grey roofs of the factories, its white belly glittering in the sunlight. In the distance a speck of metal angled east over the bay; the sky rumbled. She found a spot, two blocks away. Kids had sprayed the walls of a large Federation terrace with the same scratchy tag repeated a dozen times. Eno Eno Eno. She went up the front steps of her house, violet plumbago flowers grabbing at her hair. Grime coated the window ledge. She jammed the key in the door, busting now. She ran down the hall and out the back. Gritting her teeth as she urinated. Hot pins and needles. Kicking off her shoes, she straddled the bathtub and washed herself. In the kitchen she dissolved the contents of two sachets of Ural in a glass of water, sprinkled cold drops from the running tap down the front of her bra, feeling hot and grimy as if she'd been working in a used tyre factory.

She thought about that cop coming into her class. No idea of how to talk to foreign students. Mumbling out of the side of his mouth like Marlon Brando as he described the stolen red Toyota 4 Runner found at the entrance to the National Park. Had anyone seen a similar vehicle in the vicinity of the college? The big-shouldered detective having to ask them twice, slowly. All the students struck dumb by his presence and possibly the words *vehicle* and *vicinity*.

Turning to her, saying: "Do they understand anything?"

She saw the frightened look in their faces, the terrible realisation that Ling Ling was dead. Someone they'd sat next to in the language lab, someone they'd shared their rice cakes with. In the corridor Nickie bailed the cop up as he was leaving, determined to get an answer from him. "I don't understand." She shook her head. "I mean, why kill her?"

"Who knows?" Dedovic said bluntly. "Maybe she could identify somebody. Maybe he did it just for the gratification."

Nickie filled the kettle with water and left it on the stove to boil. There was a coppery taste in her mouth and she wanted to wash it away with a cup of camomile. She'd have to go to the clinic, be put on a course of antibiotics. Sure now that she had cystitis again. In the living room she fell into the Ikea couch, her eyes seeking out the vermilion, Prussian blue and bottle green on the Vlaminck print she'd bought at the Fauves exhibition three years ago. She tried to immerse herself in the soothing colours, but the image of Ling Ling's crushed little face lingered at the back of her mind. A dull thump overhead caught her attention. "Hiro, that you?"

No answer.

She went to the foot of the stairs. Her hand tightened around the bannister knob. "Hiro?" She heard the noise coming from his room. Like furniture being dragged across the floor. "Hiro!"

The dragging sound stopped. She crept up the narrow staircase, trying to rein in her imagination. "Hiroshi Yamaguchi." She rapped on his closed door, took two quick steps back, ready to flee.

The door opened and Hiroshi stood there in his Mambo boxers and Ralph Lauren polo shirt, a fuzzy sound coming from the small black pair of headphones clamped to his ears.

"What are you doing?" He looked guilty and for a moment she thought he'd been masturbating. Not wearing headphones surely?

"Nickie, we need to talk."

The last thing she wanted to do was talk. "Can it wait?"

Hiro removed his Sony headset and she could hear Dylan singing "Blowing in the Wind".

"Easy to understand the words," Hiro explained when she rolled her eyes. "Very clear pronunciation."

"Why don't you try to use a whole sentence when you speak?"

Hiro pointed his index finger at his nose. "Me?"

"Yes," she said. She knew she was being discourteous. But she felt like taking her anger out on somebody and he was the only man in sight.

"I have something to tell you." Hiro tapped his chest. "Very very important news." His /v/ sounding like a /b/.

"I'm not in the mood, Hiroshi. Let's talk tomorrow."

He pressed the door wide open with his slipper. Two leather suitcases guarded his futon. Hiro said, "I leaving tomorrow."

"You can't! What about the rent?"

"I make up my mind," he said. "Pay you two weeks notice. Already find another place in Bondi–"

"Well, that's just fabulous." Nickie slumped against the wall. Everything was falling in on her.

"What's wrong?"

She turned her head away.

"You cry?"

"No." She sniffed. "I'm not bloody crying." She felt the whole awful day welling up in her chest and throat. She tried to hold it back but it burst through the dam, a great torrent of tears that emptied her lungs of breath.

"I sorry, Nickie," Hiro was saying. "I can stay extra week if you want?"

"No no." She wiped her nose, face turned to the wall.

"Please don't cry. Nickie san." He laid a hand on her trembling shoulder. "In Tokyo I read many many times about Bondi Beach. When I arrive Sydney first thing I buy is Aloha." He pointed to the long waxed board propped in a corner of his room. "But never get to use near airport. Never see water. I want to ride the surf. Get filthy air."

"You mean clean air?"

"No, filthy." Hiro waved both hands to demonstrate a gigantic wave. "I want to go off."

She nodded, not knowing what he was talking about. "I'll miss you, Hiro."

"I miss you too, Nickie, I very happy with my landlady." He gave her a little bow and she smelled mousse in his hair.

"I apologise for that remark about your English."

"No no." Hiro shook his head firmly. "You right. I have lot of shame for my English."

"It's much better than my Japanese."

"You speak good Japanese. Just need to go to Tokyo, practise more."

"I want to," Nickie said. "I want to travel, I want to have children, I want to do lots of things, but I'm tied down with this fucking mortgage."

Hiro looked at her.

She thought of the fourteen hundred and forty dollars she'd have to come up with every month on her own and started to sob. "I've had a terrible day," she said. "One of my students was murdered."

"In your class?"

"Not *in* the class. From my class."

"Oh," Hiroshi said, nodding at her kindly. A plane flew low over the house. The muscles twitched at the corner of his eyes. "Too much noise," he said. "Make me sad."

"Me too." Nickie blew her nose and poked the damp tissue down her sleeve. Hiro looked away quickly. There was a new crack above the architrave so thick you could stick a bread knife in it. She didn't know how she was going to cope here on her own. Her kettle was screeching downstairs. It had cost her a hundred and forty-five dollars from David Jones and instead of a whistle it sounded like a cat having its throat slit. She ran down to the kitchen and scooped the shiny kettle off the hotplate, grinding her teeth as a wave of dinner-time jets swept over the suburb.

"A man rang for you," Hiro said, following her into the living room two minutes later. "Some policeman. He say you know who he is."

"That all?"

Hiroshi nodded, standing in the doorway in his immaculately pressed Thomas Cook uniform eating a cherry blossom mochi.

"I'll see you before you leave, won't I?" She sank

into the couch with the hot cup of camomile clasped between her fingers. At least the airport was close for his work, she wanted to tell him. It was going to be much harder driving back and forth from Bondi every night. She'd miss her Japanese friend. Hiroshi was clean, polite and as sweet as bean paste. A part of her regretted that she hadn't slept with him when he'd asked her at Easter. The front door clicked and she let out a sigh that rustled the paper lantern. She held the card Detective Dedovic had given her up to the dim red light, reading the after hours number. A mobile by the look of it. She'd never heard of cops giving out cards before. What next? The garbage man leaving one on your Sulo bin. He hadn't taken much notice of her at the college, eyes reserved for Mona. She liked his forearms, the muscular sinews above his wrists; his well-made hands. She clunked down her cup and sat up, cross with herself. She shouldn't be thinking about the cop; she should be thinking about Ling Ling. Anything at all that might help, he'd said. She reached for the phone, cradled the receiver under her chin.

There was one thing.

# 15

Dedovic killed the lights and sat under the shadows of the silicon steel arch, staring out across the harbour at a pair of small black tugs escorting a long white liner towards the Heads. A train rumbled along the steel-plated deck of the bridge. Dedovic saw a thick-chested figure loom in his side mirror. He wound down the fast glass. Detective Sergeant Raymond Doull wearing a checked shirt and black trousers leaned an elbow in the driver's window.

"Not in the car, Terr," he whispered. "I don't trust talking in cars."

Dedovic climbed out and locked his Commodore behind him. The lights from the glassy office towers glistened indigo blue on the water's edge. He followed Doull up the grassy incline to the base of a huge granite-faced pylon. Remembering when he'd first met the Ringmaster. Back in Darlinghurst station in 1981. How much he'd been impressed by the older man in those days, the way the hardest crims on the street feared him. Under the street lights Doull's face was flushed blood red, his moustache hung down over his top lip and his breath smelled of hard liquor. He peered nervously over his shoulder towards The Rocks and said, "The dogs are everywhere. Fucking green Camry followed me a coupla times today."

"Me too." Dedovic nodded.

"Got an aerial on the left, one on the right hand side. BBK something–"

"701. That's it. Was parked in the street outside my house when I dropped in on Gab."

"How is she?"

"She's good, she's solid. How's Barb?"

"Barb's shitting herself, mate." Doull leaned on the granite-faced block and lit a Camel. Sucked blue smoke into his lungs and flicked the burning match into the night air. "We received a Section 6 notice yesterday."

"You're kidding."

"They've subpoenaed my financial records – tax returns, house deeds, car repayments. Even got my kids' fuckin bank accounts. They're gunning for us."

Dedovic felt the skin on the back of his neck prickle. The breeze off the harbour moved the hairs on his arms like grass in a field. He could see drops of sweat hanging off his old partner's thick black eyebrows.

"I got a quarter-acre block, down Jervis Bay, lovely fuckin place on the water. I gotta set that right. It's in Barbara's name, thank Christ. The brother-in-law might be able to cover a bit of that, but I've got holes all over the place. What about you?"

Dedovic shook his head, eyes fixed on a Showboat paddling under the bridge, decked out with yellow party lights.

"You'd have something put away surely?"

"Nothing," Dedovic said quietly, "You know what it costs to raise a family."

"Tell me about it. I had to have Brett's teeth done last month. Fifteen hundred bucks. They should be investigating dentists I tell yer, and those wigs up in

Phillip Street, you think they never got a free bottle of Grange in the locker. Mate, I'm spewing over this, these pricks—"

"I know, Ray, I know."

"They're trying to snowjob us. Trying to tear down everything that a copper has built up over twenty-five fuckin years."

"So where's it coming from?"

"That's what I've been trying to figure. Is it coming from Charlie?"

"Kratos wouldn't talk, would he?"

"Not Charlie, he's a pretty tough cunt."

"He's not going to roll for them."

"No, he's a tough cunt, mate."

"So who have they got? They gotta have someone on tap."

Doull rubbed at his eye with the knuckles of his fist. "Just our little kickboxing friend. Whisper from a highly placed source in I. I. is that he's been seen down at the Avery Building."

Dedovic said, "I know Stevie. The guy's a champion, but he wouldn't take a piss on his own. He wouldn't have the nous to go downtown for this."

"That's what I figure," Doull said. "What can Bia fucken tell them. He can't tell them shit. We hold the line, mate, we're sweet. That's all we've gotta do. Hey – that your mobile?"

Dedovic listened. He could hear the clunk of tyres on the bridge overhead and a phone ringing faintly from the direction of his car.

"You expecting anyone?"

"Nuh."

"Leave it. We've gotta go have a talk to the prick. He's working at the Love Box. But we can't touch him up there. That's where the dogs'll be. Think we'd better contact Albert. Have a word first. Maybe he's heard somethin. I've made an arrangement where I can meet him. All I gotta do is ring his number and say two o'clock. Can you make it tomorrow?"

"I'll try," Dedovic said. "The shit's hit the fan at the Task Force with this new Asian killing—"

"Mate, our little matter's gotta have priority."

"Yep, alright."

"Now I'll ring you three times. Just say the place. Nothing else. We've gotta put this baby to bed." Doull reached out his hand.

Dedovic took it; it was clammy to the touch. He saw the web of tiny red veins at the edge of the older man's nose.

"Mate, don't worry."

"You've really put the shit up me, Ray. Know that?"

"We'll sort this thing out. Everything'll be sweet, we stick together. Now I'm shooting off this way, okay."

Dedovic watched Ray Doull cut across the hill towards the Harbourside Brasserie. He clambered down the slippery incline and stood next to his car. A ferry glided beyond the spiked railing, its red light blinking rhythmically, and the water rippled black and shiny in its wash. He stared up at the huge cross girders. The continuous arch of the bridge. The weight of it bearing down on the two three hundred tonne steel bearings which spread the load of the arch through the concrete foundations and down into the solid sandstone rock. He could feel the heavy deck pressing down on the arch, the arch pressing down hard on those steel hinge pins.

He leaned an elbow on the roof of his car, looking out over the city lights and rubbed two fingers into the muscles at the back of his neck.

# 16

"You're late, Dedovic."

"Sorry, sir." He elbowed his way between a bunch of thick-set investigators in rolled-up shirt sleeves and stood beside a platform ladder at the back of the squad room. The aluminium housing to the air-conditioning had been unscrewed; coloured wires and corrugated piping poked out from a missing panel in the ceiling. Eleven Task Force detectives and seven support personnel were fanning their faces and fingering the collars of their shirts and blouses. Dick Rainey looked across at him and winked, mouthing the words: *In the shit again, Vic*. Dedovic wished the windows could open and that Rainey would slip out one of them. The squad room smelled of sweaty nylon socks, fast food breath and dead air. Chief Inspector Winch tapped at the whiteboard with a pen marker.

"Alright, let's get this over with." Winch wiped his brow. "Kua Ling Ling." He looked over at Detective Chen for confirmation of his pronunciation and wrote the name in red ink under a blown-up photograph of the murdered girl. "Cause of death – manual strangulation. Large amount of bruising and extraneous matter found inside her mouth, vagina and anus. No traces of semen or foreign blood. Wrists bound with own underwear. No prints. Excision of flesh on the chest consistent with a small serrated knife or saw, possibly a pocket knife. Teeth marks on the neck, labia and right breast were conical shaped without a cutting edge. Definitely not human and comparable with certain kinds of lizards, particularly the genus *Crocodylus*. No trace of saliva or animal bacteria found in the wounds and the unofficial opinion of the pathologist, and I stress opinion here–" Winch waved a sheaf of typed notes in front of him "–is that the bite marks were inflicted by the teeth of a dead reptile, probably *Crocodylus porosus*."

"A stuffed croc, sir?"

"Traces of methylated spirit in the puncture marks suggest that may be the case, Detective Rainey. Forensic, however, are understandably reticent when it comes to supposition." The Chief Inspector handed a wad of detailed photographs to Detective Chen. "Here. Pass these around."

"Sir, when will they fix this friggin air-conditioning?" an overweight detective at the front asked. "We're barbecuing in here."

"The technicians say they'll have it up and running by five o' clock today." Bob Winch glanced at his watch. "Okay, pay attention everyone."

Dedovic took the photographs of Kua Ling Ling and examined them closely. The necklace of teeth marks and that once pretty face, now collapsed like putty. There were a lot of jobs he could see himself doing if he had to leave the Service. Working in Glebe morgue wasn't one of them.

"What are the similarities here – Dedovic?"

"Sir."

Dedovic pushed through to the front. Took the red board pen from the Task Force Commander and pointed at the other two photos. "Mo Ching Wan. Lin Lu Pei. Kua Ling Ling. All three were foreign students aged between nineteen and twenty-one. All studying at private English colleges on student visas. All enrolled or about to enrol in further studies at university. Detective Chen informs me that the three victims spoke Mandarin and were ethnic Chinese, although they came from Taiwan, Malaysia and Indonesia respectively." He looked to Chen who signalled her confirmation.

"Anything else?"

"All three went missing between late afternoon and early evening, sir. We know that Mo Ching Wan was abducted near her home in Lane Cove. The bus driver remembers dropping her off. Lin Lu Pei was taken only minutes after she left Chatswood train station. We don't have any details of Kua Ling Ling's whereabouts between four o'clock when she left the South Pacific International College of English and seven o'clock when her homestay family, a Mr and Mrs R. Abbott, noticed she hadn't turned up for dinner."

"Any mud on these Abbotts?" Winch indicated Rainey.

"Mr and Mrs Average, Chief. Two kids, a cat, dog. He works as a sales rep. Always on the slog. The wife works in the local creche. Both can account for their movements on the day. They liked the Indonesian girl, said she was quiet, studious. Only complaint was the food. The dead girl didn't go much on the meat and potato diet Mrs Abbott dished up. Apparently she'd put in a request at the college to be moved to a rice-eating family. The Abbotts had asked for a Japanese student, their eldest daughter is doing Japanese in the HSC. So they weren't perfectly matched there either."

"Anything else?" the Task Force Commander asked Dedovic.

"One other similarity, sir. All three victims were virgins." Dedovic saw an instant flicker of interest on the faces of the older and more hardened detectives.

"Okay," Winch said. "I want you all to know that this Kua Ling Ling's father is an influential businessman. Well-connected in government circles. Department of Foreign Affairs have briefed the top brass, so there's going to be a lot of downward pressure on this. We have to pull out all stops. Dedovic, Chen, go back to this English College and have a word with its Managing Director. Rainey, see if you can dig up something on those tent pegs. Everybody else consult with your team leaders." The Task Force Commander rustled his papers; chair legs scraped on the floor, a photocopier started whirring. Detectives began to disperse in all directions.

"Hold it – one more thing." Winch lifted his hand abruptly. "All media inquiries are to be channelled through me. Nothing, I repeat, nothing is to be discussed with anyone. I don't want this crocodile business getting further than this muster room. Understood?"

"Maybe I should go up to Byron Bay, Chief. Interview Hoges."

"You think this is the time for levity, Rainey? A nineteen-year-old girl butchered in the national park and you want to make infantile jokes."

"Just a release of tension, sir."

"This is not the time nor the place for smart-arsed comments."

"I apologise for the remark, sir."

Dedovic looked over at Rainey and grinned.

"Everybody back to work," Chief Inspector Winch barked. "Dedovic – in my office."

Dedovic followed Winch in and shut the door behind him. Stood near the three-speed industrial pedestal fan, drying the triangular sweat patches on the front of his pink Polo shirt.

"Where were you this morning?" Winch sat in his swivel chair, mopping his forehead with a neatly ironed handkerchief.

"Family problem at home, sir. Had to get security bars installed and the wife –"

"I don't want to hear about your domestic problems, Dedovic. I've had the deputy Premier and the Chairwoman of Ethnic Affairs up my arse all morning. And you're fiddling around with security bars."

"Worried about my daughters, sir."

"Professional Integrity rang and want to interview you. I told them they'd have to wait. We've got too much on right now to be bothered with outside inquiries."

"Thank you, sir."

"Don't thank me, Dedovic. Just do your job. Detective Chen, how's she coping?"

"No complaints about her work as such. She's a bit PC that's all. Does everything by the book."

"Maybe if you'd followed her example, Dedovic, you wouldn't find yourself up to your gills in shit. Next time you're late for a briefing, you're off the squad. Understood?"

Dedovic nodded, moving his lips silently.

"What was that?"

"Nothing, sir."

Dedovic went and checked the message pad on his desk. Two phone calls from Ms Nickie Taroney, one at 8.30 and then 10.45 a.m. He pictured the feisty little Greek woman ringing him from the language college. Those big brown eyes, frizzy black hair and the faint moustache that she bleached. He found her strangely attractive in a fervent way, though he'd bet anything she was as straight as the Nullarbor. He scribbled down her number in his police notebook, glancing at the three-word message from Sergeant Doull. *De Costi's Fish*.

Dedovic checked his watch, wondering how he might get Chen to cover for him for a couple of hours. If Winch got wind of it he'd be in uniform patrolling the beat at the SupaCenta. Dick Rainey and three detective constables from his team were scrummed down around the fax machine. Dedovic went over and stood next to Chen.

"Miss anything special this morning?"

"Only the autopsy." Chen was studying the running sheets and there was no trace of irony in her voice.

"Sorry about that," he said. But secretly he was glad. Seventeen years in the Service and he had not the slightest desire to watch another autopsy at the IOFM in Glebe. Most detectives became inured to it, but Dedovic never had. He disliked the antiseptic smell of the place, the chilly air in his kidneys. He disliked having to watch a power saw cut through the front quadrant of a human skull and the brain being scooped out like Aeroplane Jelly. Most of all he disliked watching some stranger's scalp being peeled away from the bone until it hung inside-out flapping over the lower half of the face like a rubber mask. In Darlinghurst he had acquired a reputation for being sensitive. Not that having feelings precluded anyone from being a good cop.

"Guess what they found jammed inside her?" Rainey said.

Dedovic shook his head.

"Chopsticks. Can you beat that? Pair of fucking chopsticks."

"Mate, that is off," one of the younger detectives said. "That is really off."

Dedovic looked to Chen who nodded seriously and he felt a wave of nausea pass through his stomach. He leaned a hand on the fax machine. The idea of a nineteen-year-old girl being abused like that. He thought of Giselle and Lucy and was glad he'd had steel bars installed on their bedroom windows. One of the workmen had drilled right through the double brick leaving a mess of red dust and plaster on the floor in Lucy's room that he'd had to clean up himself. If anyone went near his daughters–

"You alright, Terry?"

He looked over at Chen's face and let go of the fax machine. On the top were three dents in the plastic where he'd gripped with his fingers. "Need a drink of water?" someone asked. Rainey and the younger detectives were staring at him as if he had white froth coming out his mouth. He wanted a drink alright. But not water.

"Do you have any health problem?" Chen asked.

"I might just duck out to the chemist. Grab some codeine." Dedovic glanced up at the clock. "Can you mind the fort?"

Chen placed both hands on her hips like an intern, eyeing him suspiciously.

Dedovic pushed a path between Rainey and his team and walked quickly down the corridor, past the intelligence room. Thinking of that girl pegged out on the rock. Thinking that he'd had a gutful of this kind of work. After all these years. Time to get out. Do something different. He was only thirty-seven. There was a limit to how much cruelty even a cop could take.

He moved through the crowd, treading carefully on the wet concrete floor, listening to the shouts and the clink of ice and cash registers. Women wearing gumboots and black rubber aprons wiped fish scales from their hair and held up bright red lobsters and spanner crabs and green blue swimmers. They scooped kilos of tiger prawns from beds of ice and slapped twitching flathead and bream and red emperor into sweaty bags. A long swordfish lay chopped and bleeding on a wooden board and Dedovic breathed in the strong fishy smell. He watched a Chinese family select their dinner from a deep black tub filled with hundreds of live mud crabs, their claws tied with green twine and legs crawling all over one another. The Chinese man picked up two fat crabs and dropped them wriggling and foaming into his carry bag. A hand clamped Dedovic's right shoulder and Ray Doull was standing behind him wearing a beige shirt and blue polyester slacks.

"Mate, I love coming here," Doull yelled above the din of excited voices. "Look at that." He pointed at a tub overflowing with pink baby octopi, all bulbous heads and inky tentacles. "Makes you wonder if there'll be any fuckin fish left in another twenty years. Won't worry me. I'll be gone." Doull moved closer to the tray of Sydney rock oysters bedded on the half shell, surrounded by wedges of lemon and flecks of shaved ice. "Give us a dozen of them beauties," he said to the girl, who wore a little white cap over her pinned-back hair and yellow rubber gloves. "Throw in a coupla forks too." Doull took the white paper parcel and they walked down past the loading docks. Stood by the edge of Blackwattle Bay, away from the fishmongers and the jostling crowds.

"Tuck into these," Doull said. "Best oyster in the world."

Dedovic speared one with his fork. It tasted cold and fleshy on his tongue. A pack of seagulls hovered at the end of the jetty and the white mast of a fishing trawler bobbed quietly on the water. "So where's Coyle?"

"Late change of plan," Doull said. "Something big's come up at the Bay. Albert wants us to go see him in his office tomorrow."

"I can't. I'm tied up all week."

"Mate, have another oyster. Go on."

"There's a flap on at the Task Force." Dedovic checked his watch, then reached over with his fork. "Have to get back now."

"Listen, I got pulled in today . . . "

"Who by?"

"The Regional Commander."

"You're joking."

"Transferred to Bankstown."

"You what?"

"Transferred to Bankstown as of Monday."

"They can't do that."

"They're doing it, mate."

"What'd he say?"

"Said he didn't think I had a real problem at this stage. That it was all rumours and innuendos, but you know the thing's gonna be far-reaching and could come back on the Department, blah blah blah. Took me aside . . . "

"This is, this is . . . "

"The AC himself. Said he was proud to have me in his region or anywhere else I wanna go. Said he'd place me anywhere I wanted next year, but until this current investigation blows over I've gotta keep my head down. See they're paranoid about keeping the right image because of the Crime Commission and the new leaf and all that bullshit. So go and have a rest, he says, in the Bankstown Patrol."

"In uniform?"

"Yeah, uniform. I said, Fuck that. You won't catch me wearing a uniform. Like some fuckin bus driver."

Dedovic stared at the older man's thick jowls and grey crinkled hair. His head carved out of granite. After all these years he didn't know how old Ray Doull was exactly, but guessed he'd be touching fifty. "So what are you going to do?"

"Told you I had a mate down in Internal Investigations?"

Dedovic nodded.

"We go back a fair while. Got him to take a look at the TIMS file they're running. Saw my name there alright, and yours . . . "

Dedovic stepped backwards into the shade, wiped sweat from his forehead. He could smell barbecued octopus frying on a hotplate somewhere and rubbed at his jaw.

"And our little kickboxing friend got a mention."

"You sure?"

"No doubt about it, Terr."

"What we going to do?"

"We got a problem."

Dedovic squinted into the sunlight.

"So we have to correct the problem. Here, have this last oyster."

"No you have it."

"Take it, mate," Doull said.

"No."

"Go on. It's yours. Ten o'clock alright?"

Dedovic squeezed the remainder of the lemon juice over the grey fleshy meat, forked it out of its slate blue shell and let it slide, soft, sweet and briny, down the back of his throat. "Can't think of anything I'd rather be doing," Doull said quietly, "than standing around eating fuckin oysters."

Dedovic threw the empty shell out over the water and watched the pack of hovering gulls converge in a shrieking feathery swoop.

# 17

Nickie drove down Broadway, tiny particles of soot from the traffic stinging her face. Her car had been broken into last night. Local youths had screwdrivered the lock. The only thing taken were her new Ray-Bans. And why not? They were probably worth more than the car. She sped past the old Fairfax news factory and the giant Carlton brewery, engine rattling as if a handful of steel bolts were loose under the hood. One hundred and ninety thousand Ks on the speedometer. If she had any money, she'd get rid of this Corona tomorrow. But all she had was four hundred and ninety-three dollars in her account, and her bank charged a fee for every transaction below five hundred. It was going to be tight. She shifted her shoulders, cotton blouse sticking to the seat cover. The temperature gauge was showing red.

She pulled over to the kerb, got out, and inspected the radiator. Bone dry. Refilled it with lime-green coolant from the boot; the metal lip hissed and spluttered. She bent under the chassis, looking for a leak. A car tooted its horn and Nickie straightened, pulled down her skirt. She got in behind the wheel, fanning her wet blouse and drove off quickly. In Surry

Hills the temperature gauge lurched towards high. She parked in a side lane between the Sydney City Mission and the Police Centre, walked half a block until she found the V-shaped hotel on the down side of Oxford Street. The lounge bar was decorated in scarlet and black with lots of mirrors and men who looked like footballers squeezed into suits. Cops, she thought. Detective Dedovic extracted himself from a group of them and came over. "Glad you could make it," he said. "Can I get you something to drink?"

"Mineral water. Carbonated." She took a seat near the window, wondering why she had agreed to meet him here. It was very unprofessional. A little bald man in a tux was running around with a tray of savouries. Cops in polyester suits were grabbing two and three party pies at a time, juggling schooners of beer and dropping flakes of pastry on the unhappy carpet.

Detective Dedovic placed a bottle of Perrier in front of her and an ice-filled glass with a purple straw in it. The whites of his eyes were bloodshot. His dark hair cut close to his scalp. Something about his ears bothered her. "Sorry about this," he said. "There's a function on for the local sergeant and I didn't want to miss you again."

"I've been trying to contact you for two days."

"We're flat out at the moment, Ms Taroney, as you can imagine." He took out a Papermate pen with a silver heart on the clip and a black notebook. Stared coldly at her.

"I read that paragraph in the *Herald* this morning. About Ling Ling's body being found. There was no name."

"Full details are not being released until her father arrives from Indonesia. Now you said on the phone there was something else you remembered?"

"Yes," Nickie said.

Dedovic clicked the top of his pen expectantly.

"Well on Tuesday afternoon I took my class into the language lab. Ling Ling was going to give a seminar the next morning and she'd asked me for a list of resources. She was quite excited about giving her seminar. She took it all very seriously. Not many of the students do. As I was locking up the lab she came up to me and said she was going to the library. She asked me how to get there."

"What time was this?" Dedovic asked.

"Just after four. I thought she meant the university library in Quay Street, but then I realised that she was talking about the Mitchell Library. I told her to take the train to St James and walk up Macquarie Street."

"You didn't mention this in your statement to Detective Chen?"

"I forgot," Nickie said. "Students are always coming up and asking you for directions. I remembered it when I was taking a shower. You know how a shower often refreshes your memory?"

Dedovic nodded as if she was some old lady with Alzheimers. "Do you remember what she was wearing?"

"A Minnie Mouse T-shirt and a black woollen skirt."

"You're sure it was wool?"

"I'm certain. Have there been any developments on the case yet?"

"Nothing concrete, but we're working around the clock."

Nickie watched the little man in the tux bring out two plates of that yellow cube cheese publicans always prefer. A bunch of five cops had their arms around each other in a beery embrace and were singing "The Green Green Grass of Home".

"These detectives here," she inquired, "they from your Task Force?"

"One or two of them, yeh." Dedovic tilted his jaw defensively.

Nickie looked out the window at the fumy traffic. She wasn't too impressed so far. She could feel Dedovic's eyes fixed on her face. It really irritated her when men stared. She turned and glared back at him.

"You frown a lot," he said.

She touched the lines on her forehead with a finger.

"Know what happens if the wind changes?"

"I was under the impression that we were here to discuss Ling Ling's murder," Nickie said. "To tell you the truth, I don't like the police very much."

Dedovic looked at her.

"In fact I don't think many people do right now."

Dedovic consulted his notebook. "Anything further you wish to add to your previous statement, *Mz* . . . "

She hadn't intended bringing the matter up, but all of a sudden it spilled out of her: the threatening phone calls, the ambulance coming to her door. She told him every grubby little episode that had occurred since she had witnessed that cop expose himself in the dirty public bar.

Dedovic listened to her in silence, working his tongue around under his lip.

"He was about your height and weight and he was blond and his name was Terry just like yours," she said breathlessly.

"Have you registered a complaint?"

"With the Police Service *and* with the Ombudsman. They say they're investigating it, but I haven't heard anything yet."

"It takes a while. If you like I can make some discreet inquiries."

"Would you?" She picked up her drink and rattled the ice around the rim of the glass. A fan was blowing frantically overhead and the other cops had bunched together at the far side of the bar under the noisy TV set. So why was he offering to help?

"You have to understand," Dedovic said, "that p'lice are under an enormous amount of pressure these days."

The way he pronounced it – *pleece*. "You're not saying he was justified?"

"No. I'm just saying we all make mistakes."

Nickie raised her eyebrows. She had the feeling that Detective Dedovic was trying to tell her something. The doors swung open and a woman strolled into the lounge. Her red satiny dress fitted her figure like paint on a postbox. She walked over to where the detectives were drinking and greeted each of them with a smile. One of the cops fetched her a drink. The rest encircled her. A couple of younger detectives had their mouths wide open. The woman was moving her right hand up and down and then she tossed back her perfect blonde hair and laughed, and the detectives laughed along with her, shoulders bobbing.

"Who's that?" Nickie said.

"Drink up." Dedovic snapped his notebook shut. "I'll walk you to your car."

Nickie saw the blonde coming towards them, the bounce of her breasts and the curve of her waist.

"Dedo, you old fucking wanker!" she yelled from two metres away.

"Hello, Wendy," Dedovic said quietly. "Long time."

"Not going to introduce your little friend?"

"Nickie, this is Wendy Lee Burke."

Wendy Lee regarded Nickie for a moment and then removed something from between her teeth and deposited it in the glass ashtray. "Nicorettes," she said, "taste like shit."

Nickie stared at the woman. She had a sweet Barbie Doll face and a voice that could strip enamel. "So what's the story on these fuckin Asian killings, Dedo?"

"You'd better talk to Bob Winch about that," Dedovic said.

Wendy gave a dismissive laugh. "I wouldn't trust that cocksucker to tell me it was daytime."

Dedovic's ears reddened and Nickie realised what was odd about them: they were pointed at the top and had no lobes. Another detective came over and joined their table. He smelled strongly of cologne and cigarette smoke. Wendy Lee wrapped an arm around his thick bull neck. "My favourite little Dick," she said and laughed. The detective winked at Dedovic. "Let me buy you coppers a big cold drink," Wendy Lee said. "I don't think the public appreciates our hardworking police officers quite enough." She looked to Nickie with a grin.

Dedovic stood up quickly. "We're outta here."

Nickie couldn't tell whether it was pills or the woman's personality, but Wendy Lee was grinding away at her back molars. She followed Detective Dedovic out into the night air, waved at Wendy Lee who started nestling her cheek against the left ear of the stocky detective. The city thrummed with sirens and the clank of an industrial garbage compactor. Two red-nosed men had dragged a stained brown mattress into a factory doorway and were sharing a yellow wine sac on top of it. Nickie felt dwarfed by Dedovic. His big splayed hands swinging like moulded weights at his side. She looked up at the starless sky, the city lights stamped blue and red along the rims of the towers. "That woman," she asked. "She a friend of yours?"

"Na, she's a journo. Don't you read the papers?"

"Not much," Nickie said. "I prefer the radio." She stopped beside her rusted mustard Corona and saw the detective glance at it disparagingly. All of a sudden she felt ashamed to be driving a vehicle like this. It showed she hadn't worked near hard enough. "I'm saving up for a new car," she found herself saying. As if it were any of his damned business.

"Yeah?" Dedovic arched one eyebrow. "What sort?"

"I like those Saabs," she said. Choosing a model right off the top of her head.

"Nice one." He nodded slowly, as if he were recalling some personal detail. "You remember anything more," he said. "Ring me, okay?"

She could feel him close to her, his strong male scent. She shook his big rough-knuckled hand. And then he turned and walked away swiftly, heavy footsteps echoing on the concrete pavement.

Nickie sat in her Corona with the doors locked, sweat trickling down between her breasts. She wondered whether she had reached that invisible age when men ignore you completely. Even though he was a cop, there was a part of her that had wanted him to like her. To notice her as a woman. She couldn't rationalise the primitive feeling. All the time at the hotel he'd kept glancing at his dopey watch as if he was in a hurry to be elsewhere. She wondered if it had anything to do with this investigation. The thought of little Ling Ling being murdered made her skin crawl.

She gripped the steering wheel tightly, watched a man lurch along the shadows of the dark-faced terraces. She switched on her headlights and saw the man was handicapped, his left leg withered below the knee. She drove off through the back streets of Surry Hills, spinning the wheel, wondering whether Detective

Dedovic was serious about making those "discreet" inquiries. Suspecting this was just another police brush-off. She didn't want to see him again. From now on she had to concentrate on her own problems. First she had to find someone for the spare room. And there was something else she'd neglected to do. The thought buzzed around her head. She drummed her fingers on the dashboard, looked down and saw her temperature gauge glowing bright red.

# 18

Dedovic stood on the corner of Oxford and Darlinghurst squinting into the pool of liquidy lights from the traffic. The air smelled of charcoaled meat from the Balkan grill across the street. Two men wearing tight bicycle shorts strolled past, heels tick-ticking on the pavement, voices arguing over rent money. A silver Ford Fairlane braked at the kerb and Dedovic jumped in. "Nice LTD, Ray. Where'd you score this?"

"Take a look in the glove box," Doull said.

Dedovic opened it, found the certificate of registration made out to a Mr James S. Wilcox of Killara. The name vaguely familiar.

"Got a panelbeater mate on the lower north side. Lends me a vehicle from time to time."

Dedovic looked over at Ray Doull wearing a checked jacket, pink shirt, his silver hair catching the laddered lights from the street. They cruised down Darlinghurst Road. "Hey," he said. "Not Jim Wilcox?"

Ray Doull grinned through his untrimmed moustache.

"You're kidding," Dedovic said. "Let me off at the corner."

"Mate, what could be safer than this? We're spotted nobody's ever gonna believe it. I'm telling yer."

Dedovic shook his head. He should've known better than to get mixed up with Ray in the first place. Too late for regrets now. Three months after he'd been designated a detective he'd gone out on his first big drug bust. Two CIB detectives and Ray Doull who even then had a hard rep on the street. The tough Irish publican at the Tradesman's Arms calling him Mr Doull. The uniforms boys thinking yeah, that's who I wanna be. Smashed their way into a Stanley Street dive. Five Maoris dealing pure white. In a wardrobe Dedovic discovered twenty-five grams of H in a Dunlop shoe box and five thousand dollars in cash. Handed it over to the team leader. Detective Sergeant Doull. The next day twelve hundred and fifty dollars in cash turned up in his locker in a brown OHMS envelope. Two words scribbled on a piece of police notebook paper – *Meal allowance*. Dedovic was in. And once you were in there was no going back. Even if it meant driving around fourteen years later in a Supreme Court judge's car.

Doull nosed the Fairlane into a space on the point overlooking Elizabeth Bay. Eased the silver .357 Magnum out of his shoulder holster. Checked the cylinder. The same Colt Python that he'd seized from a convicted gang rapist and heroin-dealer years ago. There weren't too many crims who would face Raymond X. Doull down. "What you have for tea, Terr?" Doull asked.

"Crackers and cheese," Dedovic said. "I'm working a multiple murder case. Haven't had time to breathe."

"Had me a pan-fried barra. At this new swish place in Crown Street."

"Yeah?"

"Nice thick chips. Lovely green salad. Not too much batter on the fish. You'd like it." He tossed Dedovic a pair of cream cotton work gloves. "I'll spring you a meal when this is all over."

Dedovic slipped them on, carefully wiped down the door handle of the Fairlane and the glove box knob. Cracked the door open and stepped out into the heat of the night. The harbour black as squid ink. Followed Ray Doull across the road to a well-maintained block of art deco flats. Stood outside the barred security door, hands in his pockets, looking up and down the esplanade. An elderly couple shuffling towards them. His mind flipping back fourteen years to that Thursday night he'd taken the twelve fifty home and dumped the envelope on the kitchen table. Thought about giving it back to Sergeant Ray Doull. All night turning it over in his mind. He and Gabby staying up to dawn discussing what he should do. If he gave it back it meant he didn't want to be in the squad. He'd be ostracised. Wherever he went in the Force the word would be out – *Don't trust Dedovic*. Either he went along with it, or else he left Plain Clothes altogether. There was nothing he'd wanted more than to be a good detective. In the end he and Gabby agreed: keep the money and keep their mouths shut. He watched the elderly couple unlock the security door and then Ray Doull stepped forward, flashing his badge under their noses. "Police officers. We don't want to alarm you, sir, but there's been a report of a gang of cat burglars operating in this area."

Wide-eyed, the well-dressed couple ushered them in.

"Climb up the drain pipes in these old buildings they do. You see anything suspicious, madam, you call your local police."

The couple hurried breathlessly towards the lifts. Dedovic could feel the humidity in the air, like a balloon about to burst. "I'm sweating like a pig in this jacket," Doull said. Down the corridor they went to number three, ground floor apartment. Doull took out a bunch of strange-looking keys. Tried two before the lock clicked. "Got these skels when I was working the Breakers," he whispered. "Best squad I ever worked."

Dedovic went through the door first. Heard a faint scratching sound. Like claws on wood. The deadlock clicked shut behind him. Standing in the dark, sensing another presence in the apartment. Not human. A low growl and something heavy slammed into his leg. Threw him against the wall. He heard a dull clunk and then a whimper. Flicked on the switch and saw a white patch of fur stretched out on the hall runner, chest heaving, blood trickling from its torn right ear.

Ray Doull kneeling over a pit bull terrier. "Nice doggie." He holstered his .357 Magnum. "You right, Terr?"

Dedovic examined the rip in his CR trousers, wet puncture marks in the skin. He was going to need a tetanus shot. "What sort of a prick would keep a dog in an apartment?"

"Mate, you were lucky." Doull carried the pit bull through into the toilet, shut the door. "These things get a hold of you, they don't say die."

Dedovic went into Steve Bia's living room. Bay windows, digital TV, JBL studio speakers and an enormous red Persian carpet spread over the honey-coloured pine boards. Stared down at the intricate peacock pattern woven into the thick lush carpet.

Doull started turning over cushions on the sofa. "Let's get to work," he said.

In the kitchen Dedovic bathed his bites in cold water. Of all the cops he had ever worked with only a select few were as cool as Ray Doull under pressure. Especially when dealing with hardened criminals. The trouble with most crims was they were plain stupid. He opened the cupboards, felt around the back of drawers, down behind the fridge. Dipped his hand into the flour cannister and the sugar bowl. When he picked up the bread crock he knew he'd found something. Hidden under three slices of flat Leb bread was a .22 Colt automatic with a loaded clip. He dusted off the crumbs and holding the pistol by the grip, carried it through to the living room. "Look at this," he said. "Weevils in the bread tin."

"Wanna bet that's had a long history. Stick it on the sofa where it can get a bit of an airing." Doull flipped through a large video library. "Seems like our little Stevie's a cinephile."

Dedovic examined one of the cassettes. Two pubescent girls. Baby-faced. Spreadeagled in what appeared to be a schoolroom. German text underneath: *Willkommen meine kleinen, geilen Kinder.*

"Mate, if this stuff's been classified," Doull said, "I'm a rock hopper penguin."

Dedovic dropped the cassette on the floor. In the old days he'd always had a bit of time for Steve Bia. Lent him a hand when he was working the Drug Unit. Put a call though to the Club if shit was happening. But no more. All the misgivings he'd felt earlier about coming here with Ray Doull were gone. Now he had to restrain himself from smashing the furniture.

"Take a look at this stuff, Terr. I mean that is disgusting."

Dedovic shook his head firmly. He didn't want to see. Get the job done and get the hell out of this grub's apartment. "You know what they should do with these pricks?" he said.

"Mate, I know. I got kids too. It's right out of order." Ray Doull slipped a hand into the inside pocket of his checked jacket and took out a sealed plastic bag containing a granular light coloured powder. He sprinkled a good half of the powder along the edges of the red Persian carpet and tucked the remainder of the bag underneath the loaded pistol sitting on the sofa. "Thirty-five grams," Doull said. "Seventy per cent caffeine, acetylcodeine, monoacetylmorphine and thirty per cent diamorph."

"Where'd you score it?"

"Rescued it from the police incinerator. Been through a few sets of hands already. Way I look at it, Terr," Doull said. "Justice is a little old blind lady you gotta help across the road." He went over and picked up the phone, punched a call through.

Dedovic stood by the mantle, eyes fixed on the framed photographs of a lean muscular man with his skull shaved. Leaning against the ropes, taped hands holding up a gold trophy over his head. NSW Kick-boxing Champion. Printed on the back of his red silky cloak the words: Steve "The Cobra" Bia.

Ray Doull hung up the phone and turned to Dedovic. "Right," he said. "We're outta here."

# 19

She could smell burning now, one eye fixed on the glowing temperature gauge. Driving fast down King Street, trying to think of a service station that would be open at this hour. Fingers clenching the steering wheel. She saw the sign first: 74.9 Unleaded. Swung the car into the BP service station, braked outside the pumps, popped the catch, jumped out and ran around to open the hood. The engine hissed and a wave of dry heat soaked up the sweat on her brow. She stepped back, the radiator cap too hot to touch even through her skirt. She went into the shop and bought a litre of coolant, asked the squinting young woman behind the security shield if there was a mechanic on duty. The woman shaking her triple-pierced eyebrows. Nickie could hear shutters rattling in the garage. "Please," she said. "My car's broken down." The woman called out, "Mac!" And a man came out in greasy green overalls soaping his hands with blue gel. He followed her out to the Corona. The engine smelled of hot, fatigued metal. He got her to turn it over and stuck his hands in under the hood.

"Your water pump's gone, lady," he stated flatly.

"What will that cost?" She followed him through a side door into the dimly lit garage. A pile of Goodyear tyres stood in one corner; a gun-metal Porsche up on a hoist in the other. The mechanic took out a pad. He had a pencil-thin moustache and eyes that were set unevenly in his head like headlights that needed adjusting. He told her the price and when she could pick her car up. Looking over at the pile of tyres and then back at her slyly, his eyes telling her more than his mouth was. "What's your phone number there, love?" he said. She gave it to him and left the garage quickly, caught a cab on King Street, thankful that the Omani driver had limited English, not so thankful that he had limited road skills. Her head bumped against the roof as they flew over a hump. The cab squealed to a halt on the corner of Silver Street and she jumped out, slammed the door as hard as she could. Some nights everyone she met was deranged.

She walked underneath the bottle brushes and the frangipani trees, juggling figures in her head. A hundred and fifty. She'd be living on pasta and parmesan for a week. She stopped at her gate, fingers touching the sharp iron spears and sensed something was wrong. The light in her front window. She never left that light on. Not after the last two electricity bills. A face appeared behind the slats. Blond hair, thick lips. *Him*.

Nickie stepped back into the gutter, scuffing her big toe on the bitumen. Ready to run for the highway in her strapless sandals. The face at the window vanished. She clenched her fists tightly. No, this was her house, this was her mortgage. She pushed on the gate, her heart thumping wildly. Scrabbled in her bag for a weapon she could wield: keys, hairbrush, business card. The only sound came from her own panting breath. She stopped at the front door, slightly ajar. Willing herself to cross the threshold. A red-tailed jumbo lifted off the runway, its thunderous roar rolling over the sheet-iron roofs. And

Nickie turned and ran. Up Silver Street she flew, under the path of the straining 747, its wing tips blinking. In a laneway a gang of youths were leaning against a paling fence. "Quick," she panted. "Telephone box?"

They came out of the shadows like dingoes in the night. Baseball caps pulled down over their eyebrows, wearing Stussies and Air Jordan Trainers. Underfed, rangy, reeking of reefer.

"I need a phone," she yelled over the jet's reverberations.

They looked at her coolly. One of them was spinning a long screwdriver in his hand. "Nino's got a mobile," he said. A gangly youth with shaved temples and a little skullcap of black curly hair, whipped a phone off his belt, passed it to her. She keyed in the number she'd memorised. "It's Nickie Taroney," she blurted. "There's an intruder in my house." The voice on the other end began firing questions at her: location of the residence, nearest intersection? His cop role taking over. Five minutes he promised. The rest of the St Peters crew were staring at her, stoned as mullets. One of them offered her a bottle of half-drunk Tasmanian cider. She took a long warm swig, didn't even wipe the neck. They thought that was cool. Like she was nineteen again, hanging out with the street-night set.

"Fuckin digital too." The shaven-headed youth nodded solemnly, passing the instrument to his friends as if it had now taken on some special significance. "Cost me a buck fifty a call."

"I'll mail it to you," Nickie promised. The other youths laughed. She ran back down the street and secreted herself in the shadows of a red hibiscus. The lights were off upstairs, her front door open. When she saw the Commodore cruise down her street she was relieved there were no whirling lights, no siren, no PR

121

dramatics. Detective Dedovic approached her under the branches, a steely look in his Slavic blue eyes that meant business. In a low firm voice he asked her how many entrances there were to her residence, was there a laneway? "Stay here," he murmured.

"I'm coming with you."

"That's an order."

"I'm not your wife," she said.

He drew his service pistol and went through the front door, kicking it back on its hinges. She'd just had that door varnished. He moved down her hall yelling: "Police! Don't move! Police!" Fanning his pistol in and out of doorways. Nickie stayed five, ten steps behind, her stomach churning, wondering whether it was the intruder or this detective who unsettled her more. She heard scuffling in the kitchen. A male voice cried out in pain. She raced through the archway. Detective Dedovic had a blond-haired man spreadeagled over the stove and was pushing his head down onto the hotplate with the barrel of his service pistol.

"Don't shoot. Don't shoot!" the man cried. "Japanese working visa!"

"Hiro?" she called.

"Nickie san? Please explain me."

Detective Dedovic lifted Hiro up by the hair. A red mark from the electric coil was stamped along his left cheek.

"It's alright," she said calmly. "Hiro's my flatmate." Dedovic holstered his pistol, then ran his hand quickly up the insides of Hiro's legs.

"I write you note on fridge." Hiro bucked. When Dedovic released him, he jumped away to the far side of the kitchen and rubbed urgently at his elbow.

"What have you done to your hair, Hiro?"

"I living in Bondi now," he said.

Nickie stared at his bleach job. "Don't they say anything at work?"

"Leave Thomas Cook," Hiro said. "Looking for other job." Slowly he started to explain to her how he had borrowed a van from a surfer friend to drive over here to pick up the board. "Aloha, very expensive." Hiro shook his head. "Park on Princes Highway. Can't turn right anywhere, so have to carry it back to Kobi van. Then return here to leave you note."

"What's a Kobi van?" Dedovic snapped.

Nickie could tell that Detective Dedovic had already decided her phone call had been a waste of time. "Hiro," she said. "This is important: when you went out to your van, did you leave my front door open?"

"Only gone for three minute." Hiro made a gap between his fingers.

"Did you switch the light on in the front room?"

"No." Hiro grimaced, rubbing his arm. "I think my elbow, maybe broken."

"Let me take a look at it," Dedovic offered.

Hiro waved him off. "No, you don't touch." Scowling at the detective. Nickie remembered Hiro being distraught for weeks after he'd read of the Japanese tourist accidentally shot dead in Florida while knocking on an American neighbour's door for directions. If there was anything Hiro hated more than Americans it was guns.

"Maybe you should see a doctor. It could be dislocated." She helped her former flatmate down the hall. "Why don't you stay here tonight?"

"No no. Must take Kobi van back now. My friends waiting for me." Hiro started for the front door. "I invite you over for Zaru Soba. We have lovely apartment overlooking Bondi beach. Three Australian surfer and me. Only four hundred dollars a week."

123

"How many bedrooms?" Nickie said.

"One." Hiro moved his hands apart. "But very big."

In the kitchen, she discovered the detective going through her drawers, pulling out rolls of gladwrap and alfoil, a bag of rubber bands. He stopped when he heard her and spun around. "Your little Jap mate . . ." he said.

"Hiroshi?"

"Think he means Kombi van?"

"There was someone else at my window, I'm certain. That policeman. The one I told you about."

Dedovic looked at her dubiously.

"I know you don't believe me, Detective –"

"Call me Terry."

"But I saw him." She squinted into the light. "What happened to your leg?"

Dedovic looked down at his trousers as if he'd just noticed the rip. "Got bit."

Using the American participle. "Who bit you?"

"A dog."

"What sort of dog?"

"Guard dog."

She wished he would open his mouth when he talked. Enunciate a little more. "Roll up your trouser leg." She went into the bathroom and got out the first-aid kit that she kept in an old ice-cream container under the washbasin. With a ball of cottonwool dipped in iodine she dabbed at the dried blood and punctured skin on his shin. "Looks nasty," she said. "Were you on duty?"

"I was investigating a break-in." Dedovic winced. "Subsequent to our meeting."

She listened to a convoluted story involving suspected drug-dealers and an anonymous phone tip-off. For some reason she didn't believe a word of it. The stilted diction he'd adopted made him sound as if he were addressing a gullible courtroom.

"Then I immobilised the animal and proceeded to conduct a search of the premises . . . "

She bandaged the wound and rolled down his cuff. His legs were not too hairy. Up close his body had a pleasant odour. Lemony. The smell of a man's skin, she'd always found to be a most underrated characteristic. "There," she said.

Dedovic tested his leg up and down her black and white tiled floor. "Thanks."

Her eyes locked onto his and she felt slightly uncomfortable as if he was regarding her in a new light. "I wanted to ask you a question." She clutched her scissors and elastotape to her breast. "Is Ling Ling's the only killing you're working on?"

He hesitated.

"There's nobody else been murdered has there?"

He tilted his head slightly and she met Detective Dedovic's blue eyes. "Na," he said bluntly.

She knew he was lying to her. She had the feeling that he lied often and that she would have to be wary in future of whatever he said.

"About that blond cop you seen, I'm gonna look into it."

Standing under the hall light, his big cop's paw resting on her deadlock. He flicked the door open, brushed against her shoulder and went down the steps. A patrol car pulled up, lights flashing, and a police van blocked off the other end of the street. Four uniforms got out and ran towards a wire fence in a wedge. For a moment they were lost beneath the branches of the red hibiscus and then they appeared dragging four teenagers over to the vehicles. They patted them down roughly, removing screwdrivers and butterfly knives and knuckle-dusters from their jacket pockets. Nickie snapped her front door shut, in case the St Peters gang might get the idea she'd informed on them. She wondered if *he* had called the station. In the front room she stole a look through the cedar blinds. Detective Dedovic was standing in the shadows, wide-shouldered, talking to a blond-haired man wearing a dark tracksuit.

Both men looking up towards her house.

# 20

She lay in her bed with all the doors and windows locked, listening to the distant growl of trucks on the highway. It had struck midnight and the airport curfew was in force. She stared up at the hairline cracks in the plaster. That man in the tracksuit talking to Detective Dedovic in the street tonight. That was *him*. He'd been inside her house. He'd been inside her bedroom. For some reason Dedovic was covering for him. Cops always stuck together. She wondered if they were playing some psychological game with her. But why? It didn't make any sense. Her thoughts hurried her along the edge of a cobbled path and down into a dark warm room with lead windows. Oils burned in a lamp in the corner. She undressed to her white cotton briefs and lay on the surgical table on her belly, waiting. Although she could not move her head to see, she knew he was close by. Out of the corner of her vision she caught sight of those well-made hands with their clean, squared nails. She felt the hands stroke her shoulder-blades and loosen the tension in her spine. Strong fingers travelling towards the nape of her neck, gripping her softly below her hairline. She smelled his skin as he pressed against her mouth. Tossing and turning between the sheets. Her pillowcase damp with sweat, her bedshirt twisted above her hips. Exhausted, she rolled out of bed, as if she'd been wrestling all night with a demon.

Detective Dedovic.

In the shower she tasted fresh blood on her lips from where she'd bitten down on her tongue. The 6.15 QF flight to Fiji rattled the glass panes in the bathroom window as she loofahed her legs. She could smell herself. For some reason she couldn't get him out of her mind. She didn't even like cops. The way he'd manhandled Hiroshi. The way he lied so unconvincingly. At the foot of her bed she laid out fresh pantyhose, her best blue bra and a matching camisole. Naked, she stood in front of the open wardrobe deciding on what skirt went best with her new blue Diesel top. Combinations gave her a headache. When the phone rang she walked through into the front room, opened the blinds, her feet leaving faint water marks on the brushbox boards.

A male voice said, "Get you out of the cot?"

"No, I was up already." Nickie checked the VCR clock. Seven was awfully early to be calling anybody.

"Know who this is?"

"Detective Dedovic." She still couldn't bring herself to call him Terry.

"Got it in one," he said. "Guess it's your job listening to people talk and stuff."

His accent was so broad it was almost a parody of an Australian's. No wonder her students hadn't understood him.

"That little matter you asked me about?"

Nickie could hear planes landing in the background. She rested her buttocks gingerly on the worn edge of her couch.

"His name's Terry MacIntyre. Works in the Motor Unit. Just thought you'd like to know."

"I appreciate it." She was tempted to let him know she'd spotted the two of them together last night, but let it slide.

"Constable MacIntyre feels there's been some misunderstanding."

"There's no misunderstanding," she said.

"He wants to have a word with you in private."

"I bet he does."

"Explain his actions. That type of thing."

"Look, Detective. This bastard broke into my house last night. He's threatened me over the phone. And he's supposed to be a police officer."

"Hey, all I'm doing is relaying information here."

"Well you can tell him for me, the only place I ever want to lay eyes on him again is in court when he's charged."

"Fine," he muttered. "No skin off my nose."

Nickie heard Dedovic's voice fading. "I never got to thank you properly for last night."

The word "nuthin" was buried in a short sentence. She sensed his tone softening.

"No, it was really good of you."

"What are you wearing there?" he asked.

"Pardon?"

"I just had this image of you. Wanted to know if it was accurate."

Nickie glanced down at the triangle of dark hair between her legs. Her feet were cold on the bare floor.

"What have you got on? You got on a dress?"

"That's right," she lied.

"Is it a blue dress?"

"How'd you know that?" Playing along with him now.

"Bet you're wearing a little cotton cardigan over the top. Creamy sort of a colour. Am I right?"

"That is amazing."

"Heels. I bet you got a pair of high heels to go with that dress too."

"It's uncanny," Nickie said, "how you can be so accurate."

"I'm a detective," he said. "Guess you develop a sort of sixth sense after a while."

"I guess you do," she said.

"I know women too. That helps."

"It must do," she said.

"It's a gift. That's why I'm careful not to abuse it. Right now I'm getting a very clear mental picture of you sitting on the edge of a couch. You only got out of the shower, about two minutes. And you don't have a stitch on."

Nickie swung around, saw his face pressed against her window and screamed.

Furiously, she wrenched on her top and skirt. Her hair was damp and she raked it back with her nails. When she opened the front door he stepped back a little, raised both hands in the air. "Sorry if I gave you a fright."

"If you weren't the police," she said. "I'd have you arrested."

"Not a good idea to leave your front blinds open. Attracts the wrong element."

"You should know."

He stared at her poker-faced. "I knocked earlier, but no-one answered."

She watched him slip his mobile phone into the jacket pocket of his coffee-coloured suit. Standing there on her porch, wearing a green tie covered in dinosaurs. "Mind if I look around?" he said.

"Are you kidding?" She pressed her bare foot against the edge of the door.

"Don't tell me you keep prohibited substances on the premises?"

She stared at Detective Dedovic's bloodshot eyes, the faint shadow along his pronounced jawline. Wondering if she had misjudged the man totally.

"Hey," he said, "just a joke."

It struck her that he could force his way inside if he wanted; there was nothing she could do to prevent him.

"May I?" He gestured at the door.

She removed her foot and let him through.

"Trust me," he said. "I'm a cop."

"That's what I'm worried about." She smelled his cologne as he squeezed past and headed straight down her hall.

Surprised, she followed him quickly into the kitchen, watched him lean one large hand against the sinktop and peer around the surfaces. "What is it you want, Detective?"

Without a word he got down on his hands and knees and patted around beside the stove. Came up holding a thin black plastic wallet.

"Thought I'd dropped it here." He grinned at her. "My warrant card."

She glimpsed his ID photo. "Why didn't you say so in the first place? And dispense with all this secrecy."

"Maybe you wouldn't have believed me. The public are very distrustful at times."

She tilted her head. "Are you serious?"

"Tell me," he said. "Do you like meat?"

"Actually I'm a vegetarian." She wondered where this was heading.

"Me." He shrugged his shoulders. "I'm a carnivore. I love a rare steak. I thought maybe I could spring you a meal this week. Make up for that fright I gave you just now."

Nickie rubbed at her forehead with her finger. Unsure of how to respond. There were a lot of things she liked about Detective Dedovic. His eyes, his hands, the weight of him. At the same time every nerve in her body warned her not to trust him. She said, "I'll think about it."

"Do that." He strode down the hall, fumbled with her deadlock and stepped out into the sunlight. At the letterbox he turned to stare at what she was wearing. "Nice top," he said. "Want to know somethin'?"

"What?" Nickie frowned.

"You look better with no clothes on."

To her embarassment she blushed before she could shut the door. Thinking of how Detective Dedovic would look himself in ten, fifteen years, his hair thinner, the weight shifted around his body like sand-dunes on a beach. There was something very odd about last night. Why had that blond cop walked into her house and risked being discovered? Surely he would have known someone was there. There could only be one reason. She went into the front room and checked the tall wooden rack beside her dual cassette deck.

The tape was missing.

# 21

He could tell she liked him. The way she kept looking at him out of the corner of her eye. Fascinated by his arms, his hands. A lot of women had told him his hands were special. The only part of his body that ever scored a compliment. He guessed it had been a long time between drinks for her. She was a stubborn little thing, wrapped up in herself. Too much education. Living out there under the fucking runway. She had a nice figure, well-turned breasts, olive-coloured skin. There was something about her. Maybe he should've done life drawing, instead of becoming a cop. He went up the polished staircase, trailing his fingers over the smooth worked rail and stopped in front of a wooden plaque: *Albert C. Coyle BA LLB (Hons) – Accredited Criminal Law Specialist*. He pushed on the panelled door and went in. A pair of bare feet poked out from under the reception desk and dark roots were showing through the young secretary's milky-blonde hair. When she saw him she blinked and hurriedly slid a *Who Weekly* under her manila file. "Mr Coyle's running a little late this morning, Detective. Would you like a coffee?"

Dedovic checked his watch. He had twenty-five minutes to get to the City of Sydney for the squad briefing. "How long?"

"Should be here any second," the girl said. She was nursing a half-drunk litre of Coke in the crook of her arm like someone might steal the black syrup off her. She couldn't have been more than eighteen. If that. Every time he dropped in here Coyle had a new secretary. Dedovic wondered where he got them from. Where he buried the old ones? He walked over to the window and gazed down at the pretty yachts moored in the Rushcutters Bay Marina. Two streets back was all the sleaze and noise of Darlinghurst Road and down there were landscaped tennis courts and the glittering harbour. Two streets made a world of difference in this part of town. Footsteps echoed on the stairs and Ray Doull came through the door, wearing a black and white houndstooth jacket, silver grey slacks and R. M. Williams boots. He winked at the secretary. "Get us a coffee, Trace." Ray Doull watched approvingly as she sauntered out to the machine. "Like fuckin young talent time in here, Terr," he said. "How are yer, mate?"

"Up the shit," Dedovic said. "I can't hang around all morning."

"Albert's got held up in traffic. He's on his way."

Dedovic checked his watch. Twenty minutes left.

"You'll wear that fuckin thing out. Fair dinkum. Albert's got something he wants to tell us. Something big."

"Like what?"

"Don't know yet, do I. Left a message on my beeper." Doull lit a Camel, blew smoke at the harbour. "Hear Steve Bia got done over last night."

"Who by?"

"Major Crime South Region."

"Yeh?"

"Apparently they had a tip off." Doull's expression didn't change.

"What they hit him with?"

"Supply diamorph and a coupla firearm charges. He'd have to be Houdini to get out of this one."

"Right."

"Little Stevie's not too happy about it neither."

"Well, he wouldn't be."

"No more problems there." Doull looked over his shoulder. "Tight as a nut." The secretary came through carrying a cup of black coffee. "Thanks honey," he said. "Where's Albert keep his ashtray?"

Tracey pointed to a non-smoking sign sitting on the magazine table.

"That's just for the public, Trace." Doull winked. "Not for police officers. Here, I'll use the saucer."

Dedovic stared at the lovebites on the side of Tracey's neck. He remembered Ray telling him once at Darlinghurst Station about following the rule book. "Rules are for fools, Terr. Rules are for fools."

A little goatee-bearded man strolled in through the front door wearing a grey tailored suit and waistcoat. He removed a wide-brimmed leather hat and hung it on the stand beside the door. "Good morning Raymond, Terence." He bowed slightly. "Come through." He ushered them into an expansive office filled with north-facing windows and Turkish kilims scattered over the polished kauri floor. "Take a seat." Albert Coyle sat in a leather wing chair and rubbed his small hands together. His lips and the tip of his button nose were blue in colour. Dedovic stared at the large diamond stud gleaming in his right ear.

The solicitor said, "I've received a plethora of phone calls this morning."

"What's the news?" Doull leaned back, slurping his coffee.

"Charlie Kratos was released at 8 a.m. today from the Special Purpose Unit at Long Bay."

"You're kidding." Doull spilled coffee down his front.

"Mind the chair, Raymond. It's real leather."

"I don't fuckin believe it." Doull dabbed at his houndstooth jacket.

Dedovic shook his head with disbelief. "Charlie Kratos was convicted on two counts of murder. How the hell can he get released?"

Albert Coyle smiled faintly. "The full complexity of his legal challenge would take some considerable explaining even to an experienced police officer. Suffice it to say that the law is a wondrous thing."

"The law is an arse," Doull said.

"You mean an ass, Raymond. *Equus asinus*."

"No, I mean a hole, Albert." Doull lit another Camel.

"I really won't tolerate smoking in my office."

Doull took a drag and extinguished the cigarette in his coffee cup. "Bet there'll be a lotta nervous Chief Inspectors in town tonight. So what's he want?"

"Mr Kratos is a reasonable man."

"Yeh. For a psychopath."

"Psychologists prefer not to use that label any more. As you can imagine Mr Kratos has been inundated with a great many requests by State and Federal authorities to discuss specific payments he has made to senior New South Wales individuals over the last ten years."

Dedovic saw what was coming. He watched the solicitor's hands rub together.

"All Mr Kratos is asking from his friends in law enforcement is a donation to cover the substantial legal bills he's incurred."

"Fine," Doull said. "No problems with that."

Dedovic blinked at him.

"That's very sensible, Raymond."

"Least we can do."

"Gotta go, Ray." Dedovic stood up. He couldn't believe Doull was going to sit here and nod his head to a shakedown.

"Wait for me outside, Terr." Doull held up a hand.

"Can't." He had twelve minutes to get to the other side of town.

"Just need a quick word with Albert on another little matter."

Dedovic walked out into the reception area, memories flooding back from his days at Darlinghurst and the Drug Unit. Half the guys he'd worked with had taken a drink from Charlie Kratos, or the dozens of underlings he had working for him. Every strip club, porn shop and shooting gallery in the city Kratos had a thumb in. The Greeks said he was a Turk. The Turks swore that he was a Leb. The Lebanese were positive he was Armenian. The Armenians knew for certain he was Maltese. The only thing everybody agreed on was that Charlie Kratos would have a man, woman or child killed as easily as most people would lay a bet on the trifecta.

"You alright, Detective?"

Dedovic turned, saw Tracey regarding him oddly.

"You look pale. Would you like a glass of Coke?"

"No thanks, Trace." Dedovic stared at the faint blue striae on the side of her neck. "How are they treating you?"

"Oh, Mr Coyle's really nice to me. He's very kind."

Dedovic didn't say a word.

"It's not what you think, you know."

"Nothing ever is," Dedovic said. He went down the stairs and stopped in the stone archway, staring across the road at a green Toyota Camry CSi parked four doors behind his. Two men in the front seat talking into their shirt cuffs. Rain was starting to fall and he could smell it striking the road, stirring up the tyre dust and the dog shit. He wondered what would be quickest, take the ramp down William or cut through Darlo and Surry Hills.

Boot heels echoed on the stairs behind him and Ray Doull called out, "Mate, thought you'd shot through."

Dedovic saw the grin the Detective Sergeant was wearing.

"That Albert's an oily little fucker, but it's oil that makes the wheels go round." Ray Doull slid a slim brown envelope into his jacket pocket.

"Those two." Dedovic jerked his head at the Camry across the street. "Where they from?"

"Who knows." Doull shrugged. "ICAC, NCA, PIC? We got half the letters in the alphabet chasing us."

"So what are we going to do about Kratos? You're not really going to pay the prick?"

"Mate, you fuckin kidding? You think I'm going to give good money to that bag of shit?"

"I didn't think so." Dedovic checked his watch. Five and a half minutes.

"Even if I had it I wouldn't give it away. So what do you reckon we do?"

"Don't know." Dedovic rolled his car keys around in his hand. "You can't load up a guy like Charlie Kratos, that's for sure."

"Terr," Doull said quietly. "There's nobody in this world you can't load."

## 22

Dedovic rolled his shoulders like a boxer trying to loosen up before a bout. He took the fire escape, shoes ringing on the concrete stairs. Ten minutes late already, but if he could sneak in the back way it might look as if he'd been in the building since nine. Bob Winch ran Task Force Jarrah like an Australian League coach. Late for one weekly briefing and you could find yourself transferred out of first grade. Dedovic hit the side door and went into the muster room. Empty, except for Detective Chen poring over a large yellow map of the City of Sydney.

"Where is everybody?" He checked his watch, peered out through the tinted glass partition. Computers whirred on vacant desks.

"The Commander just rang. He want to know if you were in yet."

"What's going on?"

"I told him you weren't."

"You ever hear of lying?"

"Not to the Chief Inspector, Terry." Wai Yi Chen shook her head seriously.

"Christ." He had the feeling that something huge was going down. Except for a couple of support personnel roaming the corridors, the entire fifth floor was deserted. "Where's Winch got to?" It was well-known in the Task Force that the Commander never left the building in office hours except for lunchtime visits to the Malaya.

"He's at College Street."

"The Commissioner's office?" Dedovic chewed an old ring scar on his lip. What was Winch doing there? Maybe there'd been a breakthrough?

"He sounded very angry." Detective Chen marked a cross on her map. "Have you seen the newspaper this morning?"

Dedovic walked over to the whiteboard, scooped the tabloid off the desk. Headlines jumped up at him:

### LING LING'S CRUEL MURDER
By a Special Correspondent

Police today are hunting a sadistic killer after the body of Indonesian student Ling Ling Kua was found last week dumped in the Royal National Park. Ms Kua, 19, had been strangled and is the third foreign student to be murdered in Sydney in the past eleven months. A reliable police source said all three murders are "definitely linked".

An exceptionally talented and vivacious language student, Ms Kua is believed to have been brutally assaulted. Today her distraught father, Mr Kua, pleaded through an embassy official for anyone with information on his daughter's killer to contact police. A special

> police taskforce code-named **Jarrah** is investigating the triple murders which now threaten to jeopardise Australia's $3 billion overseas student industry. **Continued Page 2**

Dedovic dropped the paper onto the desktop. Winch would have someone's head on a plate for this, if the new Commissioner didn't remove his first. It was a major cock-up and Dedovic had no doubt who the cock belonged to. You didn't have to be Sherlock Holmes to read between the lines. *A reliable police source* was code for pillowtalk. Wendy Lee Burke had screwed more cops than the Wood Royal Commission and she didn't seem to give a damn who knew it. On page two there were references to strange marks found on Ling Ling's body "comparable to crocodile bites" and details from the pathology report which no police officer in his right mind would reveal to a member of the media while a murder case was under investigation. The New South Wales Police Service prided itself on its secrecy and Dick Rainey had managed to spill his beans.

"You see this?" Dedovic whistled. There was even mention of the chopsticks and the story had pushed the release of Charlie Kratos back onto page three.

Detective Wai Yi Chen marked a second cross on her city map. "It is very bad."

"Bad, it's fucked. We might as well write a letter to the killer telling him everything we know."

"Why do you think it's a he?" Chen looked up from a line she was drawing between two crosses. There was something different about her today.

"Cause it's obvious."

"You don't believe a woman is capable of murder?"

"Sure a woman's capable, but everything about this one – the underwear, internal bruising, the manual strangulation – everything tells me it's a man. There's a different sense of cruelty."

"I agree with you," Chen said.

"Well that makes me feel good," Dedovic replied, but his sarcasm went straight over Chen's head. "I tell you what else too. These are not haphazard killings. The Kua murder scene was very organised, the way he'd pegged her out, the position of the body, everything was done with precision. The freak just didn't drive down to that national park on a whim. He planned it all."

The phone started ringing on his desk. Dedovic ignored it. "See, I think our man hangs around outside language schools, selects his victim like you or I would select a fresh chicken fillet, maybe comes back in a week or so with masking tape and a length of fishing line, picks her up in the street."

"How?" Chen asked.

"Asian girls are very trusting. Maybe he asks her directions in English. He's polite, friendly. Acts interested in her nationality, all that bullshit. Teachers are always telling their students to practise the language with native speakers."

"You think he's an Australian?" Chen blinked.

Dedovic nodded slowly. "Else he's been here a long time. He knows the city. Knows its back streets. He knows where you can leave a van unlocked for five minutes. My bet is he lures his victim down a side alley to his Hi-Ace or his Mr Whippy van, overpowers her, throws her in and duct-tapes her mouth, wrists and ankles. Then he drives somewhere quiet and peaceful. He's in no rush. He's calm. Everything's been thought out in advance. He waits until dusk and then he starts in on her. He enjoys his work. He's slow and methodical like a good surgeon. When he's done with the body, he cleans his tools thoroughly."

"Why do you say this?" Chen's round face watched him closely. "You have a reason for your theory?"

The phone kept ringing on his desk. "Yeh," Dedovic said. "I got a reason." Intuition, hunch, whatever you liked to call it. It was something you picked up after years on the job. Ray Doull had explained to him one time that being a detective was no different to being a carpenter, that after a while you developed "an eye" for your work. Whenever he visited a crime scene he got a picture, hazy at first, and then bit by bit he built on that initial image. He'd learned to trust his senses. There was no way he could explain it rationally to someone like Chen, but he knew the freak was driving a non-descript van, knew it like a carpenter knows where to cut a piece of timber without even measuring.

"This guy is organised, very controlled and particular in his methods. I think he's a one-man band with a big wrap on himself. Sure as hell he won't get caught, but he leaves little messages to us just the same. Or to God, or to Judas Priest, or whoever he's into. Like the chopsticks in the girl's uterus. I mean what's that telling us?"

"He doesn't like Asians?"

"Or women."

"Or both," Chen said.

The phone was still ringing on his desk; other phones were going off at the other end of the squad room. Every detective in Task Force Jarrah had fled the fifth floor before the shit hit the fan. Press would be swarming all over the City of Sydney entrance – TV crews, photographers, those big dopey sound recordists. It was the sort of news the media liked best, a bizarre killing with sexual and cultural undertones. If he and Chen had any sense they'd slip out the backstairs now, follow up on yesterday's running sheets.

"It could be the Commander, Terry."

That's all he wanted. Take the brunt of Bob Winch's anger for this mess. He leaned across his own desk bulging with ring folders, boxed files and photographs of the three deceased victims. Snatched up the receiver. "Dedovic," he said.

A cop's voice came on the other end: Terry MacIntyre.

"I'm afraid she won't talk to you, MacIntyre," he said. "Says she'll see you in court first." He listened to the constable's whining voice on the other end, staring across the squad room at the air-conditioning pipes dripping water into a plastic bucket. Some of these government contractors should be given life sentences.

"Listen MacIntyre," Dedovic said. "My advice to you is to lay off. You go near that woman again and I'll arrest you myself. Understood?" He slammed down the phone. Grubs like MacIntyre were a disgrace to the service. He should never have been let in as a cop. He was a drunk and a loudmouth and Dedovic shouldn't have agreed to intercede for the prick in the first place. "Now, what was I saying?"

Detective Chen looked at him oddly.

"Details, that's right," he said. "We look for details. We ask ourselves, what is the offender trying to achieve here? What is his message? Every murderer leaves a trace, a mark where he's been. It's like quantum mechanics, the Heisenberg principle, you can't observe the particle without disturbing the equation."

Chen's eyes widened. "You know quantum physics, Terry?"

"Na, I'm just raving that's all. Trying to get a fix on our man."

"You want me to build a profile?" Chen asked.

He stared at the woman's green eye shadow. She was a plain little Jane who smelled of roast duck meat. He said, "What's Chen mean in Chinese?"

"It means great. I have an idea," she began. "Of course I'm only new at this job and I haven't had your wide experience . . . "

"Go on," he said. Flattery always worked with him.

"These two crosses here," Chen tapped a small white finger on her map of the city, "indicate where Lin Lu Pei and Mo Ching Wan were taken – Lane Cove and Chatswood."

"Right."

"And Kua Ling Ling lived with her homestay family in Artarmon. A weekly train ticket was found in her bag. Now if Ling Ling was not taken in the city, but somewhere, say, near to Artarmon station . . ." Chen marked a third cross on the map with her red felt pen.

Dedovic nodded. It made sense to him. It was much easier to snatch the girl in the suburbs. Closer to home, she'd be more relaxed, more trusting of strangers.

"And if we connect these two line we have a triangle. The murderer's centre of gravity."

"His what?"

"The area in which he operate. His geographical territory."

Dedovic stared at her isosceles triangle shaded in red. Mapping an offender's patterns was nothing new to him. Detectives did it all the time, it was just the textbook language that Chen used. "Where'd you get this centre of gravity stuff from?" he asked.

"I study behavioural science at university."

"In Beijing?"

"No no, in Sydney," she said. "I came here 1985. My parent want me to study medicine, but my TER

145

result not high enough. My father very disappointed when I became policewoman."

Dedovic slapped her on the back, heard her cough. "You done well, Chen."

"Call me Ida." She beamed brightly.

Dedovic nodded. The north shore had one of the largest concentrations of Asian migrants in the city. The freak probably hung around the train stations over there at dusk in his windowless van. But why were his victims all foreign students? Or was that just coincidence? Maybe he was after any attractive girl of Asian appearance. He had the feeling that finally they were getting somewhere. Narrowing it down. "There is one thing that's been bugging me all along."

"What's that, Terry?" Chen's eyelids flickered with interest.

"Whoever's doing these murders has a very high forensic awareness. There's no prints at the scene, no fibre transference of any significance, no blood, no semen, no DNA samples. Forensic services has come up with nothing whatsoever."

"Perhaps he is a very experienced criminal," Chen suggested.

"Well he certainly has a sound knowledge of modern forensic procedures."

"Perhaps he's worked as a morgue assistant or in an analytical laboratory?"

Dedovic listened to the phones ringing in the empty squad room, fluorescent strips glowing above the vacant desks. "Or perhaps," he said softly, "he's worked as a police officer."

# 23

Nickie sipped cautiously at her bowl of laksa. There was nothing she liked more than soup; the way it opened your airways, warmed your chest. She sat at the low round table with eleven other teachers, the popping of plastic containers and fizz of soft drink cans interspersed with calls of, "Where'd you get that sushi from?" "Is that eggplant?" Everyone glancing with curiosity at each other's lunch boxes. The smell of fried dumplings mingled with the aroma of cheesy pizzettas, prawn rolls, fish tempura, tofu-burgers, sweet potato patties and hot steaming noodles. An elderly male was spilling curried egg from his salad roll onto the floor. Two married teachers unpeeled gladwrap from thick home-made sandwiches. A dieting twenty-year-old lingered over a spotty banana, chewing each pulpy mouthful diligently. For thirty brief minutes the celebration of food dispelled the grief that had spread through the language college like a London fog. From the far end of the staffroom came the clunkety-clunk of photocopiers churning out lessons for the afternoon. Nickie waited patiently for the newspaper to make its way around the circle. Even though she was a senior teacher she never pulled rank. She took the paper, grease-stained at the edges, and read the headlines: LING LING'S CRUEL MURDER.

The journalist had transformed a real flesh and blood person into a "city story". It was like she was reading about someone she'd never met. Sentences leapt out at her. *Third Asian student murdered. Three murders definitely linked.* So Detective Dedovic had lied. She had suspected that there was more than just one killing. Only someone evil would think of harming Ling Ling. Nickie finished her soup, staring at one word that stood out like a beacon above the rest – *strangled*. She pictured Detective Dedovic's large hands with their sweep of fine black hairs and dropped the paper.

"Strangled," she said. All the teachers stopped chewing and stared at her. "It's a shocking thing," a woman whispered. "Ling Ling was such a sweet child." Nickie got up from the table and walked down the corridor, past the maze of cold air-conditioned classrooms. Students milled around the Coke machine and in doorways, short-haired boys and long-haired girls with the sleeves of their sloppy sweaters pulled down over small fingers, clutching Mickey Mouse bags and coloured folders plastered with stickers of Madonna and Michael Jackson. They had come to Australia because it was safe, but nowhere was safe any more. The whole world was dangerous.

Voices were yelling from the Director of Studies' office. Nickie stopped in the doorway. Laurie Limacher was jabbing two fingers at his ex-wife's chest, his neck corded. "I saw you," he said. "I know what you're doing." Laurie spun around and stared at Nickie in the doorway. His eyes were wild. She stepped to the left, he stepped to the right. Up close he was good-looking in an intense, electric sort of way. Nickie killed the thought.

She wasn't getting involved with another of Mona's cast-offs. She smelled the sweat through his plaster-streaked T-shirt as he pushed past. Mona was squeezing the back of her chair.

"You alright?" Nickie went over, touched her bony arm.

"I can't get rid of him."

"You should go to the police."

"They're useless. He won't let go."

When Mona had first arrived at the college, Nickie had taken her under her wing, shown her the resources, and though never intimate friends, Nickie was the only teacher that Mona had invited to her wedding. She had bought them percale bedlinen, a pair of Egyptian cotton sheets that cost her three days' pay and when the happy couple split after nine unhappy months, Nickie had strongly regretted the expense. She had hoped that Mona might return the sheets unused, but of course she didn't and when she heard in graphic detail about how the relationship had soured, she began to feel sorry for her workmate. Over coffee she listened to the stories of fights and abusive phone calls and after Laurie moved into the block of flats next door to harass her, Mona started picking up young men from The Oaks, attempting, as she revealed one damp autumn morning, "to wipe that bastard from my mind".

Mona stepped away from Nickie's hand. "The agent just faxed me through," she said. "Twenty-five Taiwanese nurses cancelled this morning. That makes sixty in two days."

Nickie thinking, *strangled*. Why would anyone want to murder foreign students? Did Dedovic have any idea? How good a detective was he anyway? Funny that he and Mona knew each other. He didn't seem her type. She wondered if Mona had slept with him.

149

"I'm afraid there's going to be some downsizing," Mona said.

"Downsizing?"

Mona walked over to her desk, sat down. "We have no choice. Either the college lays off teachers or everyone takes an adjustment in salary."

"What sort of adjustment?" Nickie followed her to a chair.

"One or two days a week. But I'll do everything I can for you. I know how tight money is in your present circumstances."

Made her sound like an invalid pensioner.

"It will only be until enrolments recover. I wanted to tell you first. Because you're the union representative and we're such old friends."

"Well, thanks," she said in a hollow voice. She hadn't realised they were such old friends.

"I know it must be hard. Me being younger and getting this promotion–"

"No, no," Nickie said. "I'm glad you got it."

"I feel you're one person I can talk to."

Despondently, Nickie touched the stack of crisp white business cards in a little ceramic shoe on the desk: *M. Limacher (Dip Tefl)* DIRECTOR OF STUDIES. It still galled Nickie that she had been overlooked for the job. She had travelled the world. She had learned Mandarin, Japanese and Spanish; she'd lived in Shanghai, Sagamihara and Salamanca. She spoke Greek fluently. She had a BA (Hons) in psychology, an MA in applied linguistics and had abandoned a PhD in typological linguistics. She knew the phonetic alphabet and could explain the difference between alveolar and pharyngeal articulation or voiced plosives and voiceless non-sibilant fricatives. She loved the complexity of human language. She had written a paper on lexicostatistical glottochronology (criticising it) and given seminars on lexical diffusion. And here she was, approaching thirty-five in a minor language college sitting opposite a woman seven years her junior who had slipped past her in the inside lane.

Somehow she had been unable to transfer this store of knowledge into the one substance valued in the community – money. For years she had disdained the accumulation of wealth and now she found herself brooding on bills, walking an extra two kilometres to save a dollar-fifty bus fare, scanning the prices of cereal in supermarket shelves. Her budget so finely balanced that the cost of a water pump could set her finances back for a fortnight. She had no vices, except for yoga, her weekly Russian class, the occasional bottle of cheap red, and the four cigarettes she allowed herself each day. Her mortgage drained her like a leech. She envisioned herself becoming a thrifty old Greek-Australian woman counting out coins in the canned food aisle of Franklins. Of course she could always get lucky. She could win lotto, she could meet someone wonderful – man or woman. "Detective Dedovic," she said suddenly. "What's he like?"

Mona shrugged. "Hardly know the man. He tried to pick me up in a gym, but I wasn't interested. Not my type. He must be in his late thirties."

"So you didn't–"

"Good God no. Anyone over thirty is far too old for fucking."

"I'm thirty-four," Nickie said.

"Men, I'm talking about. That's when they start watching the State of Origin in their dressing gowns. One of my jade earrings went missing from my gym bag. I'm sure he took it."

"Stole it?"

"They do worse than that every day. Anyway he rang me up later, said he picked it up on the carpet somewhere. I didn't believe a word."

"How did he get your number?"

"He's a police officer, isn't he?" Mona said. "Have you noticed the size of his hands, he has the biggest hands I've ever seen on a man. If I were you, I'd stay out of his clutches. You fancy him, don't you?"

"I think he's a brute," Nickie said. "I just hope he's clever enough to catch this killer."

"So do I," Mona said. "For all our sakes." She leaned forward in her chair and her voice dropped to a whisper. "This is in the strictest confidence." Her green eyes darted to the doorway. "If another Asian student is murdered, this college will have to close."

Nickie caught her breath.

Mona leaned back, pulling at a black strap under her blouse. "That's not to go any further than this office."

"I understand." Nickie stood up. "Thanks." She walked out of Mona's office, her thoughts running ahead of her like startled mice. A group of Indonesian girls looked at her, doe-eyed and jittery. If only she could do something. She was going to lose her job, her home. They all were. Was it ethical to keep this secret from the other teachers? She went into the empty staffroom, cleared a half-eaten pizzetta and a bowl of smelly green curry from the low table. Threw open a window and breathed in carbon and nitrous oxides. She needed to think. She gazed down at the black-haired students waiting on the pavement to be picked up by uncles and cousins and elder brothers.

A white Mitsubishi van stopped on the corner outside the college. Nickie watched the driver ask a pigtailed girl for directions and then the van accelerated slowly towards the heart of Chinatown. She pressed her nose against the aluminium frame. It was crazy, but she believed that she could help find out who'd murdered Ling Ling. She had taught Asian students for years, she understood human psychology. Of course Detective Dedovic would just laugh at her offer, but Nickie didn't care. What did she have to lose now? She slammed the window shut.

The worst she could do was fail.

# 24

He stepped out into the street and saw them bunched together on the wet black pavement. TV reporters weighed down with cables and boom mikes, plastic sheeting draped over the lenses of their heavy cameras. They moved towards him in a flying wedge, shoes pounding through the puddles. "Any leads on these Asian killings?" someone yelled.

Dedovic shook his head. Chen and he striding towards the squad car parked outside the City of Sydney station. Print journalists, struggling to stay alongside, thrust slim black recorders up under his chin. "What can you say about the marks on the girl's body, Detective?" "Is it true she was mutilated on a sacred Aboriginal stone?" Dedovic brushed a leather-jacketed photographer aside and opened the car door. "No comment." A hand reached out and grabbed his elbow. "Dedo, you old fucker." He swung around. Wendy Lee Burke's sharp features zoomed in close. "Want me to help your career, Senior Constable?"

"Like you helped Dick Rainey's?" He took the business card she was holding out, saw the shiny lipstick moving on Wendy Lee's red lips. "Dick's a fat-arse slob, but you've got brains. Together we can crack this. Give me a ring!"

He slammed the car door shut. Chen was talking to a TV celebrity on the driver's side and when she hit the accelerator, the tyres splashed the man's Drizabone riding coat with brown slush from the gutter. "Know who that was?" Chen said excitedly and flicked the wipers on. Rain was slanting across the wired canopy of Darling Harbour and dancing on the oily black bitumen.

Dedovic ripped the card Burke had given him in half and poked the pieces into the ashtray. He felt sorry for reporters. They were just like cops. Had to hang around the courts all week, wearing out their shoe leather waiting for a break. Guys who wore ink-stained shirts, dandruff-speckled suits and suffered lower back pain from sitting all day on the hard wooden benches at Central Court. He got on with them. But the TV world, that was different. That was feudal. All those poorly fed gaffers and gophers humping around hardware while the haircuts paraded in front of the judges' chambers in cashmere jumpers and linen suits. Guys who wouldn't know their dick from a hot dog if you fed it to them with barbecue sauce.

"Used to be on *Current Affair*." Chen thumped the wheel with her tiny fist. "Then went to *Today Tonight* show and marry that actress woman from the gardening program. You know the one?"

"What are you talking about?"

"Very famous TV interviewer. I see him on the billboards and buses. He ask me how to spell my name."

"Why?" Dedovic said.

"I tell him we're going to the north shore area to pursue further inquiries. Was that indiscreet?"

"Two bits of advice, Ida. Never tell a reporter what *they* want to know; just tell them what *you* want them to know. Second, never give your real name; always say 'a police source'." Dedovic looked out his window at five broken umbrellas lying on the steps of the Town Hall like dead black birds. They drove through the glassy heart of the city, the rain releasing the smell of hot rubber from the tyres on the road. Against the grey concrete buildings, people were bright smudges of colour. Detective Chen had the driver's seat pushed right under the steering wheel and her chin peering over the top. "I hope I have not disappointed you, Terry," she said. "My father very disappointed with me."

"I think you mentioned that," Dedovic said.

"Whatever I achieve I can never do enough in his eyes. He always want a son, you see. I'm the only child."

"Lucky he didn't drown you," Dedovic said. "They do that in China. Drown the little girls. Keep the boys. I've read about it."

"That is only in very remote countryside. Not in the cities."

"Lucky you weren't born in a village then," Dedovic said. In the distance a train rattled along the bridge and cars were herding themselves into the narrow lanes, blinking their yellow indicators and blaring their horns. The light was fading across the sky and silver flecks of rain swept between the thick dark girders. The phone rang in his pocket and he fished it out, held it up to his left ear. "Dedovic."

"Terr, we gotta talk a.s.a.p."

"Can't, Ray. I'm on a job right now."

"Don't you fuckin switch that mobile on? I been ringing you all arvo."

"I was at work."

"Mate, I tried the Task Force five times. No answer. We gotta stick our heads together now. Where are you?"

"On the bridge. Northbound."

"Headed where?"

"Artarmon station."

"Meet me in fifteen minutes. Corner of Berry and Walker. One more thing."

"What?"

"Your phone's O double F."

Dedovic slipped the mobile into his jacket pocket and stared out the window at the blue domes of the insurance towers on the north side. He'd never heard Ray Doull sound so rattled before. Something wasn't right. If they were under investigation, all phones were off. Only an idiot would assume otherwise. He wondered if Ray Doull was losing it. Like a pro boxer there came a time when a detective just didn't have that edge anymore. Dedovic rolled his neck from side to side. He had to ring Gab, see if everything was alright at home and then somehow he had to cut loose from Ray Doull. Things were falling apart.

"Anything wrong, Terry?" Chen looked across at him. The sky had turned into a swirling black wash and hundreds of thousands of tiny white lights glowed like fireflies around the shores of the harbour.

"Something's come up," he said. "Old police business. Going to have to cancel tonight."

"I still want to go ahead."

"I don't think that's such a good idea, constable. Not without back-up."

"We're over this side of the city now," she insisted. "Besides, I've gone to all the trouble of getting changed."

Dedovic remembered waiting for Chen outside the toilets on the fifth floor, but had been so entangled in his own problems he hadn't even noticed what she was wearing. Slowly he ran his eyes over her salmon-pink Ken Done top, the word SYDNEY in bright orange letters emblazoned across her small flat breasts. A multi-coloured Benetton bum bag was secured around her waist above a pair of ironed blue jeans and her small feet were shod in Nike sports shoes. She reached into the back seat of the police vehicle for a mini vinyl backpack, her digital phone protruding from a side flap.

"Know something," Dedovic said. "I think I've underestimated you."

Detective Chen blushed as red as the tail-lights in front. Streams of traffic stretched bumper to bumper along the freeway. "I just look in the shop window and then hang around the platform for half hour or so."

"You see anyone suspicious, do not engage. Understood?"

Chen straightened the glasses on her nose and nodded seriously.

"If you strike trouble, you know what to do?"

She unzipped her Benetton bag, pulled out a snub-nosed five shot S&W .38, checked its load, tucked the revolver back inside her bag and zipped it shut.

"I think you're going to make a fine detective, Ida."

"Oh no, Terry." Chen shook her head. "I still have much to learn about good police work."

Huge glass towers loomed above them, lit up from within like radioactive mounds. Dedovic stared at the hundreds of fluorescent strips burning on every level, the red and blue neon. He loved the city, the sparkling coloured lights that spread their liquid glaze over the harbour. Driving between the clean office blocks of the northside, the smell of salt water mixing with the sharper bite of traffic fumes. Car tyres hummed on the wet shiny road; the skyline dipped and shops and flats jostled for the eye's attention. Chen pulled up in the shadows of a row of pine trees and massaged her forehead with two fingers. Beyond the pines, Artarmon station nestled in its suburban quietness.

"You alright?" Dedovic asked.

"Just a headache." Chen squinted. "It's gone now."

"I get those," Dedovic told her. "Look, I'll be back here in two jiffs–"

"No, my father expecting me to cook dinner tonight. I look around and then catch the train home. I just want to get a feeling of where the offender operates." Chen stepped out of the driver's door; threaded her arms through the straps of her mini backpack. Her straight black hair was tied in a ponytail and all that was missing from the outfit was a pair of earphones.

"Whatever you do don't get into any strange vans," Dedovic said.

Chen shook her head. "I'm not stupid, Terry."

"Be careful." He followed her with his eyes as she passed the village green and disappeared down the tunnel that led under the platforms. He got in the driver's side of the unmarked police vehicle and adjusted her seat back. He didn't feel right leaving Chen alone, but she'd worked undercover in Cabramatta for two years before she'd been designated a detective and the chances of her finding anything untoward at Artarmon railway station at eight o'clock on a Tuesday night were pretty remote. He drove back along the northern line, past angophoras and blocks of concertinaed units that rose up from the sandstone subfloor. Thinking how long it was since he had been as enthusiastic in the job as Wai Yi Chen. A good while. Ten days after he'd found that first brown envelope stuffed into his police locker, he was invited out "for a feed" by Ray Doull. He knew then that he'd passed some kind of test. They'd called into a small expensive Italian place off Darlinghurst Road where he'd tried pan-fried calamari with radicchio salad for the first time in his life followed by lobster with rice and washed down with two bottles of German Liebfrau wine. When he'd gone over to the cashier to settle up, the manager had refused his money, waving his hands in the air like he was offended. "Mr Doull's guests don't pay here." And it wasn't so much the free meal, but the way Detective Sergeant Doull didn't say a word. Dedovic realised that his education was to be a silent one. That the way things worked in the plain-clothes section were as much to do with what was not said, as what was said. And he understood that junior detectives were expected to look and to listen but to ask no questions.

Later that night he followed the Ringmaster into a strip club on Roslyn Street that every cop in the city knew was frequented by the state's heavier criminals. The lights were dim and coloured liqueur bottles glistened behind the velvety red bar where identical-twin Tongan bartenders were squeezed into tuxedos and black bow ties. Doull disappeared into a backroom marked PRIVATE and Dedovic watched three strippers gyrate on stage while school-aged waitresses glided between the red-topped tables with canned beers and fake kangaroo pouches. The strippers grew bolder and the customers got drunker and through a gap in the PRIVATE doorway, Dedovic saw his sergeant laughing with a large man wearing a black suit and black riding boots. The man's face was turned away from the light, and his voice was thick and guttural. Leathery ears stuck out on either side of his big shiny head. Dedovic stepped back from the doorway as Ray Doull came out straightening his jacket.

Speeding home in the squad car afterwards, Dedovic asked Doull about the man in the club: wasn't he the one the newspapers referred to as Sydney's Mr Big?

"Yeah well, don't believe any that horseshit, mate. If the papers said it was raining, I'd leave my umbrella at home."

Dedovic smelled hair oil on Sergeant Doull's coat.

"Na, Charlie's just a businessman. He was a bit of a tearaway in his youth. But I tell you what. He's got some great ideas for this city." Doull braked outside a block of red-bricked flats in Concord West and Dedovic climbed out, looked up at the porch light that Gabby had left on for him.

"Hey," Doull called. "For a bloke with a family on the way you should be more careful."

"Why's that?" Dedovic turned around.

"Dropped this out your back pocket."

Dedovic stared at the two fifty dollars bills in the outstretched hand.

"Mate, get yourself a nice little wallet."

For a moment Dedovic stood there in the driveway and then he reached out and took the money and walked up the iron stairs to his flat, closed the door behind him and waited for the police vehicle to drive off. When everything was quiet again and all he could hear was the ticking of the fridge he went down to the bedroom and woke his pregnant wife.

Stunted trees and ferns were growing in a speckled concrete tub behind the plate-glass window and Ray Doull stood outside on the steps pulling on the remains of a cigarette like it was his last. Dedovic hit the horn and waved. Four lanes of traffic swept down the hill towards the bridge and light drops of rain were clicking on the car roof. In the next street he found a space and strode back up to the corner, ducking under the office workers' umbrellas. Ray Doull was wearing a brown jacket over a green Lacoste shirt. His grey lined face was creased and rumpled and he hadn't shaved too well. When he saw Dedovic coming he looked away.

Dedovic stood underneath the curved glass and metal canopy with his back to Doull and stared down towards the harbour. "What's up?" he said.

"I'm off the fuckin job. Suspended from all police duties."

"You're kiddin'–"

"They raided me at six o'clock this morning. Frightened the shit out of Barb and the boys. Gave the dog a fuckin heart attack. It's bad, mate. A mess. You rung home?"

"Christ no."

"Give her a buzz, right now."

Dedovic flipped out his phone and punched in the number. His heart was thumping in his breast pocket and the coloured lights of the city pulsed in time. "C'mon c'mon," he said, listening to it ring; there was a little metallic click and Gab's voice came on with the same message she'd laid down on that day two years ago when he'd moved out. "Not there," he said.

Ray Doull was chewing at the ends of his thick grey moustache, flicking ash onto the clean marble steps of the Nippon Meat building. "Na," he said. "I think you're sweet. You woulda heard by now. They hit Lance Bullmore, Scotty Dwyer, Hargraves, Bill McJannett today – the old fuckin unit."

"Who did?"

"Integrity."

"So what are you gonna do, Ray?"

"My health's out the window. I lose my fuckin pension and I got nothing. Simple as that."

"You got the place down the coast. You got a four bedroom house in North Ryde. That oughta be worth something."

"Twenty-five years I put into this town. For what – forty-five Ks a year, a crook back and clapped-out knees. Okay, so we took a fuckin drink. Who hasn't? You think it's only cops doing it. There's guys in the morgue stealing the shoes off dead people. Everyone's on the fiddle. It's fuckin human nature."

Dedovic watched the older man take out another Camel, give it a real hard look like he knew it was poisoning him, then flip it into his mouth and clamp down tight on the end with his teeth. The flame from Doull's yellow lighter revealed the bags under his eyes, his skin the colour of wet cement.

"Everyone's rolling," Doull said. "This whole town's rolling. We gotta stick together, not like these young punks. I want you to go see Kratos."

"No. You go see him."

"Mate, if I go anywhere near the prick, I'd knock him. I wouldn't trust myself. I'm not authorised to undertake any police business. It's gotta be you."

"Why, for Christ sake?"

"He won't let me, or Bull or Dennis Hargraves, any of the hard arses go near him. But he'll trust you, Terr. You're not a big hitter. Kratos is swanning it up right now in a five star Jap suite in Macleay Street. He's got subs, chits, receipts and diaries going back fifteen years. He's asking seventy-five up-front."

"What about Albert? Send him up there."

"Mate, we gotta go through the front door. We gotta go direct. Albert's only got one loyalty to one client and his surname's Bill and first name's Dollar. Na, we gotta fix this ourselves. We gotta fix it fast. I'm not going to be stood over by some pyschopath. Charlie Kratos wants us to square up with him. Yeah, alrighty, we'll square up with him."

Dedovic shook his head. "I won't be involved in that."

"Terr, it's too late in the day to start growing a conscience. All you got to do is talk to the fat prick, get him to a meet, then you don't need to know nothing else."

"Can't Ray, I'm working a triple homicide."

"We got a major meltdown here and you want to concentrate on some looney who's knocking off fuckin Asians."

"He's killed three girls. Three."

"I know that, and my sympathy goes out to the families and to the tourist bureau, but this is *us* we're talking about, Terr. Blokes you used to work with, blokes you still drink with."

Dedovic leaned against the thick glass base of the tower, staring at the traffic. Cars wailed along the freeway and water glistened like black oil in the gutters. He glanced over at a double-parked red Mitsubishi with twin aerials and then at Ray Doull's bulky jacket. City lights were flashing in front of his eyes and a voice was whispering in his ear to bail out, bail out. He said, "Can't help you this time, Raymond."

Doull ground his Camel out on the marble step with his shoe and rubbed at his stubble with the back of his hand; the sound it made was like sandpaper scraping on hard wood. "Mate, I never thought you'd let the team down. Fair dinkum, I'm real disappointed."

"I'm not in the Drug Unit no more. I'm in the Task Force now and I want to run my own race. I want to put all that other shit behind me."

"You can't run away from the past, mate. Nobody can."

"I'm not running, Ray. I'm walking." Dedovic went down the steps of the Nippon Meat building and stopped at the lights. He didn't look behind him, but knew for certain that Doull was watching. He could hear the traffic thrumming and people in suits were streaming out of the electronic glass doors of the building opposite, smiling and chattering like prisoners who'd just been released. The lights flashed green and he stepped out onto the road, hurrying his feet along, the sounds of the city hammering in the back of his head.

# 25

Pulling into the driveway, Dedovic braked and snuffed the lights. Gravel slurred underfoot as he crossed the drive. He pounded up the concrete steps, tapped on the dimpled glass with his knuckle, waiting impatiently for the door to open. Giselle answered wearing a blue chenille dressing gown, a faded lemon towel wrapped around her hair. "Dad. What are you doing here?"

"Where's your mother?" He clicked the door shut behind him and went down the hall checking rooms. Picked up the phone and heard a high-pitched shrill on the line. "I been trying to get through for an hour."

"Sorry Dad, I was on the Net."

"When you're finished sweetheart, I've got to make some business calls. Everything been alright? No strange visitors?"

"What's wrong, Dad? You're really pale."

"Just some trouble at work."

"You're not being investigated are you? Mum said if you were investigated we could lose the house."

"Giselle." He grabbed her in the crook of his arm. "Nothing's going to happen to me or the house. Where's your mother gone?"

"Dad, lemme go." Giselle tried to extricate herself from his grip. "I gotta switch the modem off. Da–add!"

Dedovic sniffed at his daughter's wet hair. "You still smoking?"

"I haven't had one for five days. Honest."

He sniffed her hair again; toasted marshmallows. Giggling, Giselle slipped out of his headlock.

"Tell you what," he said. "You give up the cigs for a month and I'll wipe that two-fifty you owe me. Deal?"

She readjusted the towel on her head. "Deal."

"And no dope either. Can I trust you?"

"Course you can. I'm your daughter for Chrissake."

"Don't blaspheme."

"You do it."

"Yeah, but I'm a police officer." He walked down the hall and looked in on his youngest. Only times he ever saw Lucy lately she was sleeping. Her room smelled like a little marsupial's cave. He stood in the darkness listening to her soft breathing. For the first nine months of her life they used to worry themselves sick over SIDS, go running to her cot every five minutes. His dusky mouse daughter was the quietest breather he knew. He tested the steel bars on her window. Solid as a rock. Glad now that he'd had them installed. In the bathroom he rifled through the medicine cabinet, checking Gabby's beauty potions. Once a detective, always a detective, she used to say back when they were cohabiting. He urinated in the bowl, examining himself under the fluorescent strip. At primary school he was the only uncircumcised male in the class. Came home one evening after seeing all the Anglo kids in the shower and asked his father if it was too late to have his done. His father leapt from the dinner table brandishing the meat knife, saying, "Boy, I cut it off now." His mother dishing up cevapcici yelled,

"Branco, that's not funny, you'll frighten him!" Dedovic zipped up his memory bag. Families.

With his own daughters he tried to lighten up, not come across as the heavy cop father. You did the best you could with your kids; the rest was up to them. He came out of the bathroom, sat at the table and picked up the phone, the red light on the machine flashing. Relieved that he'd been spared a dawn raid, the humiliation. Giselle floated past, pretending she was busy, when all she really wanted to do was talk. "Did Mum tell you about the rat?"

"What rat?"

"We had a rat." Giselle rubbed at the ends of her flaxen hair with a towel. "Mum said it had to be a rat, because possums don't go under houses."

"When was this?" Dedovic jumped up from the phone table.

"Early this morning."

"Stay here." He ran down the hall, slammed the front door behind him and flew down the steps. In the garage he switched on the light with his left hand, gripping the butt of his Glock pistol with his right. Ran his eyes over the lawnmower, stepladder, the array of rusted garden tools and Lucy's old cot covered in blue plastic sheeting. Nothing out of the ordinary. Ducking his head he went up under the house, scraped his scalp on a beam. At the far wall he dug out the tobacco tin, ripped the lid off and felt the thick bundles of notes with his hands. Four left. He stuffed them into his trouser pockets and shuffled back towards the light. Stood under the naked bulb, straightening his bones and touching the new bump on his head. Sure that someone had been in here. He studied the oil patches on the bare concrete floor, the white electrical cord looping and snaking under the house. Then he saw it on the step, half-filled with a red brownish liquid. He stared at its sharp glistening spike. Carefully, he picked it up with an oil rag, carried it outside and placed the used fit in the glove box of the police vehicle. He locked the car doors and went inside the house.

"Dad, you're tramping mud in everywhere."

He took off his shoes, soles caked with thick yellow clay. "Where's your mother?"

"She went to the movies. Why, what's wrong?"

"I want you to answer me truthfully, Giselle. You ever shoot up?"

"Never."

"Any of your friends inject?"

Giselle shook her head firmly. "No, Dad. Did you find something in the garage? It wasn't a rat?"

"I'm pretty sure it was," he said.

"Did you see it?"

"It's not there at the moment, hon. Looks like we're going to have to set a trap."

"You mean kill it?"

"Why don't you make us a strong coffee, sweetheart. I could really use one and I need to put through a call."

"Dad, I'm not a child. I know you're in big trouble. You can't fool me."

"I wouldn't even try to, Zel." He picked up the receiver, waited until his eldest was in the kitchen. Unsure of who he could trust now. He had to keep his wits about him. The garage door had not been forced, the window didn't open. Either Gabby or the girls had forgotten to latch the roller or some stranger had picked the lock. In the seven years he'd worked the Drug Unit he'd turned over thousands of users. It could be any one of them, but he didn't think so. Sticking your dirty works under a detective's house could only have one desired result. It was meant to really piss him off. He pressed the play button on the machine, heard Ray Doull's flat emotionless voice: *Mate, there's a shark in the bay. It's biting everybody. So take your boat out.* Dedovic touched the twenty grand in his pocket. He'd have to find somewhere safe to deposit his cash. There was still a chance they might hit him at dawn tomorrow, but he was hoping the investigators were after bigger fish than a lowly senior constable. Disco music came on the machine and a man said, *Watch your step, Mr Dedovic. Get the message.*

The tape clicked and rewound; he played it again, trying to pick the muffled voice. He wasn't certain whether this was a threat or a warning. He removed the tape and slipped it in his shirt pocket. Like most detectives he had a silent number. His address wasn't on the electoral roll. There was no way someone from outside could get this close to him. Apart from family, the only people at work that he'd given the Meadowland Avenue number to were Bob Winch, Dick Rainey, Ray Doull and Wai Yi Chen. Even Ray wouldn't be that devious. No, it had to be Kratos. But how did he get this number and why stir up a cop's nest? What good did that do him? There had to be a piece missing. Something he didn't know. He went through into the kitchen and sat at the long round pine table with his yellow fluffy-haired daughter. "Sorry Dad, there's no coffee left. I had to make you tea."

"I hate tea, hon," he said, "but I'll drink it just for you. What time's your mother get home? She ever stayed out this late before?"

"It's only half past nine," Giselle said.

"That's pretty late for a weeknight. Who'd she go to this movie with?"

"Dad, I think it's better if you ask Mum yourself."

"It's her therapist, isn't it? He should be struck off." Dedovic glanced at a new oil painting on the wall: bananas and black cherries in a blue starfish bowl. "I'm going to sleep here tonight on the couch."

"Mum won't like it."

"I'm worried about leaving you and Luce alone."

Giselle said, "It wasn't a rat downstairs, was it? It was a man."

"You get a look at him?"

"No, but I saw a car outside last Tuesday night. Two men staring at our house."

"You sure it was a car. Not a van?"

"I think so, it was dark." Giselle rubbed at her nose. "Why are they investigating you for, Dad? My friends asked me if you were like those police you see on the news."

"Not all cops are bad, Zel, only a very few."

"How do you tell the bad ones?"

"Well, they beat their daughters."

"Dad, I'm not Lucy," she said. "I want an adult answer."

Dedovic reached across the sugar bowl and touched his daughter's hand; it was still warm from the cup she'd been holding. "Sometimes police have to enforce laws that are not very smart, Zel. Sometimes they make mistakes, but mostly they do their best. You don't believe I'd ever do anything bad, do you?"

"No." Giselle played with her teaspoon and saucer. "I just wanted to hear you say it." She stood up and cleared the cups away. Dedovic checked his watch. He'd have to stop by the bachelor flat early, grab a change of clothes. He had no desire to sleep on the hard springless couch, but he couldn't leave his family alone now. Tomorrow he'd ring the local uniforms, get them to keep an eye on the place. He wondered whether he should inform Bob Winch; it depended on where this was coming from. It had to be Kratos; no-one else would have the front. The phone rang and Giselle slipped down the hall before he could stop her. "It's for you, Dad," she said. "Work." He grabbed the receiver out of her hand. "Who is this?"

"Detective Senior Constable Dedovic?" A gruff male voice said.

"Where'd you get this number from?" he demanded.

"I'm Ron Cheers, the Divisional Sergeant from Lane Cove Station. You know a Constable Wai Yi Chen?"

"That's right, why?"

"I'm ringing from the Accident Emergency Unit of the Royal North Shore Hospital. I think you'd better get over here right away, Dedovic."

"Christ," he said. "What's happened?"

"Looks like someone's tried to crack her skull open with a hatchet."

# 26

Turning into Oxford Street, Nickie rolled her window down and let out a great sigh of relief. Finally it was over. Four years they'd been going out and he couldn't commit himself to their relationship. He spent hours examining his own psychological stools. He was heterosexual; he was homosexual. He was happy; he was unhappy. "Look, if you are gay, I can accept that," she said. "I just want to know one way or the other. Do you want a family or not?"

"I can't decide. I need more time."

"I know you're a Libran," she said, "but this is ridiculous." She'd gone out to the Corona and removed the sheepskin seat covers he had given her on their third anniversary. Bundling them under her chin, she stormed up the steps of the large terrace and dumped them on the polished oak boards in the gallery. "There."

"Are you insane?" he said. "You'll get dust everywhere."

She looked around at the drying plaster dugongs trapped in nets, fake seaweed washed up on the floor. Polystyrene mirrors encrusted with fish bones and shark fins, and tiny desiccated sea horses hanging from the walls. She had often imagined herself moving into this 1.3 million dollar house. She loved its wide rooms with their old-fashioned pressed-tin ceilings, Federation fireplaces and rough sandstone walls. His Jersey Road terrace was so huge it made her own tiny place seem like an outhouse. Though legally it wasn't even his. It was still his mother's who kept him waiting for his inheritance like Prince Charles. Forty-three years of age and even the old blue Merc he drove was registered in her name. "It's finished." She stepped over a lump of driftwood. "The relationship's off."

Calmly Garth continued unpacking his colour catalogues. "Fine," he said, "but I hope you're still coming to opening night." Standing there, slightly stooped, with that grey streaked hair and his back towards her as she walked out.

Lightheaded, she drove through Paddington, glancing in the tinted windows of the boutiques. Esprit, Dotti, Attitude. She had never realised that breaking off with someone could be so empowering. A heavy load had been lifted from her shoulders. In a day or two depression would sink in and dark thoughts would circle her pillow but now she was glad to be rid of him. To be on her own. She leaned her head out the window and drank in the night air. Rain glistened on the blacktop like lubricating jelly and people were spilling out of the bookshops and cinemas and coffee houses. Taylor Square buzzed with the roar of cars and voices and boombox music. This was her favourite part of town. Cruising down Oxford Street. Billboards and curved concrete towers rising up to block out the starless sky. Cranes leaned out into space. A lone headlight from the car behind shone in her mirror and she angled the glass away from her eyes. She must have bumped the mirror when she was unhooking those seat covers. The car behind was sticking very close to her. Turning into Wentworth Avenue she stole another look at it. Some kind of early model Chrysler, its single headlamp shining on full beam, its big clunky body drifting into the corner like a river barge. She put her foot down, accelerated through two sets of orange lights, the radio soothing her nerves. A black female voice singing about relationships. This was her third in ten years. At the time she hadn't seen Marcus, Lewton and Garth as failures, but in retrospect that's what they'd been. Maybe her mother was right. Maybe she'd always gone for the wrong type; cold, analytical. She'd wanted a partner to be her intellectual equal, but so many men were frightened of a clever woman. And the ones she liked physically, well most of those you couldn't talk to. Guys like Detective Dedovic. Something about the man she didn't trust.

She pictured his strong hands, his lying blue eyes and pulled on the wheel sharply, steering the Corona back into its proper lane. Twice this evening she'd tried to ring him on his mobile, but her calls were diverted to an answering machine. "You've reached Terry Dedovic at Task Force Jarrah. I'm unavailable at the moment, but if you'd like to leave a message..." Not much good if you were being murdered, Nickie thought. She wanted to talk to him about Ling Ling. She had this idea. Whoever had picked Ling Ling up had to be someone she knew, someone she trusted. She would never have got into a car with a stranger. She was too wary of Western men. No, it had to be some kind of authority figure.

Nickie braked at Cleveland Street and the smell of hot Lebanese bread drifted in her window. Meat was cooking on a rotisserie spit in a kebab house and the aroma of roasted young lamb mingled with the bus fumes. She glanced in her rear-view and saw it right behind her, the Cyclopian headlight. Two people in the front seat, a man driving and beside him a big solid figure with long hair. Nickie jumped the lights, swung down Cleveland, engine straining as she whipped through the gears, shoes digging into the worn rubber mat. Her thoughts skimmed across the surface of her mind. People didn't get followed in real life. Why would anyone follow her? But the Chrysler was still there, two, three cars back. She couldn't miss it in the flow of twin white lights. This was crazy. She'd gone over what had happened to Ling Ling time and time again. Could there be any connection to her own life? Aside from the fact that Ling Ling was her student. The two other victims were Chinese, the papers said. It was all too tenuous. The only possibility she could think of right now was the blond cop. But why would he follow her? He knew where she lived. She headed south along City Road, the dark shapes of fig trees in Victoria Park weighed down with rain, the wet black road slippery under her smooth radials.

Traffic slowed at the bottleneck in Newtown and the smell of curried chicken seeped out of the doorway of a Thai kitchen. She hadn't realised until now how hungry she was. She was tired of the inner city with its sharp edges, harsh concrete surfaces and blaring sounds. Some days it wore her down to the bone. She tried to imagine what sort of person would strangle a nineteen-year-old girl weighing no more than fifty-three kilos. It had to be a man of extreme violence, a man of limited education and great upper-body strength. Someone who could entice a wary non-native speaker into his car in the heart of the city. A man who would blend in anywhere, who Ling Ling would trust.

A police officer.

She checked her mirror and saw the Chrysler moving up fast behind her, its V8 engine rumbling over the top of her Corona's little motor. She felt the hairs standing up on the back of her neck and realised that she was out of her depth. With a wrench of the wheel, she turned into Silver Street and braked outside her house. She ran up the steps, keyed open her front door and deadlocked it behind her. Threw the chain on the latch. In the front room she prised open the cedar slats and watched as the Chrysler pulled to a halt in the shadows across the street, its exhaust clouded with blue smoke, its long aerial quivering. The headlight switched off and the driver's door opened with a creak. A man climbed out and stood there on the roadway looking up towards her window.

The blond-haired cop. Terry MacIntyre.

She grabbed the phone off the couch and dialled Task Force Jarrah. "Detective Dedovic," she breathed into the mouthpiece.

"Dedovic ain't in. Call back tomorra morning."

"It's urgent."

"Yeah," the bored male voice said. "Well, you could try his mobile, if he ever switched the damn thing on. What's up?"

"My name's Nickie Taroney. I've been followed."

"Look, I'll try and page him. Want me to send a squad car over?"

Nickie hesitated, listening for a sound outside. "No," she said. "Just get him to ring me at home. Soon as he can." She hung up the receiver. She was tired and hungry and she'd had enough of being scared. Footsteps scraped on her front step and knuckles rapped on wood. She went and stood in the dark hallway, determined to face this coward on her own. "What do you want?" she called out.

His voice came muffled through the door. "Need to talk to yer."

"I've called the police," she said. "Go away!"

He banged with his fist.

She switched on the porch light. Through the dimpled glass she could see his blurred yellow shape standing there on her property, holding something dark in his right hand. "You got me all wrong," he said.

"Get off my porch!"

"I got somethin here for yer."

She could hear his slurred consonants. That aggressive male tone. Anger burned inside her at this man, that he could impinge on her life like this. She saw herself running to the stove and boiling a pan of hot water, grabbing the sharpest knife from the drawer ready to stab him in the liver. She was not going to hide in her own house. She was not going to be bullied. Trembling, Nickie unhooked the chain. She could feel her breath coming in short shallow bursts; she gripped the knob with her fingers, hesitated for a long second, then stepped back and threw open the door.

# 27

Above the ambulance bay, red neon letters a metre high spelled out the word EMERGENCY. Dedovic pulled into a handicapped space and jumped out of the police car, walked across to the two uniformed police officers smoking near the doorway. "I'm Wai Yi Chen's partner," he said to the senior sergeant.

"Go on through, mate, she's in a right bloody mess."

The electronic doors slid open and Dedovic strode across the green lino, his eyes flicking over a row of wheelchairs and white towels piled high in metal baskets. A sign on the desk instructed him to turn off his pager and mobile. He checked that they were shut down and flashed his ID at the triage nurse who waved him through to the Resuscitation Room. A nurse's aide rushed past carrying a bundle of goo-stained towels and a cleaner in a green uniform was vigorously mopping up blood and other fluids from beneath the trauma bed. Dedovic had the feeling that he'd come in at the end of something hectic. A short athletic man in a pale blue surgical gown approached him, peeling off a pair of transparent latex gloves.

"You the doctor?" The guy was handsome and freckled with sun-blond hair swept back off his forehead. "I'm Terry Dedovic from Task Force Jarrah. How is she?"

The doctor rubbed at his fingertips; they were wet and wrinkled at the nails. He shepherded Dedovic over to a pair of stools beside the phone. "Okay," he said. "Here's the situation." He leaned in close, using his hands as aids to help him explain. "She's been intubated and ventilated and we've just scanned her. The CT shows an extradural haematoma. That means there's blood in between the skull and the brain."

Dedovic listened carefully.

"She's got a very severe head injury with skull fractures, bleeding within the skull leading to compression of the brain tissue and possible loss of nerve tissue. Her condition has stabilised but our main priority right now is the bleeding."

Dedovic watched the doctor's hands move together.

"The skull is like a box, so we have a very confined space and nowhere for that blood to go. We're going to drill in two burr holes to relieve the pressure."

"When can I see her?"

"The trauma team are preparing Ms Chen for surgery now. She's heavily sedated." The doctor slid off his stool, checked his watch as if he'd already wasted too much time. A grey-haired nurse came through the twin plastic doors and nodded at him urgently.

Dedovic grabbed the doctor's elbow. "If she survives," he said, "will there be any permanent damage?"

"We can't be certain, Detective. We won't be able to assess any neurological sequelae for several days." And turning on his heels, the doctor hurried out of the Resuscitation Room.

Dedovic stood there for a moment with his fingers pressed against the bridge of his nose. If Chen died he'd wear this on his conscience for the rest of his life. He'd warned her about taking unnecessary risks, but he shouldn't have let her play detective on her own. It was all this other business. He hadn't slept right in weeks. His mind wasn't on the job. If she'd been attacked out in Cabramatta he might have expected it, but Artarmon was safe middle-class suburbia. She must've stumbled onto something connected with the murder inquiry, IDed the man they were searching for. Chen had been certain that the Artarmon area was the offender's home ground; it looked like she was right on the money.

He strode past the triage nurse out into the busy ambulance bay. Paramedics and uniformed police officers milled around Senior Sergeant Ron Cheers who was arguing on his mobile. "Wake the prick. Get him out of bed, I don't care who he's with." He looked up at Dedovic. "Seen her?"

"She's gone under the knife."

"Well, she weren't a pretty sight I can tell you. Two skateboarders heard screams, went to investigate and found her lying in the tunnel at Artarmon station with half her scalp hanging off." Cheers chewed his lip. "Blood everywhere."

"They find the weapon?"

"Right beside her toes. One of those little hatchets. Brand new, $5.95 sticker on the handle. Diamond Brand. Made in China."

Dedovic held his breath.

"Yeah, yeah, okay, rightyo, Cole." Cheers took the mobile away from his ear. "Police Rescue have been called in to do a line search. Video Unit's at the crime scene now. We got every man and dog combing those bushes."

"Skateboarders see anything?"

"One kid saw a man but the other kid said it could've been a woman. Usual fuckin story. About as helpful as a poke in the eye with a burnt pin."

"How'd you get hold of me?" Dedovic asked.

Ron Cheers rubbed at his fat, freshly shaved neck. His skin was pink and smooth and apart from the spiky grey eyebrows there was not a hint of hair on his glabrous head. "Found her notebook. Had your number innit and a bunch of others. Rang 'em all, except the Chinese names. Leave that to your CI."

"I want to take a look in that notebook."

"Forensic Services took everything at the scene, backpack, clothes, hatchet, even her service revolver. That's when we twigged she was one of ours."

"Was it fired?"

"Never even got it out of the bumbag."

"Her mobile," Dedovic said. "Check if she made any calls in the last hour." He glanced at the long white vehicle pulling into the hospital car park, Dick Rainey behind the wheel of a Ford Fairlane LTD. Two shapes in the back seat. The LTD parked in the ambulance bay and Bob Winch climbed out with an older man wearing a peppermint green blazer. Chief Superintendent Darcy Clout, District Commander of the Sydney Region for the NSW Police Service.

"Shit." Dedovic shifted his feet, eyes flicking around nervously as the two senior officers strode towards him.

"What the hell's going on, Dedovic? You're supposed to be her partner. Where were you? What was Chen doing dressed up in that ridiculous Ken Done outfit?"

"Off duty, sir. She was going home in her normal city apparel."

"Bullshit." Winch stepped right into his face. "She was working a lead and you let her drift without a line.

I know you Dedovic. I know your fucking reputation. You've been running around town with bad meat for years and you wonder why there's an awful stink sticking to your shoes. Well not on my squad. You don't let a team member down, you don't let 'em get their fucking head chopped off."

The Inspector's finger prodded his chest and Dedovic stepped back instinctively, rolling his neck from side to side. He imagined ripping a short hard right in under the man's rib cage. He felt bad enough about Ida without Winch adding to his load. Warm spittle showered his cheek and he thought of his childhood, the old man blowing up like this time and time again. Paramedics standing by the ambulances were watching open-mouthed as Bob Winch went off his head, his lips quivering, his face boiled red, the words *fucking idiot* used three times in two staccato sentences.

"Alright Bob." Chief Superintendent Clout stepped forward. "The lad's been given a decent bake."

Dedovic breathed out. A pair of alert black eyes studied him intelligently from a craggy sandstone face. On the District Commander's green blazer pocket was stitched President RBBC and underneath that a smiling bowling ball. "What's the prognosis, Senior Constable?"

"Serious head injury, sir, penetrating into brain substance. I just talked to the emergency specialist. She might not pull through."

"Detective Constable Chen's an extraordinarily brave police officer. No doubt she was acting on an anonymous tip-off to attend the Artarmon area?"

"Sir?"

"Quite possibly made a significant breakthrough into a major murder investigation." The DC tugged at a large leathery ear. "Media been notified?"

"Not yet, sir."

Clout turned to his Chief Inspector. "Get onto them, Bob. We've got a female officer from a non-English-speaking background badly injured in the line of duty. I think Constable Chen deserves all the approbation this city can bestow on her. Now let's have a word with this RMO chap."

Winch turned to Dedovic and spoke through the side of his clenched teeth, "My office. Tomorrow. Eight a.m. sharp," then followed Chief Superintendent Clout, Sergeant Ron Cheers and two uniformed female officers through the electronic doors of the Emergency Unit. A paramedic blinked his eyes and snapped into action, stowing a stretcher in the back end of a red and white checked ambulance. Dedovic rubbed the ball of his thumb into the bony part of his neck and shook his legs until the muscles in his thighs stopped twitching. He never should have left Chen there all alone. She was onto something, but he couldn't see it. He was just growing to like his pocket-sized partner and now she was going to end up a vegetable. He stared at a lone casuarina in the car park, its delicate foliage weighed down with drops of water. The sky overhead was as black as tar and the lights of the city glowed like a fire in the distance.

Dick Rainey sidled alongside and leaned a stocky shoulder on one of the metal poles supporting the ambulance bay. He offered his pack of Longbeach 40s, struck a match and cupped both hands under Dedovic's chin. The two men smoked in silence, staring above the carpark at the smudged night sky. "Thought you were going to drop Winchless cold there, Vic. Fair dinkum, he was way out of line. You don't carry on like that in front of the ambos."

Dedovic breathed out smoke, sparks falling from his fingers.

"Got to hand it to Darcy stepping in. He's a canny old Scot. Survive anything, that old boy."

"I let her down badly, Dick. I was the senior investigator. I should've looked after the kid."

"Don't blame yourself, mate. She went off on her own steam. It's not a job for lone rangers, it's a team effort. You know that."

"She was one of the best partners I've had."

"Hey, Vic, don't be like that," Rainey said. "You know I couldn't afford to have Integrity tailing me round. When they're off your back, we'll team up again. You and me, mate. Like the good old days."

"When were they?" Dedovic said. He extinguished his cigarette with a hiss against the wet pole. "Why don't you give Wendy Lee a buzz? Get her over here. She'd appreciate the scoop."

Dick Rainey looked over one shoulder nervously. "God help me, Vic, don't say a word to anybody. I just got carried away that night."

"She's an attractive woman, Dick."

"Mate, she's gorgeous. Bad Catholic girls – I can't say no to them. Talking of which," he said, "I fielded a phone call for you tonight. That little Greek piece you brought into the pub, one with the Mediterranean hair and those big brown eyes. Well she rang. Actually there were a couple of callers. Some cop wanting your home number."

"Which cop?"

"That drunk MacIntyre. Didn't give it to him. Told him to go ring information."

"Nickie Taroney – what she want?"

"That's the one, yeah. Said she was being followed. Would you give her a buzz at home. Soon as you could."

"How long ago was this?" Dedovic snapped.

"Half hour maybe. Was trying to get hold of you when all this other fucking drama broke."

Dedovic moved across the bitumen. Coloured streetlights were strung together over the hospital entrance and his shoes crunched on broken glass. He could feel the damp night air cutting through the thin cotton fabric of his shirt. He worked the mobile out of his jacket pocket and jabbed at the buttons with his right thumb. By the time he reached the car door her phone was already ringing.

# 28

Nickie saw him framed in the porch light, a lick of blond hair dangling rockabilly style over his narrowed eyes, thick wet lips and a chin that was starting to slide into fat. He was wearing a white rugby top with sweat stains under both arms, blue track pants with a Puma cat on the left thigh and paint splotched Reeboks. She hadn't seen him this closely since that night in the small seedy Newtown bar. Her eyes didn't leave his face, determined that whatever he did she'd be able to pick him out of a line-up. She felt a sudden anger flare inside her at this beefy individual. He stepped towards her, angling something sharp at her breast. "Here," he grunted. "This belongs to your friend."

She looked down at the black leather wallet. "Where'd you get that?"

"Take it."

"No," she said. "That's evidence."

"What are you talking about, evidence?"

A big solid figure was watching her from the passenger's window of the Chrysler and something moved in the back seat. "You stole it," she said. "Now you're trying to return it. Well it won't work."

"Listen," he said. "There's been a misunnerstaning." He leaned forward and she could smell a stale beery odour. "They caught this woman at the Prince Hotel. She was trying to pass off a man's gold Mastercard in the bottle shop. The publican rang me."

"What woman?"

"This Abo woman. Been drinking steadily in there for a month."

"That's a lie. I know that woman."

"Told me she found your friend's wallet on the bar floor. Reckon'd she was going to hand it in when she got round to it. No cash left, but the plastic's all here. You can press charges if you like."

"I don't believe you," Nickie said.

"Ask the publican."

"You broke into my house and stole my tape. I saw you."

"I never broke in nowhere," he said. "I was coming over to return this wallet. Saw your door wide open so I investigated and then rang the station, but I don't know nothing about a tape."

Nickie looked at him, her fists resting on her hips. She was not going to be fooled. "What about the phone calls?" she said. "I know you made them, because I recognise your voice."

"Okay, okay, so I made a couple of calls. I've been under stress."

The same broad, fast delivery, that aggressive tone.

"Do you think it's proper that a policeman should ring up a citizen, threaten her over the telephone –"

"No, it was stupid. I regret it now."

"Then send an ambulance round to her home?"

"Look, I didn't want to lose me job –"

"Do you think it's right that a policeman should expose himself in public?"

"I . . . I've been going through a real hard time. The doctor's got me on medication."

"You don't have much of a future in the police service do you, Mr MacIntyre?" Nickie said. She watched him turn away and lean his weight on her iron railing. She saw his shoulders heave and at first didn't comprehend what was happening. Only when she heard the extraordinary sound resonating from his throat did she realise.

He was sobbing like a seal.

Nickie felt the anger dwindle inside her. She had never witnessed anything like this before. The low choking noise he was making as he gripped her rail. She reached out a hand towards his bobbing shoulder and then drew it back, uncertain of what to do. The Chrysler door creaked open and a bulky woman climbed out, tousled brown hair falling to her shoulders. From the back seat she picked up a child and clasping it to her breast walked across the road, up the front steps and put her arm around MacIntyre's waist. "Honey,'" she said softly. "C'mon, honey. Let's go home."

The little boy was no more than three with pale pinched cheeks and his breathing was laboured. Nickie waited for the woman to explain herself, but she simply guided her big lump of a man down the steps onto the footpath. "The wallet," he said brokenly. "Give her the wallet."

A jet approaching from the west grew louder and louder and flew low and fast over the chimney tops as if it was striving to beat the curfew. Its blinking tail lights illuminated the front yards and the sash windows in Nickie's house rattled. The woman was saying something to the man. She came up the steps. She had thick padded arms with small tapered hands like flippers. She held out Garth's wallet and Nickie hesitated.

"You must excuse him," the woman said. "He's not a bad man. Since we moved down to the city, things haven't turned out right for us. Our little boy has a rare blood disorder and every day's been a struggle . . . "

Nickie took the wallet. She wanted to help, she wanted to invite them in, do something concrete. Saliva was running down the front of the woman's blouse from where the child's mouth was pressed against her breast. She said, "Could I make you a pot of tea? I've got apple juice."

"No, no," the woman said, embarrassed. "We have to go."

Nickie watched from her porch as they walked over to their clunky Chrysler, got in, MacIntyre's head cupped in his hands, his wife behind the wheel, the child harnessed in the back. The phone was ringing, but Nickie ignored it. She went inside and sat on her couch. She had never seen a policeman cry before. It wasn't a pretty sight. She wondered if he was telling the truth. She didn't believe him about the Koori woman, felt sure he was covering for somebody else. She got up and walked over to the wooden cassette rack, ran her fingers over Beethoven, Mozart, Vivaldi. In between Jane Rutter and Patsy Cline she found the tape lying on its side. *Asking People to Do Things*. How the hell had she missed that sitting on her shelf? She must've knocked it over when she was cleaning. She touched the plastic sleeve as if she doubted her own eyes. Her mind was spinning. At the very least she'd have to withdraw the complaint she'd filed. Constable MacIntyre needed treatment, but it looked like he hadn't broken in. She'd convinced herself that he was responsible for Ling Ling's murder. It just seemed so perfect for the killer to be a cop. Now she didn't know what to think. The doorbell rang and she hurried to answer it. There was only one person it could be.

Detective Dedovic was standing on her porch wearing a rumpled grey suit and that same green tie with the long-necked dinosaurs roaming over it. Soon as she saw him she felt her heart jump. She stared at his hard city features, the broken bridge of his nose, those deep-blue eyes and saw none of the weakness she had seen in MacIntyre's face.

Detective Dedovic was in a different league altogether.

"Got your call," he said. "Whassup?"

Firing the words at her through a half-closed mouth. She wondered what criminals thought of him, had the feeling that most men would be wary. She led him into her front room without responding. She could sense something was wrong; his tie was pulled away from his throat, his eyes were bloodshot and the skin stretched over his cheekbones was dry and lined. A smell of antiseptic clung to his clothes; Nickie wondered whether he had come directly to her from some ugly crime scene. She said, "I had a visitor."

"MacIntyre huh?"

Watching his reaction while she blurted out her story. She wasn't telling it well. She tried to describe the animal sound and heard him mutter the word, "pathetic". His mouth was curled up at the corners as if he'd swallowed a bad oyster.

"Don't you feel sorry for him?"

"Guy's a grub and a drunk." Dedovic shook his head with disgust. "Sooner he's dismissed the better." He rubbed at his jaw with a large restless hand; the rims of his nails were milky white. Nickie watched his hands closely as he tried to settle them, pressing them against the gold buckle of his belt. She remembered her masseuse telling her that a person's hands represent what they want. She felt her heart beating in her chest, the blood rushing through her veins. He was standing right in front of her, eyes roving around her walls.

"Any news?" she said.

"Nuh." His tone was distant. Like something heavy was weighing on his mind. She wanted him to touch her, to run his fingers across her skin.

"Wild beasts," he said.

"Pardon?"

"The Fauves." Staring up at her Vlaminck poster on the wall. "Always liked 'em."

"About that dinner you offered. I've given it some thought."

Detective Dedovic nodded.

"And I'm ready to eat."

# 29

Driving through the city with the smell of vinyl clinging to her bucket seat and the black road hurtling past her window. She had never been in a police vehicle before. She could feel the power of its special V6 engine, the buzz of excitement as if she had stepped out of her own quiet life into something more dramatic. The Philips radio crackled. God, was she hungry. She hadn't eaten since lunchtime. "Will there be anywhere open at this hour?"

"I know of a little place," Dedovic said out the side of his mouth. "Friend recommended it."

"A police friend?" she asked. She had the feeling that Detective Dedovic wouldn't have too many friends outside of work. He pulled into a bus zone a hundred metres from the corner of William Street. Yellow lights shimmered from the top floors of luxury hotels. Well-dressed couples were sitting behind plate glass staring out at the nightlife on the streets.

"Do you like fish?" he said.

"Not much, no."

"You're kidding," he said. "I love fish."

"I thought you loved meat?"

"Meat, fish, I'm not exclusive."

She realised he was the kind of man who liked to control the car, the food, the evening. Normally she would have protested, but tonight she was riding a wave and she didn't care where it landed. She watched Dedovic attach a blue and white police sticker to the front of the unmarked Federation green Commodore and followed him through the glass doors. Sirens were singing in the distance. A teenage waiter came up to them shaking his head and Dedovic had a word in the boy's ear. The waiter ran down and spoke to another man in the open kitchen. "What's the problem?" she asked.

"No problem," Dedovic said. The waiter and the older man came back, smiling, and guided them to a table. A second waiter produced a menu and wine list while a waiting couple in black stared resentfully from the bar.

"You know the owners here?" she asked.

"Never set foot in the place."

There was a dark aura hanging over his head, his big hands twisting at a red serviette while waiters bobbed like corks around them. When they were alone, Nickie said, "Something's happened tonight hasn't it?"

"What makes you think that?" Downing his wine like water.

"Those other murdered students," she said. "Were they strangled too?"

"I can't reveal that information."

"I don't know how to take you, Detective."

"Call me Terry," he said.

"One minute it's all jokes and laughs, then you shut down. I want to help find out who did this to Ling Ling."

"We always welcome assistance from the general public."

"But you're not going to tell me anything, are you?"

"I wish I could."

"When MacIntyre was following me tonight, I thought maybe he was involved in these murders somehow. Ling Ling was a very cautious young woman, she would never have gone off with just anyone. It had to be a person she'd trust. Who better than a police officer?"

"But you don't think that any more?"

"No," she said, "not after tonight." She watched Detective Dedovic squeeze lemon over his grilled baby octopus with cracked black pepper. The couple at the bar were still staring at them and Nickie wondered if it was because she was wearing jeans. The place was packed with suits and pearls.

"I ran a check on MacIntyre," Dedovic said. "He stands up. Unfortunately he's just one of those cops who should be in another line of work. Hey," he said, "what are we talking about this stuff for?"

He filled her glass to the brim.

Nickie could feel the blood pulsing in her neck. Men were so unsubtle. He didn't need to get her drunk. All he had to do was reach out with those well-made hands and stroke her arms.

"So why don't you eat fish?" he said.

"Oh look, it's a long story." She played with her salad. Rocket with shavings of parmesan and vine-ripened tomatoes. "If you tell me about this investigation," she said. "I'll tell you about the fish."

"You don't give up, do you?" He guided a white boney piece of octopus to the edge of his plate. "Okay," he said. "But none of this is to go any further."

Nickie smiled at him across the table, took a sip of wine. "I grew up in a tiny fishing town just south of Ulladulla. My father owned..." She stopped.

The couple in black were coming over towards them. The woman had a determined look in her eye and was clutching a glossy theatre program. "We've been waiting here for an hour," she said. "You jumped the queue."

Nickie blinked at her, mouth full of lettuce.

"You stole our table," the woman said. People were staring at them.

Dedovic turned to the man. He had a little horseshoe of grey hair, red framed glasses and looked like a banker. "You're not from Darlinghurst," he said in a quiet firm voice. "So why don't you take your wife back to the bar and buy her another drink?" He hooked the flap of his jacket open with a thumb. "There'll be a table along shortly."

The man gripped his wife's arm and led her quietly back to their stools.

"Do you always flash your holster like that?" Nickie said.

"Actually it was my handcuffs. I find they have a stronger psychological effect on the public. People don't believe you'll shoot them, but they sure have a fear of being cuffed," he said. "Now you were saying, your father had a fish and chip shop, right?"

"No," Nickie felt her face blush. "He owned two fishing boats." All along she'd suspected that Detective Dedovic had stereotyped her as a Greek girl from the corner takeaway. "My father came from Skiros," she said, "but my mother is fifth-generation Australian."

"Look, I didn't mean any ethnic slur. We're all wogs deep down. My mother's from Serbia and my father's a Croat. They used to get on like a house on fire. I grew up in East St Kilda and then moved here when I was twenty. Joined the force. A lot of my Sydney friends still call me Vic."

"Is that right?" She looked at him sideways.

"Yeah, I'm a Melbourne boy at heart." He began skilfully removing the flesh from his freshly grilled snapper as if his main intention was to get to the skeleton underneath.

"How did those other girls die?" Nickie asked.

Dedovic gripped the fork in his right hand, his left hand busy with the wine glass. "Mo Ching Wan was suffocated with a plastic bag. Lin Lu Pei was stabbed and then strangled with her own underwear..." His voice trailed off.

"All three students were sexually assaulted?"

Dedovic nodded. "One involved genital intercourse and the other two involved penetration with a blunt object. If my Inspector found out I was discussing this investigation with you I'd be dismissed."

"I appreciate you talking to me, Terry."

"There's a lot of pressure on p'lice right now. We're expected to get down in the sewer but still come up smelling of violets."

There was a long silence before he asked, "So how's your pasta?"

"The tortellini's good. They've used real spinach. What about forensic evidence?"

"Negligible," he said. "Mostly non-specific clothing fibres. No semen. A small amount of foreign DNA material was found under the fingernails of Lin Lu Pei and Kua Ling Ling. Forensic tried to compare it using the latest STR technique but the match was weak. A lot of guys in law enforcement think DNA profiling is foolproof. Me, I'd rather have a signed confession. You get one expert in the box contradicted by a second expert for the defence. We consulted two of the leading forensic psychologists in the country for a profile in this case. Both from Melbourne. Only thing they could agree upon was that this bastard is likely to strike again."

Dedovic pushed his plate away with his hands, the white cleaned bones of the snapper sitting like a perfectly formed fossil on the blue china plate. Nickie was amazed at how quickly he'd finished eating.

"Most people don't realise what the bulk of p'lice work entails. You're tapping on doors, you're talking to people, you're wearing out the shoe leather. So far we've checked and cross-checked the alibis of every sex offender in this state. We've interviewed over two thousand people, searched more than a thousand houses and residences . . ."

Nickie played with her ear-shaped pasta. "What's wrong?" she said.

He was twisting the silver foil from the garlic bread in his big slow hands and rolling his shoulders as if something heavy was troubling him.

"Has something happened?"

Dedovic looked across at her with those harbour-blue eyes. He pressed down on the table. "You know that little Chinese cop come in with me to the college?"

Nickie remembered.

"She was attacked tonight with a hatchet. Multiple skull fractures. She's in a critical condition at Royal North Shore right now."

"Was it the same–"

"Odds on it was," he said. "Chen's a good little investigator, she's smart, cluey. I let her trail off on her own."

Nickie went to say something, but Dedovic shook his head as if he only wanted her to listen. "When I joined up I was like her. Keen as punch. Everything's black and white at first and then the edges blur and there's no longer any lines to tell you where to walk."

Nickie nodded, unsure of what he was saying. His hands had stopped moving. She reached out and touched the back of one. "It's not your fault."

Dedovic jerked away like he'd been bitten. "I'm sorry for dumping on you like this," he said. "Aren't you going to finish that pasta?"

"I don't think I can eat any more. You want it?"

"Na, I never eat off a woman's plate on the first date."

"So this is a date?" Nickie asked.

"Either that or you're filling in for my psychiatrist," he said. "Nothing worse than going out with someone who whinges over dinner all evening."

"I understand how you must feel. You worked with her."

"How about I get the bill?" he said. Shaking his head at himself.

"We're going to split this."

"I like a liberated woman but I owe you a meal." He raised a hand in the air.

Nickie glanced at the other diners. Black cocktail dresses, black jackets and white T-shirts. People were still queueing at the bar and diners were lingering over coffee as if the importance of this place was not to eat, but to be seen. She tried to read the bill as Dedovic took out a thick wad of fifties, counted four notes off and tucked them under the saucer. "Well, thanks for that," she said. "Now I guess I'll have to sleep with you."

He looked at her sharply.

"Only joking."

They stood up and the theatre couple at the bar leapt off their rocket stools. In the car she wished she hadn't tried to be funny. Maybe he didn't find her so attractive. She was thirty-four and he was what – thirty-seven, thirty-eight? Maybe he only liked teenagers. He'd liked Mona alright, she knew that. She smelled the vinyl and stale cigarette odour in the police car. The streets of Darlinghurst were quiet as if only the well-off and the homeless could afford to be out this late. They drove in silence through the sleeping city, her body sending out urgent messages, the blood in her throat beating so fast and so loud she was sure he could hear it. She watched him out of the corner of her eye, brooding over his Chinese detective while he gripped the wheel. She wanted him to touch her, to wrap his arms around her tight. She wanted to make him forget everything.

"I love the city," he said.

"Pardon?"

"I love the city." He was looking up through the top half of the windscreen. "I love concrete."

"Nobody loves concrete," she said.

"I do, I love the smell of the cars, the coloured lights, the whole box and dice."

She wondered whether he was trying to be poetic or whether he was just a little stupid. She didn't mind that so much in a man. There were far worse things. He pulled up outside her door, kept the V6 engine running, the twin headlights shining down Silver Street making the trees and poles look sinister. She didn't know whether to invite him inside or not. What if he said no? She could smell his skin, the Aramis cologne he wore, a faint fish-oil smell on his breath. The police radio crackled. She hesitated, her left hand touching the plastic door handle. He was waiting on her to say something. She cracked open the door, turned her head towards him and said in a flat, dispassionate voice, "Would you like to come in?"

He looked at her obliquely. "I thought you were never going to ask." And switched off the engine.

# 30

Planes woke him early, streaming overhead at intervals of two, three minutes, each with its own distinct sound. He lay on his side listening to the whines and roars and rumbles. The only ones he could pick were the jumbos. They really rocked the roof. He wondered how long a person could live here with the noise. He slipped out of bed and barefooted it down the stairs. It was dark inside the tiny terrace and he had to use the electric light to wash her smell from his hands. In her cabinet he found a stick of shaving cream and a blade that looked like it had been out of work for some time. He cut his face in a few places and bled into the bowl. The blood thinned and chased the cold water down the drain. It was not a fluffy bathroom, he was glad of that, it was spare, practical, with diamond-blue tiles and a bath large enough to stretch your limbs. He cleaned up his mess, carefully wiping down the basin and all the items he had disturbed. The stairs groaned under his weight as if they had been used to a much lighter step. Her thick black hair was sprawled across the pillow, her body perfectly still underneath the sheets.

He dressed quickly, in a hurry to get away, throwing on his holster and suit jacket. His shirt smelled of yesterday. Downstairs he checked the front room carefully, patted his coat pockets. His eyes swept over her furniture, the bolt on the window, the steel chain on the front door. Outside the sun warmed the terraces on the western side of the street. The rain had ceased and the bitumen had gone from black to light grey as if it had been stone-washed. Her side of the street was still in shadow and he got into the Commodore quickly without being seen by any of the neighbours and peeled away from the kerb, doing seventy, seventy-five along the Princes Highway, nobody out except a few early morning hackers and a clanging fruit-juice truck. He switched his pager on, thinking about Chen, whether she'd been able to give a description of her attacker. Wai Yi was certainly a lot tougher than he'd given her credit for.

On Broadway he stopped by the flat. A four-storey warehouse that had been converted into two hundred and seventy-five lock-up units. Ray Doull had got him a very good price on a north-facing one-bedroom apartment from a realtor acquaintance who owed him a big favour. The place was clean, close to the CBD and secure. There was only one drawback. Dedovic rode the lift to the third floor; his unit still smelled faintly of paint and silicon sealant. Windows looked down towards the rising city. He changed his shirt and suit and put on a fresh blue tie, checked the messages on the machine. A familiar voice said: "Ring me, two o'clock today. Urgent."

Dedovic wiped the message. He was not getting involved in that. He knew what Doull wanted him to do and he wasn't doing it. The risks were too high. Downstairs he passed an Asian woman struggling with four bags of airport luggage and two tiny children. He held the security door for her. She thanked him in

Mandarin or Cantonese, he wasn't sure what. So far he had not met a single person who spoke English in the apartments. The two hundred and seventy-four other units had all been sold off-the-plan to Malaysian, Indonesian and Chinese investors. The city was changing at a frenetic pace, buildings going up and buildings coming down, and a Detective Senior Constable had to be very careful not to get caught between the bricks. He fired a call through to the hospital and asked the ICU nurse for any news on Detective Wai Yi Chen. She was still under sedation, the nurse said, and they didn't expect her to regain consciousness for several hours. He had a bad feeling about this. He had to get out there, start doorknocking, see if the local police had compiled an image.

The City of Sydney station was packed. Every member of Task Force Jarrah had been called in as well as additional units from the Dog squad and Rescue. Dedovic squeezed between a bunch of younger leather-jacketed constables and went into Winch's office. The TF Commander gestured at him with a finger to shut the door and stood up, banging the edge of his desk as if Dedovic was about to cop another blast. Dark folds of skin hung under Bob Winch's eyes. It was common knowledge on the fifth floor that when Jarrah had been created under the Crime Commission Act, after ten attacks on Asian students and the murder of Mo Ching Wan, Winch had seen his appointment as Commander of this politically sensitive investigation as a direct stepping stone to a District Command. Eleven months down the track with three dead foreign students and a critically injured officer on his plate, things weren't looking so hot for the Chief Inspector. One thing Dedovic knew for sure was that someone was going to have to take the fall.

Winch leaned across his desk. "Last night, what went down between us two."

Dedovic stood by the pedestal fan, waiting for the shit to fly.

"Let's put that behind us, Senior Constable. There's no doubt now in my mind that Constable Chen was responding to an anonymous tip-off and wandered off on her own bat."

"Sir, is this some kind of apology?"

"We've all been under enormous pressure these past few months, Dedovic. This attack may be just the breakthrough we've been waiting for. We've got some good information coming in of the AK being seen last night at Artarmon station."

Dedovic stared at his Chief Inspector's bloodhound jowls and long pointed nose. Detectives who had worked with him over the years swore black and blue that Bob Winch could smell out a criminal in a crowded room.

"Sir, I'm real keen to get out to Artarmon. Start working on this."

"No doubt Constable Chen was onto something. She's exhibited extraordinary courage, despite her inexperience. But I want you to go back to that English College. Talk to the teachers, students, management–"

"We've already talked to them, sir."

"Then talk to them again. Everyone from the cleaners up. Take their statements." Winch tapped his needle nose. "We're going to crack this bastard wide open."

"Sir, I'd prefer to work directly on the Chen assault."

"Is there something bothering you, Dedovic?"

"No sir."

"You're not running your own race here are you?"

Dedovic shook his head firmly.

"Good, because this a team effort. There's no individual players in my squad. We work as a unit, investigators get assigned a task and they go do it." Winch lowered himself back into his chair. "Well, what are you waiting for?"

Dedovic touched the black notebook wrapped in a plastic exhibit sleeve on the edge of the Commander's desk. "Is this Constable Chen's?"

Winch looked at him.

"Do you mind if I take a copy?"

"You read Chinese, Dedovic?"

"No sir, not a word."

"Well, that's why we're getting it translated. Seems Constable Chen liked to write things down with Chinese characters." Winch picked up the phone and with a tilt of his hand indicated the existence of the door.

In the squadroom plain-clothes detectives and uniformed police were filing towards the lifts, an air of excitement in the echo of their hurried footsteps. Dedovic sat at his desk and pushed his mouse around. For some reason he was being deliberately excluded from the Chen investigation. Winch was sending him out on a wild fucking goose chase. A yellow Post-it note with Ray Doull's home phone number and a message was stuck to the edge of his monitor: *Ring me*. He screwed it up in his fist and palmed it into the basket. Someone had once told Dick Rainey that women liked the scent of cologne on a man and he had taken that advice to heart. Dedovic could smell him coming down the corridor like a human stick of Old Spice. "You know what's going on here?"

"Nah." Rainey shook his head. "Secret women's business. They still got me on tent pegs. Been out to every camping store in this city."

Dedovic glanced around. The place was quieter

than a morgue. Through the glass partition he could see Bob Winch talking excitedly on the phone. "Something's happening."

"Nobody trusts nobody these days, Vic. You got more investigators watching the investigators than you got watching the crims."

"This has to do with you doesn't it, Rainey? You and your big dick. Winch's got it into his head that one of us two breached security. I oughta fill in him on who's been pillowtalkin'–"

"Vic, you promised to keep that under your chin. Wendy's getting a personal briefing from them anyway. They want her onside now. She gave me the flick this morning, no more egg McMuffins for breakfast."

Dedovic spotted a cop he knew vaguely from the old Scientific Investigation Section going into Winch's office. "A sad story, Dick. Is that a new flyspray you're wearing?"

"Nah, just the Old Spice. You don't like it?"

"No, I do. It's . . . it's strong."

"Wendy says she'll always think of me whenever she smells this."

Dedovic got up and walked across to the young constable emerging from the CI's office. "Ballistic, before you go. I need a copy of that."

The Scientific squad constable turned around, holding the police notebook in its plastic sleeve. "The Chief Inspector didn't mention it."

"Probably forgot," Dedovic said. "There's a machine down the corridor. Run me off a copy while I duck downstairs. I got something for the lab." He went down the lift to the squad car, opened the glove box and, careful not to spike his fingers, wrapped the used fit in the oil cloth and carried it back upstairs where he placed it in a double plastic exhibit bag and handed it to the young expert. "Get this checked for prints and have the contents analysed."

"Looks like blood to me." The Scientific squad constable peered through the blurry plastic. "You filled out a form?"

"This is a personal matter."

"Still got to fill out a form."

"Ballistic, do me a favour. Take this over to the lab, phone me with the results by two o'clock today and I'll owe you a big one."

Squinting, the young constable scratched his pear-shaped head. "A big what?"

At his desk Dedovic copied the microcassette onto a high-quality Sony tape, played it on a listening device machine that reduced the background distortion. *Watch your step, Mr Dedovic. Get the message.* He could make out the Bee Gees singing "Staying Alive" and was pretty certain the voice in the foreground belonged to Steve Bia. He listened to it again keeping one eye on Bob Winch's office and ignoring the persistent queries from the neighbouring desk. "Whatcha doing there, Vic? This to do with the AK case?"

"I'm moonlighting."

"Uh huh." Dick Rainey nodded perceptively. For the past three years he had been the junior partner in a private investigative agency with two former North-West Region Major Crime Squad detectives. Dedovic suspected that from time to time Rainey was called on to access the COPS database. It was hard to make do in this city on a senior constable's wage.

Bob Winch came out of his office rubbing life into his telephone ear. "You still here, Dedovic?"

"Just going, sir." He stood up and bundled tapes and papers into his suit pockets. Downstairs in the street he ran into Wendy Lee Burke accompanied by a stocky photographer with two Nikons strapped around her neck. Wendy Lee was wearing a scarlet V-neck top that accentuated her 1950s bust, a tight black and white checked skirt, flesh-coloured stockings and high heels. Her fingernails glinted shiny red in the sunlight.

"My favourite copper," she said.

Dedovic nodded coolly.

"Heard your little Chinese partner got scalped?"

"That's not funny, Wendy."

"Oh, I know. It's a tragedy. That's why we're here, to convey pathos to the public. I've been waiting for you to give me a ring."

"I thought Dick Rainey was giving you one."

Wendy Lee smiled. "You and me, Dedo, we should team up. We're not so different under the skin. I know what you like to do to a woman."

"Yeah," Dedovic said.

"I can read it in your eyes." She fingered the tiny glass crucifix around her throat. "I tell you one thing. You wouldn't be disappointed."

Embarassed, the photographer turned away, fiddling with her zoom lens and Dedovic felt Wendy Lee move in close. Her breath was warm, her lips were shiny red as if they were enamelled and he wondered what it would be like to open her door.

"I'd be worried I might talk in my sleep," he said.

Wendy Lee flicked back her blonde hair; even in the wind it didn't move. "We wouldn't be sleeping," she said.

He held her gaze for a long moment and then looked over to the freckled photographer studying her chunky black diver's watch.

"By the way," Wendy Lee said quietly. "I'd watch your back."

"What do you mean?"

"When you're an award-winning police reporter, you hear all kinds of rumours on the street."

"So?" Dedovic shaded his eyes from the blinding sunlight off Darling Harbour.

"Thing about rumours." Wendy Lee brushed her hand against his wrist. "A lot of them turn out to be true."

# 31

Nobody was at the front desk. Dedovic picked up a pamphlet and recognised several inky characters from Wai Yi Chen's notebook. A Vietnamese girl came out of a doorway and he told her who he was. Bewildered, she stared at him until he flashed his ID and that seemed to get the message across. When she was gone, he checked his reflection in a photograph on the wall; against the white sails of the Opera House his hair looked wild, manic. He tried to tidy it with his fingers. A shadow moved behind him and he turned. She was standing there in a black tailored jacket and skirt, as thin-legged as a wading bird and looking more corporate than he could ever have imagined.

"You wanted to see me?" Her voice was icy cool.

"Long time, huh?" he said.

She gestured him into her office. A charcoal-grey Toshiba laptop sat on her bare desk and a brass plate screwed into the desk top announced her position in the college. DIRECTOR OF STUDIES. Dedovic looked around the walls for something personal of hers to latch onto.

"I'm extremely busy," she said. "What is it you want?"

"I need to talk to the students and staff."

"You've already done that. Your female assistant took everybody's statement."

"There's been a further development in the case."

"Has anyone been charged?"

Dedovic shook his head. "We're working on it."

"What the hell are the police doing out there? This industry is bleeding to death."

"I appreciate that, Ms Limacher." He met her green eyes across the desk. "That's why we need your full cooperation." It was hard to square this woman wearing the tailored suit and designer reading glasses with the wild sweaty gymnast who had led him back to her Crows Nest apartment.

Mona let out a sigh. Her long red hair had been cut short around her neck like a bathing cap and she looked different. Everything about her was older, snappier, more up-market. Dedovic had seen it happen in the Drug Unit. A transformation in guys he had worked with closely over the years. Once they were promoted beyond sergeant they no longer wanted to know about the bad old days. It was a joke in the squadroom that a significant promotion was the best way to erase a senior constable's memory.

"I need a list of everyone who's worked for this college over the past five years," he said. "Administrative staff, cleaners, tradesmen and teachers, part-time, casual and permanent."

She got up from her desk and walked over to the china blue filing cabinet, shaking her head at the inconvenience. Dedovic watched her sorting through personnel files, leaning over the drawers on her long thin tapered legs. He remembered kneeling between those legs and touching her smooth white skin with his lips. He remembered the noise she had made in the back of her throat and the way she had gripped his furniture.

"Here," she said, pulling sheets of paper out. "I'll have to copy them." She went over to a white machine in the corner and punched in buttons. "Whoever has murdered these Asian students, Detective, I can assure you of one thing. He's certainly not from this college."

"Why's that?" he said.

"Because it could only jeopardise his future employment, that's why."

"Maybe it's someone with a grudge. Any staff been laid off?"

"Dozens of them," Mona said, "but only *after* Ling Ling was murdered." She passed him a sheet filled with names and addresses. "I don't think you police fully comprehend the consequences of these killings. We're going to have to close our doors."

"I got something for you." He removed his left hand from his coat pocket and held it out, palm upwards. "Been meaning to return this."

Mona snatched her jade earring from his hand.

"Found it on the floor," he said.

"In my flat."

"So you remember, eh? I thought you'd forgotten."

Mona dropped the earring into a drawer and closed it with a bang. "I'm extremely busy right now, Detective. Is there anything else?"

He got up out of the chair. "Might have a word with your boss."

"Mr Lipmann's not in yet," she said. "He doesn't arrive until lunchtime. Nickie hasn't come in today either and that's most unusual. She always rings in if she's sick. Have you spoken to her lately?"

"Why?"

"She fancies you. She's more your type."

Dedovic caught a glimpse of the Director's sharp white teeth. He said, "I hope we can still remain friends."

Mona moved her jaw slightly. "One fuck does not make a friendship, Detective."

Dedovic strode into the corridor, breathing through his nose. The woman had used him. She'd picked him up, she'd borrowed his skipping rope and now she was treating him like dirt. He didn't much like it but he couldn't understand her motive. Was she just one of those people who don't want to know you after they go up in the world? Or had he really been that awful on the couch? He kept walking, hearing a chorus of heavily accented voices from the warren of flimsy classrooms. Students were chanting in English, tape-recorders were playing and a nasal teacher was enunciating the days of the week: "Mon-*die*, Tues-*die*."

Dedovic peered over the perspex walls and stood back from the open doorways staring at the scores of dark-haired Asian girls, slender of bone and delicate of frame. Several of them were wearing the Muslim veil and others from Japan or Hong Kong wore very short skirts, their lips painted pink and cherry black. They weren't all girls, there were males too, big brawny Koreans in the classes, but Dedovic ignored them. He had eyes only for the brown-eyed females, the ones who would return his gaze and then look away timidly. The ones he knew might respond to a stranger's call in the street, might hesitate momentarily when a man leaned out of the window of his white delivery van and said, "Excuse me. Do you speak English?"

"A little bit."

"Wonder if you could help me? I'm trying to find Darling Harbour."

Dedovic understood how simple it would be. A man stepping out of the driver's seat clutching a street directory, a concentrated frown on his clean-shaven face, one hand resting on the door handle while he asked her to show him – if she would be so kind – exactly where on his map. Then quickly, roughly, bundling her inside the van, binding her wrists and ankles, throwing a plastic tarp over her small writhing body and driving through the city at a steady sixty kph to a quiet secluded barbecue spot.

To be a good detective you had to imagine the worst, to put yourself mentally and emotionally in the shoes of a killer. The best cops Dedovic had worked with had been able to do that. Think like crims. Some of them had been able to do it perfectly. His pager beeped in his pocket and he checked the number, then rang the Analytical Lab at Lidcombe. "Thought you'd like to hear the latest on your hypodermo," Constable Ballistiros said. "No prints but the blood's human alright. The lab boys are going to run tests for AIDS and hep B, but we won't know the results for a week."

"Ballistic, I owe you big time." Dedovic flipped the mouthpiece closed, walked over to the window and touched the double-plated glass with his fingertips. Some rat had got in under the fence at home and left a filthy junkie's fit as a message, but he wasn't sure who and what they'd have to gain. Steve Bia had been kicked in the head so many times at training it could've been him, or else it could've been Doull who was cunning as a fox. The only thing he could do now was to set a trap. He looked down at Chinatown, at the cheap noodle cafes and the busy parking stations. A bell rang from within the bowels of the building and students burst out of the doorways like bullets, tossing their bags over their shoulders and yelling in foreign tongues. Dedovic watched the Asian girls, their slim hips.

"Excuse me, Detective."

Dedovic turned side-on.

The Managing Director was leaning out of a doorway; he beckoned Dedovic into a large untidy office, desk and cabinets covered in files and folders. "Mona mentioned you wanted a word with me," he said. Silver-haired, Roland Lipmann had the dry wrinkled skin of a sun worshipper. "Mona is doing a tremendous job as DOS," Lipmann said. "Of course we're hurting, financially and emotionally at the moment. Now where have I put that phone?"

Dedovic watched him root around underneath an enormous pile of papers. "Do you know of anyone at all who would wish to harm Asian students, sir?"

"Can't say I do. There's a distrust of Asia at the moment which I believe is political. Of course the idea of Asia itself is a Western construct. Ling Ling would never have regarded herself as Asian. She was a Cina Indonesia. We're terribly ignorant in this country of neighbouring cultures. When I was in Telukbetung . . . "

Dedovic waited for a break in the traffic, but Roland Lipmann was off on a overland route, travelling from Medan to Krung Thep to Mandalay to Allahabad, across the Kush to Mashhad, up to Baku and Izmir where he paused briefly on the shores of the Mediterranean.

"Well, thank you for you help, sir."

"I don't know if I've been *that* much assistance really, Sergeant, but I'll let you in on a secret. I always wanted to be a detective myself. I've maintained a personal interest in forensic casework, particularly in the development and validation of STR profiling techniques . . . "

Dedovic made it out of the office and down the lift. After all his years in the Drug Unit he could tell at a glance the types of people who were attracted to prohibited substances. Old dope smokers were the easiest to pick.

Outside, the midday heat was baking the thin crust of the pavement. The smell of garlic and fried dumplings drifted out of a steamy hot kitchen. He stood on the far side of the street, staring at the bare-legged girls from the South Pacific International College of English. A horn blew twice and a black Commodore SS V8 pulled up in the middle of the traffic. Dedovic hesitated, one shoe touching the road.

"Get in, get in," Ray Doull said from behind the wheel.

Dedovic got in. "Whose car's this?"

"Terr, you're always fuckin worried about whose wheels you're sitting in. Where do I go here, quick tell me."

"Straight, go straight."

"It's a dead end."

"Do a u-ey then."

"Fuckin Chinatown. You can't get outta the joint. All these narrow little fuckin one-way streets. Jesus, I hate this part of town."

"What are you doing over here, Ray?" He looked at the older man behind the wheel: Ray Doull wearing a short-sleeved Glo-Weave shirt, tartan golf slacks and tan shoes. His grey cheeks were hollow and his moustache was lying over his top lip like a bull terrier that had just been fed.

"Had a king prawn sambal with Dennis Hargraves and Bill McJannett at the Malaya. Your name came up in conversation."

Dedovic buckled his belt.

"Heard about your Chinese partner. Looks bad for everyone involved when that happens. Could she speak any English?"

"Course she could."

"It's a dangerous fuckin job, that's what people don't realise. The stress. I get these sharp pains in my neck—"

"I get those too."

"Mate, they're real bad. Fair dinkum, the job's turning into a witch hunt. I got seven days to report to the Commissioner why I should not be sacked. We're talking pension, half my fuckin super—"

"I'm sorry, Ray," Dedovic said.

"A lot of the boys are dark, Terr."

Dedovic stared out the window at the huge apartment towers.

"Look, I said, Terry's in the clear. He's slipped through the driftnet. And good luck to him. We're having a drink at eight o'clock tonight. They want you along."

"I'd love to, Ray, but I'm up to my ears—"

"That's what I told 'em. Terry's working this fuckin Asian case. Dead Chinese girls popping up all over town. Hey, where's your car?"

"Back in Hay Street."

"Mate, I'll run the loop," Doull said. "Jesus it's changed round here. Pagodas everywhere." He fired up a cigarette. "Anyway, they're digging into every little job the Unit were involved in. You worked the marina bust?"

"Rushcutters Bay?"

"Yeh, that's the one. Thought you were in on that. I don't know what Kratos has coughed up so far, but Integrity are real interested in that particular enterprise. Something's got to be done pretty quick."

"Let me off here," Dedovic said.

"Hang on, hang on. Come up to the Nelson tonight."

"I can't promise anything."

"Mate, everyone's kicking in twelve grand."

"Ray, I'll try, alright."

"Make me happy. Pop in for the one." Doull pulled up outside the Entertainment Centre. Dedovic unbuckled his belt and stepped out into the heat. He watched Ray Doull tear away from the kerb followed a hundred and fifty metres behind by a green Toyota Camry CSi, two clean-cut men in grey suits in the front seat who looked like Mormons on a doorknock mission. Dedovic walked through the back alleys of Chinatown, trying to clear a path in his head. How had Ray known that the three murder victims were Chinese when it hadn't been mentioned in the papers? What had Charlie Kratos spilled so far? If the Rushcutters Bay job was under scrutiny, then why was he the only detective from the Unit who had escaped attention? Most importantly, what the hell was he going to do now?

# 32

She lay on her bed with her legs raised, letting the images of last night float through her mind like a breeze through an open window. She remembered the weight of his hand on her shoulders, his soft fingers stroking at the nape of her neck, the feel of his chest as she'd pushed hard against him. For a big man he had been careful not to dominate her, to use his strength, and what had surprised her the most about him was how gentle he'd been. Leaning over to her sidetable, she picked up the indigo glass vial her aromatherapist had sold her, removed its tiny cork and rubbed the perfumed oil into the flat pan of her belly, up and along the insides of her thighs, over her dry bony knees, her thin arms and elbows and into the backs of her hands. She rolled off the bed and stood bare-footed on her coloured mat rubbing a palmful of lightly scented oil over her ribs and kidneys and her small boy-like buttocks, rubbing it in until her body glistened and the pores in her skin opened up to drink in the liquid. She was a little sore inside, but on the outside her nerves and muscles tingled as if she had neglected her body for too long and now it was grateful for the attention.

Humming, she went into the kitchen and stood before the wilderness calendar and calculated the days backwards from last night. Fifteen. The phone rang and she answered it, making sure firstly that the blinds in the front room were closed. "Why didn't you ring in today?" Mona's voice snapped in her ear. "I was worried about you."

"I did," Nickie said. "Left a message on the answer machine."

"God that Ngoc's hopeless. We'll have to get rid of her. She doesn't pass anything on. So what's wrong with you?"

"If you must know, Mona, I've been throwing up all morning. I had some pasta last night. I think it had bad seafood in it."

"Detective Dedovic was in here asking a lot of useless questions. I don't have a lot of confidence in that man. Will you be in to work tomorrow?"

"Possibly," Nickie said. She could sense Mona veering towards the real reason she'd rung.

"Laurie's been harassing me again," Mona said.

"Why don't you move out of there?"

"That's what he wants me to do, force me out of my flat. Don't ever get married."

"I won't," Nickie said.

"I must be jinxed. When I think of some of the men I've got involved with. I mean I'm not a difficult person. You wouldn't say I was difficult would you?"

Nickie didn't answer. She let Mona talk until she was all talked out. Then Mona said abruptly she had to go, as if it had been Nickie holding her up. She'd hardly got in one word. It was always the same with talkers. She went into her bedroom and put on her blue David Jones robe. She made herself a light lunch of mixed leaf salad, a soft-boiled egg followed by pawpaw and plain

Greek yoghurt. It was so good to be home. She wondered if Terry had mentioned her name to Mona. At thirty-four she had no illusions about men; she knew what they were good for. She had come this far on her own. The thing she missed most about a relationship was not the sex, but being touched. God she missed that. When she heard the gate creak she went down the hall and opened the door just as his finger was reaching out for her bell. "You're late," she said.

"I've been out to the hospital." His face was lined and his jaw was stubbled. She looked at the blue rhinoceros tie he was wearing. "How is she?"

"No change." He put an arm around her waist and guided his left hand in between the buttons of her robe, touched her rib cage and then her breast. He said, "I want you to do me a big favour."

"Not on the porch." She looked up and down the street.

Inside she let him run his hands all over her body, removing her robe on the arm of the couch, while he nudged her knees apart. She glimpsed the white half-moons of his nails as he traced the angle of her collarbone with his fingers and then stroked her chin and throat with his knuckles. She closed her eyes, feeling him move inside her, one hand rubbing at the nape of her neck, the other hand pushing gently at her coccyx. The sound he made in his throat reminded her of a puppy she'd once had and then he withdrew from her and lay on the couch with the eye of his penis glistening. He was not circumcised, she saw, and not at all embarrassed. "You smell funny," he said. "What you got on, you got on some kind of oil?"

Her body was tingling from her neck down to her toes as if she'd just stepped out of a river after a long invigorating swim. She waited for the ripples of pleasure to pass.

"I liked that," he said. "That was nice."

The tip of his penis was strawberry red; she watched it shrink in his lap. His brown suit jacket was neatly folded across the stereo and there was a large bulge in the right pocket.

"Ever been married?" he said.

"Never."

"No kids?"

She shook her head. "I've never found anyone good enough." She pulled on her robe. "Mona said you were out at the college today."

"Yeh, I talked to your boss, Lipmann."

"Roland's very cool for his age, very erudite."

He got off the couch and grabbed at his yellow boxers. "You think cops are dumb, don't you?"

"No."

"A lot of educated people try and put p'lice down, but when they're in trouble, guess who they yell for first?"

"Is there something wrong, Terry?"

He shook his head. "Nah. I'm just under a bit of extra pressure at work." He got up and walked down the hall to the bathroom. Nickie stared at the back of his legs and then went over and felt the lump through his coat pocket. It was too soft for a pistol. She reached her hand in and felt three separate bundles each tied with an elastic band. She pulled one out and saw that it was a roll of fifty dollar notes; with the edge of her fingernail she tried to count how much was there. She dropped the roll back in his pocket as he came down the hall. Caught her standing by his clothes.

"Where do you buy these dreadful ties?" she asked quickly. She picked up the length of silk patterned with tiny blue rhinoceroses.

"My youngest daughter buys them for me," he said.

"I didn't know you had children."

"Two girls and an ex-wife."

She'd suspected all along he was a divorcee. "Do they look like you?"

"Only the daughters." He came over and put his hands around her waist. She could feel the strength he had in his arms, the power in his shoulders and it occurred to her that whoever had murdered Ling Ling was someone with similar upper-body strength. Personally she couldn't have strangled a mouse. She felt his breath hot against the lip of her ear.

"I want you to do me a favour," he said.

"What is it?"

"I want you to look at something."

He let go of her and thrust a hand into the inside pocket of his brown coat and pulled out a sheaf of papers. "Can you translate this shit?"

Nickie flicked through the lined pages. It was some kind of numbered notebook written in a mixture of English, Chinese characters and Pinyin. He hadn't said who it belonged to, but she knew it was the Chinese detective's. "My Mandarin is a bit rusty," she said, "but I'll try." He sat beside her on the couch in his boxers while she worked her way through the copy with a pencil and a large dictionary on her knee. Most of what Detective Chen had written in English dealt with mundane police matters, "*Attended IOFM 10 a.m., witnesssed autopsy,*" but the passages written in Chinese characters seemed to be more reflective in their focus. Slowly she tried to transliterate: "*Where operates the criminal the most distinctive shadow he casts.*"

"What's that mean?" Terry said.

"I told you I was rusty. A second language is like a child; you can't afford to neglect it. We have to change the syntax around." It surprised her a little that Detective Dedovic didn't ask what syntax was.

"Centre of gravity." He nodded intently. "The area in which the AK operates."

"What do you mean?" Nickie said.

"Never mind." He leaned across her and she could smell his salty skin. "What's that bit say?"

"*Australians very stupid, always talk about football, football, Chinese the best people.*"

"You're not making this up are you?" He tilted his head and regarded her from the side like a huge barn owl. "Nothing more in there?"

Nickie turned the numbered pages. "Is this an official notebook?"

"Yeh," he said. "All police up to the rank of inspector are supposed to carry one, but when you're working plain clothes you tend to use the duty book in the squad room. Uniforms have theirs checked once a week by a supervising sergeant. They're an accountable item."

"And you're allowed to write in Chinese?"

"Well, I never heard it done. What's that other stuff there?"

Nickie explained that Pinyin was a romanised spelling of the Chinese language. "Like Guangzhou means Canton," she said.

"So what's that say?" He pointed to the right-hand side of the page. Nickie tried to transcribe it as accurately as she could:

Organised
Late twenties to early thirties
White male
Technical/semi-professional occupation
Drives a van with high mileage,

driving connected with his work
Some physical/ emotional defect
Lives alone in Artarmon area?

Terry leapt up from the couch and paced the room in his boxers, rotating his neck from side to side. "Is this connected with Ling Ling?" she said. He started pulling on his shirt and trousers and then his coat. She wanted to ask him why a Detective Senior Constable would carry thousands of dollars in cash on his person, but felt this wasn't the opportune moment. "I want to know what's going on, Terry."

He still didn't answer, just looked at her with that hard city face, his lips sealed. She grabbed his elbow. "I want to come with you."

He shook his head firmly. "This is police business."

There was a determined look in his eyes and she knew that however much she pleaded with him he was one of those stubborn men you couldn't change with a bull whip.

"I'll transcribe while you drive."

"There's more?" He glanced at her suspiciously.

"Oh yes," she said. "Much more." She ran up the stairs in her bare feet and threw on her jeans and a blue Jigsaw top. She looked in the mirror. She couldn't decide whether to wear lipstick or not. Yes, yes, put it on. She could hear him pacing downstairs and his knuckles tapping impatiently against the stair rail. What about mascara? No, she didn't have time. When she came down he had his tie knotted and his keys out.

"Where are we going?" she said.

"Artarmon. You could get me sacked for this."

"I won't tell anyone if you don't." She was not going to be excluded. Not now. There were skills she could bring to this investigation. She grabbed her

225

dictionary and ran around the house checking windows and power points. She heard him say, "Take a look through these addresses. I want you to check for any members of your staff who live on the North Shore."

"Mr Lipmann lives in McMahons Point."

"Anyone else?"

"Mona."

"I know that," he said.

Nickie snapped the door behind them. "So you've been to her flat?"

He didn't answer.

"Did you sleep with her?"

His mobile started ringing. He pulled it out of his left coat pocket, leaned one big hand on the hood of the unmarked police vehicle and said in a voice she could barely hear, "I don't kiss and tell."

# 33

They sped out along Olympic Highway past miles and miles of car yards and showrooms. The sun shone in her eyes and coloured banners proclaimed sales and special deals and low hire-purchase offers. Tens of thousands of passenger vehicles and white delivery vans crammed into lots like shiny metal eggs. Nickie stared out her window at the Holdens and Fords and Toyotas and Mazdas and Mercedes parked on the footpaths and in the driveways and on the backs of semitrailers as if the whole of Parramatta Road was a Mecca to the motor vehicle. Plumes of diesel smoke and brownish-black petrol fumes swirled over the banked-up traffic. The air filled with the honking of car horns and the heat shimmered above the throbbing engines.

"Sorry about the delay." He hadn't explained to her where they were going after he received that call. All she knew was that it was some kind of family drama that had diverted them westwards. She worked the dictionary on her lap, leafing through the copied pages of the Chinese detective's official police notebook without finding anything more of interest. Somehow, if she was to retain her usefulness, she would have to string him along like Scheherazade.

"You lived in China, that right?" he said.

"Three years." Even now she could recall the pungent factory smells of Shanghai, the clanging of trucks and the crowded dusty streets.

"What was it like?"

"Like this." She indicated the heavy congested traffic. "Only with people."

"That's the problem everywhere. Too many fuckin people. Soon you won't be able to take a drive in this city."

"Here's something," Nickie said. "The last entry she made in Mandarin: *Three diamonds white van*."

"What's that mean?"

"I'm not sure, maybe she means Mitsubishi. That's their insignia. Last week I saw a white Mitsubishi van parked outside the college. The driver was asking a Chinese girl for directions."

"You get a look at him?" His hands gripped the black bar of the wheel. The police radio crackled cryptically; but not once had she seen him use it.

"No," she said, "I couldn't tell if it was a man or a woman."

"So how do you know it was a Mitsubishi then?"

"I know cars. I've been wanting to buy a new one for so long, I'm always comparing makes in the street. I tried to memorise the number . . . "

Dedovic reached for the police radio. "What is it?"

"GN something or . . . MJ . . . No, I can't remember now. It's gone." She saw his face sink with disappointment and then he removed his sunglasses and rubbed at the bridge of his nose. "But the van had lettering on the side."

"What kind of lettering?"

"Black like a business sign."

"The AK," he said.

Nickie wanted to ask him what an AK was, but didn't wish to show her ignorance. The traffic began flowing again and cars lurched forward eagerly. Dust swirled along the treeless road and vans were cooking in the yards. A long semitrailer passed them transporting liquid oxygen. For some reason Nickie thought of her fourteen-year-old neighbour two doors down in Silver Street who was suffering from leukaemia. She pressed the pad of her thumb against the inside of her wrist and felt the pulse in her veins. She said, "So why does he want to murder foreign students?"

"You've asked me that before."

"Have I?" she said. "Well the police must have some idea."

"We've got ideas." He was staring at the blinking traffic lights. "Ling Ling Kua had teeth marks that were inflicted postmortem by some kind of dead reptile. All three victims were mutilated."

"God," Nickie said. "He must be sick."

"These killings are personal." Terry turned off the highway and drove down an arterial road in silence. Nickie hadn't realised how sordid police work could be. She didn't have the stomach for this. They stopped outside a house with white-trimmed windows. Red bottlebrush trees planted along the council strip enflamed the entire street.

"Do you want me to stay in the car?" she said.

"No, you'd better come in."

In her opinion it was a little too early in the relationship to be meeting his family, but she followed him up the path, hung back nervously as he rapped on the glass. The front door opened and a short, butter-faced woman with yellow hair appeared. Nickie heard Terry introduce her and she nodded but immediately forgot the woman's name. That always happened to her. The woman didn't seem overjoyed at her presence and glowered at Terry as if he'd tramped dirt into her house. "Ms Taroney's assisting us with a murder investigation," he said.

The woman rolled her eyes. For a detective senior constable he was a poor liar, Nickie thought. She waited in the living room while Terry and whatsername went into the kitchen. It was an awkward position he'd placed her in. She could hear their raised voices through the sliding door, a faint French accent: "Are you fucking her?"

"Shut up, Gabby. She'll hear."

"How dare you bring your fluff into my home. No wonder your daughter's uncontrollable. She won't listen to me."

"Where is she?"

"She's in her bedroom. I was washing her tunic this morning—"

"Show me," he said.

"Three of them for God's sake. What are they?"

Nickie heard footsteps behind her and swung around. A girl was standing in the doorway. Instantly Nickie recognised her features. She had her mother's flaxen hair and fine dairy skin, but she had inherited Terry's nose. She was wearing a gold bracelet on her right wrist and that drew attention to her hands. Nickie couldn't take her eyes off them. Her hands were the size of a man's.

"Are you Dad's punch?" the girl said.

"Sorry?" Nickie blinked.

"Mistress, you know. His piece of skirt. Don't you read crime fiction?" she said. "I love the words they use."

"Giselle!" her father yelled. "In here, please."

"I'm in the shit," the girl said. "I'm always in the shit. Were you a wild child?"

"Once I was," Nickie said.

"But then you settled down, right? Listened to classical music."

The door slid open and Terry appeared, gesturing coldly at his daughter with a finger. "I thought we had a deal," he said.

"It isn't dope, Dad."

"I know what it is," he said. "Do I have to go through every prohibited substance with you. Do I have to spell it out like you're a kid."

"Sabrina, Crogan, all my friends have tried it–"

"If Crogan stuck her head in the toilet bowl, would you do it?"

"That's a stupid analogy." The girl shook her head angrily. Nickie watched the mother biting her lip and she wondered if parents simply regurgitated the dialogue from their own childhood. Terry extended his hand towards his daughter and Nickie saw the small, round, yellow-flecked tablets sitting in his palm. "Where'd you get these from?"

"At the Morgue," the girl answered.

"What morgue?"

"It's a nightclub," Nickie said. "Near the mortuary station at Central." Everyone looked at her as if this were a live TV drama and a member of the audience had just interrupted.

"Who sold it to you?" Terry stood over his daughter. "Answer me."

"He didn't sell it, he gave them to me."

"Who did?"

Nickie could feel the tension rising in the living room, a repressed emotional and sexual energy. The mother stepped back as if at any moment the cord between father and daughter might snap.

"He said he knew you, he told me not to tell. He

231

said that you stole money and that you were corrupt, he said that you loaded up people."

"Steve Bia – is that his name?"

"I don't know. He gets in there, he drives a Porsche Turbo–"

"Steve Bia is a liar, a pornographer and a drug-dealer."

"He said you loaded him."

"You're not to go near that place, do you hear me? Never again. Now go to your room."

No, Nickie thought. Don't dismiss her like that. Talk to her. Explain.

"Please Dad, don't tell him. My friends'll find out, if you say anything, please, Dad." His daughter had worked herself up into such a lather that the nerves on her small pimpled face were twitching and her eyes were blinking wildly as she held back tears. Terry put an arm around her shoulders and Nickie could see there was something emotionally disturbed with the girl, as if all the hormones in her body were rebelling.

"Alright." His voice was hard. "I won't say a word."

"You promise?"

He steered his daughter out of the living room and down the hall and Nickie could not help feeling impressed by Detective Dedovic's paternal concern. All of a sudden she was left alone with his little blancmange of a wife. There was an awkward silence of the kind Nickie had experienced only once before when she had woken to find herself in bed with her Spanish teacher. From the hallway she could hear the daughter going over old ground, "You won't arrest him, will you? Promise me, Dad, you promise?"

"I'm sorry you were subjected to this absurd display of *Home and Away*," the woman said with a detectable French burr.

"No, I . . . I . . ."

"They're lovely when they're babies then they turn into teenagers." She shrugged. "Do you have any children?"

Nickie shook her head.

"Well, I'm sure you will."

And Nickie wondered whether she was psychic.

In the police car she asked him was it LSD?

"MDMA," he said. "Or Methylenedioxymethamphetamine. I never realised Giselle was that stupid. A hundred times I've warned her about hallucinogens. She knows I worked the Drug Unit."

"Maybe that's why she tried it," Nickie said. He was looking straight ahead, two hands clenching the wheel, windows wound up tight and his chiselled jaw set firm as if there was something personal he'd resolved to do. The police radio crackled. Wisps of blue exhaust haze swirled over the windscreen then rose into the atmosphere. In the distance the towers of the city shimmered in the heat. When they were leaving the house she'd seen him tuck five fifty dollar notes into his wife's hand and Gabrielle, for that was the woman's name, had exchanged a look of complicity with her as if they were in on some secret deal together. She looked out her window at the backside of a bus, whizzing past traffic in the fast lane. "How long have you two been separated?"

"Let's not talk about family."

"Fine," she said. "So who's this Steve Bia?"

"You ask a lot of questions, Nick."

"I'm curious," she said. "Is that a crime?"

"Could be, I'll check." He reached over to the console for the vitamin bottle, shook out three orange tablets into his left hand and chewed on them. "Steve

Bia's a low-life. Preys on kids, teenagers. He's out on bail on a supply diamorphine and possess firearms charge."

"And he's still selling ecstasy?"

"He'd sell his baby sister if there was a buck in it. I think the public forget the kind of scum police are dealing with. If we get a tap on someone like Bia, I can't just go listen to it, I have to tell the Telephone Intercept Unit what specific information I'm after and they hand me that one page. You wouldn't believe how we're hampered by current regulations."

"What about corruption?" Nickie said.

"That's only one per cent. Most cops are straight down the line."

"Have you ever taken any money?"

"What is this, interrogation week?"

"Have you?"

"I could ask you have you ever cheated on your tax return. Or taken stationery home from the college?"

"It's not the same," Nickie said. "Have you as a police officer ever been in receipt of corrupt payments — isn't that the question they ask?"

"I've never stolen anything," he said coldly. "Now where can I drop you?" In Leichhardt he turned off Parramatta Road and cut through the side streets of Petersham driving fast, back wheels bouncing over the humps. The roar of aircraft grew louder and giant bird-like shadows were cast across pebble-creted yards.

"I thought we were going to Artarmon," she said.

He pulled up on the corner of Silver Street and removed his black wraparound sunglasses. "You got my mobile number?"

She nodded.

"Go through the rest of Chen's notebook. See if you can find anything more. I'll be back in a couple of hours, okay."

"Where are you going, Terry?"

"Just some old police business I have to attend to."

Holding her dictionary, Nickie stepped out onto the highway and watched the jade-green police car spin away from the kerb. You didn't have to be a cop to figure out this had to do with Steve Bia. Nickie remembered what his daughter had said and she felt the blood rush to her legs. There were two things she was hoping for and one of them was that Terry Dedovic would not do anything he'd regret.

## 34

Dusk was falling over Sydney Cove and the double goose-necked streetlamps flickered on. The expressway curved overhead and the road passed under the steel ribs of the bridge and down through the oldest part of the city. Dedovic parked outside a nineteenth-century rough stone terrace in Millers Point, with the grey office towers looming in his rear-view mirror and the harbour waters turning the colour of lavender in front of him. He stared at the control tower and smoked a cigarette down to the nub, flicking grey ash outside his window and thinking of all the times he used to drink here when he was in the Drug Unit. He checked his service pistol and got out of the police car. The sky was filled with bogong moths flying around in mad circles as if they had lost their way, batting their flimsy wings against streetlights and sandstone walls.

From across the road he could see five burly men sitting by the window in the Lord Nelson Hotel: Ray Doull, Dennis Hargraves, Scotty Dwyer, Lance Bullmore and Bill McJannett. The old fucking Unit. The clinking of glasses greeted him as he strode through the doors. Over the years he'd met a lot of hard crims in this pub. It was the oldest hotel in the city and those detectives who knew Sydney intimately said it was the best. He pulled up a chair at the table. Hands came at him and slapped his shoulders and patted his arms. If he hadn't known any better he would've said his old colleagues were just pleased to see him, but the hands lingered a fraction too long on the edges of his shoulders and brushed against the front of his shirt and a set of steel-like fingers strayed under his coat and touched his rib cage.

"Vic, what are you having, mate? My round."

"Gimme a Coopers."

Chief Inspector Hargraves stood up and went over to the bar. Empty pints were stacked high on the next table like a glass midden. Dedovic pressed his back against the sandstone wall and listened to the long story Ray Doull was telling, something to do with a masseuse he'd been to see. In all his years in the Drug Unit, Dedovic had always been on the fringes. For a start he was a Victorian with a wog name and he was ten, fifteen years younger than some of these senior detectives, men like Dennis Hargraves and Lance Bullmore. Both Bullmore and Hargraves had risen much higher in the service than Ray Doull ever had but there was no doubt who still carried the real weight. Ray Doull had worked all the hard-hitting squads, the Breakers, Armed Hold-Up, and Consorting, and when he spoke the other four suspended police officers listened. It was something Dedovic had never considered before, but by sheer luck or planning five of the hardest detectives in the city had ended up at one time or another in the Drug Unit.

"Then she puts on this rainforest music, this water dripping like a fuckin toilet with a bit of wind blowing through it and I'm lying there . . ." Ray Doull wet his lips and wiped froth from his shoe-brush moustache. Like the four other barrel-chested men at the table he was wearing casual clothes, a Cairns fishing shirt open to the third button and bone-coloured moleskin trousers. In his left hand he was jangling a big set of car keys on an RSL key ring that Dedovic had never seen before. "Fixed the neck right up. You oughta go see her, Terr, you get those neckaches same as I do."

"That's stress, Ray. Work load," Scotty Dwyer put in.

"Yeah, stress, mate, I should've gone for a pay-out."

"Slipped over on a fuckin milkshake."

"Hurt on duty, mate. "

"That's what we shoulda done. Fallen down the stairs at the police centre. All five of us."

"Oh yeah, everyone and his fuckin dog's tried that."

"Too late now, eh."

"We're in for difficult times, Den. An inquisition, a Spanish inquisition that's what this is."

"Yeah, you're not wrong there."

"Fair dinkum, mate, I'm thinking of fuckin necking myself."

"We'll ride it through. All they got is Kratos. Deal with him–"

"And we're sweet."

"The guy's a danger to us all."

"Yep."

"Scotty's right."

"That's what we have to do, mate. We're all in the same rowboat."

"Except Vic here."

"Hey, Vic, didn't you work the Rushcutters Bay job?"

"Yeah, mate, how come you slipped through the ropes?"

Dedovic lifted his pint glass. Five sets of eyes were looking at him and he could see the resentment in some of the older faces. He said, "Just lucky I guess." He looked out the window at the city lurking behind Observatory Park, the tip of Sydney tower gleaming like a sharp wet needle.

"Terr's working these Asian killings. Some guy running around town slicing up Chinese women."

"Hear they've pinned him down to the northside," Bill McJannett said.

"You live on the north, Ray," Dwyer said. "Could be you."

Ray Doull laughed. "Why would I run around cutting up Chinese girls? I got enough hobbies."

Scotty Dwyer and Bill McJannett grinned. Dedovic shook his head. Lance Bullmore had a pair of black eyebrows that met above the bridge of his nose. He said, "They picked up someone late this afternoon. Bob Winch's got him down at the City of Sydney right now helping with their enquiries."

"You're joking," Dedovic said. "Where'd you hear this from?"

"Lance'd have the ears on that, Terr."

"Came through Darcy Clout. Bumped into him on the way over."

Dedovic shook his head. Bob Winch had given him the run-around, sent him out to talk to nobodies while he lined up the pinch. He slammed down his Coopers and stood up.

"Sit down, Terr. There's nothing you can do about it," Doull said.

For twelve months he'd worked this case. He couldn't believe he'd been left out in the dark. "Who'd they pick up?" he asked Bullmore.

"Some Chinese gangster. Been stamping prominent

Chinese families on the northside for months. Bob Winch thinks he's their man." Lance Bullmore looked at the clock on the wall and then at Doull, who nodded.

Dedovic sunk back into his seat and stared at a wooden ale barrel roped to the ceiling. In his veins he knew that Winch had got it wrong. Whoever was knocking off these girls, it wasn't business, it was personal. He could smell hatred on this job and it ran deep.

"Bob Winch was grabbing a drink there for years," Scotty Dwyer said.

"Is that right?"

"He was in the Joint Drug Task Force, before he got the nod for CI. Then he turned Christian. Total fuckin rebirth."

"He's a brownnoser, mate. Always looking after number one."

Footsteps clunked on the bare wooden floor and Detective Superintendent Lance Bullmore was leaning over Dedovic with a full tray of drinks. Arms reached out and a platter of cheese and biscuits was lowered onto the table. Ray Doull whispered in his ear: "You're not to put your hands in your pockets tonight, Terr. This is on us." He raised his pint glass. "Here's to the good old days. When coppers had balls."

Dedovic tasted the cold bitter beer on his tongue, gripping the glass handle tightly. He couldn't get over Bob Winch. Sending him out to that language college when all along he had a bite on the line. Just because he'd worked Darlinghurst Detectives and the Drug Unit, a lot of straight cops distrusted him and the hard men, well, Dedovic looked across at Dwyer, Bullmore, McJannett and Hargraves, they didn't really trust him either. He watched Bull and Hargraves check their watches every few minutes the way older detectives do. He had the feeling all five men were waiting on him.

"Well, Terr, you going to help us out with our little bit of business?" Glasses stopped clinking; bodies leaned in over the cheese platter.

"I dunno Ray," he said. "Depends what you have in mind."

"We're counting on you," Bill McJannett said.

"That's right," Dwyer put in. "You worked the Unit, Vic."

"Mate, you're one of us."

"We don't want that Rushcutters Bay job coming to light, now do we?"

"No, mate, not that."

"That wouldn't look too good splashed across the *Herald*."

Dedovic locked eyes with Doull. "I need a word with Steve Bia on a personal matter, but I don't want to get involved in anything heavy."

"You won't be involved, Terr."

"No, mate, you're out of it."

"Just a little delivering job, take a parcel up a lift, pick up a box of papers," Dennis Hargraves said. "No fucking dramas, nothing."

"Ten minutes work, Terr, and then you're home." Ray Doull jangled his car keys in his palm.

"Okay, I'm available tomorrow."

"We need you tonight mate." Bill McJannett looked at his watch. "In fact we need you right now."

Dedovic drained his pint. All five men were looking at him intently and then Lance Bullmore produced a large manila envelope from his attaché case and bounced it on the table. "One other thing, Vic, we need to borrow ten large. Just overnight."

"That's right, Terr. You get it back tomorrow."

"Guaranteed."

The bar was quiet. Cricketers in green pyjamas flashed their blades up on the screen, but there were no gambling machines, no noisy amusement games, not even a pool table. Just a good decent hotel. The barmaid clattered cutlery in the sink. A young couple were kissing on stools at the far end of the bar but nobody paid any attention to the policemen's table. Dedovic watched Lance Bullmore, the senior officer present, collect bundles of used notes, thick wads of fifties and hundreds secured with orange rubber bands. He felt in his coat pocket and brought out two rolls of fifty dollar bills, a hundred in each roll, and waited for Bullmore to count them in front of him and write down the figure of ten thousand on a piece of paper next to his name. He patted the inside of his coat and thrust his hands urgently into his trouser pockets.

"Anything wrong, Vic?" Lance Bullmore licked and sealed the flap on the bulging yellow-brown envelope.

"Na, na," he said. He took off his coat, checked every pocket again.

"Lost somethin', mate?"

Shaking his head, he stood up and went out to the toilet. His third roll of fifties was missing. He tried to remember where the hell he could've dropped it. The car? Or back at her place? Yeah, he remembered draping his coat over her couch. It could've rolled out then. Maybe he should ring her. He took out his mobile and entered his pin number. No, he'd have to explain to her why he was carrying so much cash. She wouldn't believe that every detective he knew carried a wad. Better to go back there afterwards. Deal with the business at hand. Once this shit was over he was finished with Ray Doull. Finished with the Drug Unit. Those days were gone. The city had changed. The rulebook was being rewritten. A moth bumped its wings against the naked light bulb, again and again. Dedovic watched it expend all its energy. Some insects never learned. In the bar a hand grabbed at his sleeve as he was walking back to his table. A silky female voice said, "Hey, Dedo. What are you doing here?"

Wendy Lee Burke was sitting on a stool with a flute of champagne in one hand and a late edition of the city tabloid in the other.

"You actually read that paper?" he asked.

She uncrossed her bare legs. "So do a million other people."

Dedovic caught the front page:

## HEROINE COP IN CRITICAL CONDITION

Tonight Detective Constable Ida Chen lies in the Royal North Shore Emergency Unit after her courageous undercover work led to the first breakthrough in the triple murders which have haunted Sydney's Asian community. While surgeons battle to save Constable Chen's life, a man is helping Task Force Jarrah with their enquiries. **Continued Page 2**

"Exclusive huh?" Dedovic dropped the paper down on the bar cloth. "Bob Winch's work."

"Be careful who you drink with, Dedo." Wendy Lee tilted her head towards the five suspended detectives huddled around the low window, talking in hushed voices. "You've heard what they say about that crew?"

Dedovic stared at the large metal crucifix resting between Wendy Lee's breasts. "You're the journalist, Wendy. So you tell me."

Wendy Lee looked at him and lowered her voice to a slurry whisper. "For years Doull, Hargraves and Bullmore have been operating a–" She stopped and pulled at the hem of her short black skirt. "Of course I would love to . . . "

Dedovic felt a hand clasp his shoulder and he turned to see Bill McJannett and Scotty Dwyer standing there. "Hello Wendy," Dwyer said. "We were just admiring your legs."

McJannett said,"They're the kind of legs every journalist should have. They'd extract my secrets."

"Walkley legs," Dwyer added and laughed.

"What's happening fellas? Detectives' picnic?"

"Na, just a social drink. Hey, Vic, you want that lift?"

Wendy Lee went back to reading her front-page story and Dedovic followed his five former colleagues through the double blue doors out into the night air, the lights of the traffic running to meet them. "Loyalty," Ray Doull was saying as they moved down the hill towards their cars, "that's one thing money can't buy."

# 35

Dedovic crossed the marble foyer and elbowed his way through a party of Japanese honeymooners. Newly-wed couples wore identical Ken Done T-shirts as if they were concerned they might lose each other and need to give police an exact description. Uniformed hotel staff worked the glass doors beaverishly, greeting guests and guiding the webbed luggage to reception. Dedovic could see a parade of cabs outside. He stood in the lift bay, tucked the large manila envelope under his left arm and pressed UP.

Strange to be back in the Cross. The armpit of Sydney. In the early eighties when he first worked Darlinghurst he used to see the young toughs coming up here, straight off the train from Lithgow and Coffs and Wagga Wagga. Muscled, tattooed youths, hard as boilerplate and ready to take on the town. Nine, ten years down the track he'd see those same hard faces sitting in Belmore Park or Fitzroy Gardens with dirty jagged toenails, hands shaking as they tried to build a straggly cigarette. The city ground you down; it chewed you up and spat you out. It changed the way you thought. He remembered the first time he ever went into a club on Darlinghurst Road, freshly shaven, wearing a clean blue shirt, uniform crisply pressed and saw the lumpy middle-aged strippers and the drunks in their loud paisley shirts and smelled the cigar-filled air and he thought to himself – this is hell. And then gradually things changed and the girls started to look younger and he didn't smell the foul air so much, and the chain-smoking club managers, with their eighteen K gold ID bracelets and their diamond rings, used to approach him when he'd drop in on his beat and act as if they were tickled pink to see a twenty-one-year-old constable from Melbourne called Vic.

The lift doors opened and Dedovic stepped inside the lift with some Asian dignitaries talking into their mobiles. He pressed the seventeenth floor. He'd worked Darlinghurst in uniform until the station had closed and then he'd been transferred out west and when he'd come back to the city it was to the Drug Unit. Some days he'd be in the office and Dennis Hargraves or Lance Bullmore or one of the other senior detectives would hand him a couple of hundred in a police envelope. "That's for the Xmas shopping, Terr," Sergeant Doull might say. Or mostly they would say nothing.

Sometimes Dedovic had no idea where it came from. If you said anything to ISU or Internal Affairs, word would get out. You were on your own. You'd have no career. As long as drugs were illegal there were always going to be guys taking a drink. That's the way it worked, and it was no good just blaming coppers. For seven years Ray Doull had been second-in-charge of the Drug Unit and that meant every serious dealer in the city had to go through him. He had the power to shut them down, to allocate de facto leases and regulate business. Sergeant Doull was the man. In the Detectives' office behind a removeable partition there was even a treasure chest. The load box Ray used to call it, and gear that had never been booked up was kept there. No other squad Dedovic had worked was anything like this. There were hundreds of payments over the years and they ranged from fifty dollar sweeteners to the Rushcutters Bay job.

The lift settled, the doors slid open and Dedovic stepped out into the corridor, clutching his fat manila envelope and rubbing the heel of his thumb against the strap on his shoulder holster. He could not remember where the tip-off had come from, but Ray Doull got a call at the Drug Unit. A private yacht moored in Rushcutters Bay. Twenty metres long, silver paintwork with a tall white mast. The bar fridge crammed full of coke. Not in cans or bottles, but in clear plastic bags. Cocaine hydrochloride. Dedovic had never seen so much dust in one load. Five kilos of it. The owner of the yacht, Mr X, was a prominent city businessman and organiser of charities. Tanned, tense, and wearing a blue polo shirt with a little peaked French sailor's cap, he had made an unwise career change to get into whitegoods for his retirement and had been caught red-handed. To say he was scared was an understatement. He was shaking, sweating and the Italian naval shorts he had on were stained down the front. Ray Doull walked him up to the bow of the vessel and they had a long talk while Dedovic, Dwyer, McJannett and Hargraves stood drinking from the little mixer bottles of dry ginger ale they found at the back of the emptied gas fridge. Whatever arrangements were reached, Dedovic was never told. Things went unsaid. All he knew was that going by the new stains on the back of the man's shorts he was pleased to see them leave. A year later Dedovic saw Mr X's picture in the New Year's honours page of the

*Herald* – an AM for services to business and to the anti-litter campaign. The hydrochloride was taken back to the Detectives' office and placed in the treasure chest. "What are we going to do with it?" Detective Senior Constable Dwyer asked.

And Ray Doull had replied, "So why don't I give the big fella a ring."

Dedovic stopped outside Suite 1704 and knocked loudly. He heard the heavy sound of bodies moving around inside, and then the door opened and the Tangaluka twins stood there with their battle-scarred faces, their arms as thick as tree trunks. The only way Dedovic could tell Moses from Samsun Tangaluka was the long jagged knife scar that ran down the side of Samsun's cheek from the corner of his left eye to his Adam's apple. It was not a Tongan initiation cicatrix; in fact it had occurred outside the Mansions Hotel in the summer of 1987 when Charlie Kratos first started taking over the clubs on the strip. Dedovic had witnessed the Tongan twins at work when they had iron-barred a gang of western suburbs bikers whose birthday party at the Love Box had got out of hand. It was the first time he'd seen extensive blood splash patterns on a club ceiling.

Moses Tangaluka gestured him inside the suite and ran his hands up and down the insides of Dedovic's trouser leg, around his groin, over his waist, back and ribs. Big black hands patted his holster and service pistol, but it wasn't a firearm he was searching for. Dedovic lifted up his tie for the Tongan to check for wiring. "Thank you for your cooperation, Mr D," Moses Tangaluka said politely. It was common knowledge that the twins were the only bouncers in Kings Cross with a tertiary education and before Charlie Kratos had discovered them they were seriously considering a career in the Uniting church. Dedovic's shoes sunk into thick white carpet. The curtains were parted and huge blue finialled towers glowed with orange and yellow lights. A plane blipped silently between the fattened office buildings, a red light blinked on the hump of the bridge and the few white shells of the Opera House gleamed by the edge of the harbour. Dedovic stared hard out the window as if the restless city held a power over him. An ambulance shrilled in the street below and a voice behind him said, "You loaded me, Mr Dedovic".

Dedovic turned and saw greasy Steve Bia standing in the bathroom doorway zipping up his fly. "You fuckin loaded me."

He'd promised Giselle he wouldn't say anything to Bia. He took off his jacket and laid it down with the bulky envelope on a low black table underneath the window. He could feel his heart chugging in his chest. The city lights strung out between them. Steve Bia rushed at him making noises in his throat. Dedovic let him get close, then feinted with a left, dropped his shoulder and popped him with a big overhand right. Steve Bia buckled at the waist and sank onto one knee. Dedovic rubbed the ridge of his fist. It had been a long time since he'd hit a man that hard and it felt good, even though he suspected he'd broken at least one bone in his hand. He waited for Bia to get up, saw Moses Tangaluka shaking his head at this foolishness. Determined now, Steve Bia came at him, chopping and kicking. Dedovic tried to jab him off, but his combinations were as slow as a Sydney bank queue. Bia stepped inside a rusty hook and whacked him twice on the jaw. With a thump Dedovic landed on his coccyx on the floor. Steve Bia was standing over him grinning with hostility. "You wanna go round some more, Mr Dedovic?"

Dedovic rubbed at his jaw and tasted fresh blood in his mouth. There was grease on his knuckles and two of his bottom teeth were loose. Shakily, he got to his feet, shook the ring rust from his joints and pulled his service pistol, aimed it squarely at Bia's grinning face. "You're off," he said.

Nobody moved.

"You don't have the pump, Mr Dedovic."

Dedovic sighted his Glock semi-automatic between Bia's crazy blue eyes. He was going to shoot him here and now and hang the consequences.

"Put the pistol away." The voice came from the bedroom doorway. Dedovic swivelled one eye towards a large man standing in the shadows. The Tongans had stayed out of it so far as if manhandling a New South Wales detective was not in their contract, but they moved forward at the sound of the harsh guttural voice.

Dedovic holstered his weapon.

"I told you," Steve Bia murmured. "You don't have the pump."

"You and me aren't finished yet, Stevie."

"Any time, Mr Dedovic. Any time."

Out of the doorway appeared a large man wearing a black suit and polished black riding boots. His short hair bristled around his big fleshy ears, the skin on his face and neck was loose and leathery like some large monitor lizard. His nose was flattened at the bridge and his eyes were pouched and dark as if they were all pupil.

Charlie Kratos moved nearer the window, like something huge and nocturnal. Behind him trailed a scraggy blonde child-woman. Her skin was so tanned it looked as if it had been barbecued and she was wearing crocodile shoes and a white cotton dress. There were no lights on in the suite and the only illumination came from the red and purple neon in the distance.

"You're not a killer are you, Detective?"

Dedovic stared at the big fella. In one hand Kratos clutched a glass of milky liquid and the smell he gave off was of old-fashioned hair oil.

"That is why I ask for you," he said. "Doull, Hargraves, Bullmore, they would not hesitate to shoot. Of course you understand these men have been operating a Death Squad in your New South Wales Police for years. They would like to silence me too."

Charlie Kratos's speech was slow and thickly accented. Dedovic wondered where he'd come from originally. All he'd heard was that Kratos had fled central Europe in the late fifties as a refugee from Communism.

"Everyone knows who the real criminals are. I'm only a businessman. All I do is sell a product for which there is a great demand."

"So why did the Homicide squad find a human head in your house?" Dedovic asked.

"They had no warrant, that was an illegal search. For years I pay your squads money — Consorters, Armed Holdup, Kings Cross, Vice. I look after over fifty detectives." Kratos held up five fingers. "Ever since I come to this country your police take more from me than the taxman. Even in Europe we never have such greedy men."

Dedovic picked up the manila envelope from the low black table. He sensed the Tongan twins stir behind him and passed the bulky envelope over to Kratos who gave it to Moses who handed it to Samsun who gave it to Steve Bia. "Ray wants to know what can be done," Dedovic said.

Kratos sipped at his milk, his small dark hooded eyes fixed on Dedovic. Bia took the parcel into the bedroom suite and came back a few minutes later. He passed the envelope to Samsun who gave it to Moses who handed it back to his boss who stuffed it into the inside pocket of his suit. "Seventy-five, Mr Kratos."

"Tell me something," Kratos said. "You think this will buy my silence? Seventy-five is nothing." The big feller moved in front of the window with the skinny child-woman hanging off his arm. Her eyes were sleepy and her chin nodded on her chest as if she were struggling to stay awake. "Many times I pay your colleagues twenty-five thousand in *one* week. Do you want to know who else I pay, Detective?"

"Not really," Dedovic said. The knuckles on his right hand had swollen up like a bunch of grapes and his jaw ached. He listened to Kratos rattle off the names of judges, barristers, ministers, even a former Premier of whom there'd been inside rumours for years.

"How much did Ray Doull give you for the delivery to my home?"

Dedovic looked at Kratos's fleshy ears. The veins on the big fella's baggy leathery throat pulsated. Did he mean the Rushcutters Bay job? It was the only time Dedovic had been to Kratos's house. They'd driven out to an enormous three-storey place in Strathfield – floodlights, high brick fence, security cameras, guard dogs. A fortress. Dedovic and Scotty Dwyer in the front, Ray Doull nursing a vinyl suitcase in the back. When they got to the house Doull went into the bedroom and Mrs Kratos, a blonde buxom woman in her late forties with dark roots showing through her bleached hair and a beauty spot like Elizabeth Taylor's on the corner of her lip, took their suitcase and gave them a canvas sausage bag in return. They were only there five minutes. Back at the Drug Unit Ray Doull carved the sale up five ways. That night Dedovic took his share home and stashed it in an old cigarette tin in the garage under his daughter's bedroom. Twenty-five thousand in fifty dollar notes. "I don't remember the amount," he said.

Kratos smiled faintly and the folds of skin stretched back over his small dark eyes. "Sergeant Doull was paid two hundred and fifty for that delivery. Very pure merchandise. I hope you got your correct share, Detective."

For years Dedovic had suspected that Doull had dudded his mates, that he'd sifted the cream off the milk, but there was nothing he could do. He wasn't even angry. He just wished he had never got involved with Ray Doull and the Drug Unit in the first place. It weighed on his mind. Some mornings when he woke sweating after a hard night's sleep it was the first thing he thought of. Moneys received; briefs he'd gutted. Seventeen years in the Police Service and he had sunk to this: standing here in this fat low-life's hotel suite bargaining to save his own neck.

"I have not mentioned your name to Integrity or ICAC yet." Kratos studied him. "As you can imagine, Detective, there are many State and Federal agencies willing to speak to me over certain payments made to senior police officers."

"I'm supposed to pick up some documents," Dedovic said coldly. "A box of papers."

Charlie Kratos tapped the side of his flat, elongated head. "I keep everything in here," he said. "That way I don't lose it. Tell Raymond I want another seventy-five delivered next week."

Dedovic picked up his jacket. He wanted to get out of this hotel as quickly as he could. He didn't like the air in here. The honeycombed towers of the city soared above the Domain; a train glided low over the Woolloomooloo rooftops.

"I'd like you to accompany us to dinner, Detective."

"No thanks."

"But I insist," Kratos said. "It's not often I have a visit from a New South Wales detective these days. I buy you the best seafood banquet in Sydney."

"You've got your money, Kratos. You're on your own."

The Tangaluka twins moved forward on either side of him and clamped his arms at the elbow. "I think you have the wrong impression of me, Detective. I'm not a common criminal."

"Yeah yeah, I heard all that."

"So I don't intend to be getting into any strange police vehicles this evening. Please."

They went out of the suite bunched in a group of six and caught the lift, Dedovic bookended between the two rugged Tongans, their arms thicker than his thighs. For such big men their skin was abnormally smooth as if they never shaved. Up close they smelled of limes and coconut oil. Samsun said something to his twin in Tongan. In English he added: "Maybe you can come as far as Circular Quay, Mr D."

"What is this?" Dedovic said. "Kidnapping a police officer?" He felt eight steely fingers gripping right through the muscle into his ulna bone.

"Nothing so crude," Charlie Kratos said. "Just additional insurance."

Dedovic saw the sneer on Steve Bia's face. The girl holding Kratos's arm was smiling in a sleepy way at everyone. "Can we have some lobster, Charlie, can we have some lobster?" Whatever fuel she was flying on, it looked too good to be legal.

In the foyer another planeload of Japanese honeymooners had landed from Kingsford Smith. Uniformed porters were running to and from the coaches with quality luggage. No sooner had Kratos and Bia stepped out through the sliding glass doors than three RSL cabs pulled up in the hotel driveway. Sirens were going off in the distance and the high-pressure sodium vapour street lamps gave off a pure white light. Macleay Street was filled with well-heeled men and shiny-lipped women wandering into glass-fronted sushi restaurants.

Squeezed between the Tangaluka brothers, Dedovic was escorted towards the second cab. "Let him ride with me," the big feller said in that burred European accent. They packed him in the back seat beside Kratos and his sleepy-eyed girlfriend. Dedovic stared at the Tongans and Steve Bia hurrying into the cab behind. "Where to, mate?" the driver said.

Dedovic recognised the voice, saw the checked cloth cap pulled down over the driver's iron-grey hair and felt the skin on the back of his neck prickle. Charlie Kratos grunted the name of a harbourside restaurant. The cab pulled out into thick Potts Point traffic, accelerated down Wylde Street and cornered the hairpin bend at the bottom with a muffled screech of rubber.

"What the hell—" Kratos yelled.

The cab jounced as it left the roadway and the tyres rumbled across the iron grate of the Defence Forces car park tucked in the shadows of a huge apartment block. Charlie Kratos started to get up out of his seat as the cab braked violently but Ray Doull swung around in the driver's seat and pressed the barrel of his .357 Colt Python into the loose sack of skin surrounding Charlie Kratos's throat, jammed it hard up under his fat chin.

"Not in the cab, Ray," Dedovic cried. "Jesus, not in here."

But Doull didn't hear a word. He cocked the hammer with his thumb. "I hate squealers." He looked directly into the big fella's dark pouched eyes, and pulled the trigger.

# 36

They drove out along Botany Road with their roof-sign extinguished. Dedovic's ears were still ringing from the gunshot and Charlie Kratos was slumped against him in the back seat of the RSL cab, a trickle of semi-clotted black blood running from the star-shaped entry wound under his shattered jawbone down over his shirt collar. On the other side of the dead man the sleepy-eyed girl was chewing at a hunk of her bleached hair and whimpering. "Shut up," Ray Doull barked from behind the wheel. Industrial estates sprang up on either side of the road, tyre factories and smash repair shops; an incinerator blew out a brown toxic haze and a 747 with its belly lights blinking banked over the Kurnell refinery in the distance. Dedovic could smell hair oil in the cab and another more disturbing odour emanating from the black-suited body lolling beside him. Kratos's girlfriend was coming down fast and she started wailing, one hand covering her nose, her face and white cotton dress sprayed with blood. Ray Doull pulled off the road into an unlit service station, parked at the rear behind the customer toilets and switched his headlights off. Two more cabs drew up behind them and dimmed their lights. Dedovic saw three figures silhouetted in the first cab and four in the second. He wondered if Ray had the same fate in mind for the Tongans and Steve Bia. Doull turned around in the front seat and his thick grey moustache was wet at the ends, his eyes were bloodshot. There was a faint clicking noise as he reached an arm over towards the sobbing girl. Dedovic grabbed the barrel quickly and shoved it away; it was still warm. "Are you crazy?" he said.

"She's an eyewitness. We can't take any chances."

"I won't be a party to this, Ray."

"Go take a walk, Terr. Go on."

"No," Dedovic said firmly. His hand went under his jacket and he locked eyes with Ray Doull. In that moment there was no need for any words between them. Dedovic had never been more serious in his life. Ray Doull shook his head sadly and replaced his trigger hand on the steering wheel. "Mate, we're all in this together," he said. The girl was still crying. "It's alright, it's okay." Dedovic wiped her face. "What's your name?"

"Lisa." She sniffed. "Lisa Pope."

"Okay, Lisa, now tell me the truth. What have you taken tonight – acid, PCP?"

"Charlie's gone, he's gone, isn't he?"

"Listen to me, Lisa. You're having a very bad trip. You've taken some adulterated shit, alright."

"I want some lobster, Charlie's going to buy me some lobster."

"Forget about the lobster, lobster's off." Dedovic took out a fifty dollar note and tucked it into Lisa's small damp hand. "I want you to catch a cab, go home and when you wake up tomorrow you won't recall anything, okay?" He reached across Kratos's thickened waist and opened her door. "Go now. And remember," he warned her. "Stay away from drugs."

The door clunked and the girl in her white dress and her crocodile shoes clacked across the concrete slabs towards the city. Dedovic got out of the cab and stretched his legs. The sky was dark and bearded with brown scurf. A sign above the locked pumps said, *Bullbars and Mufflers fitted here*. The closed diner next door specialised in Food to Go. Apart from the three occupied taxis idling at the back of the garage there was not a soul in sight. Dedovic lowered himself into the front seat and slammed the door.

"Mate," Ray Doull said. "I dunno what to say."

"We're police officers, Ray. We don't kill twenty-year-old girls."

"Terr, you're right. I dunno what came over me then. Mate, I'm sorry. No really, I mean that."

Dedovic stared at the former Drug Unit sergeant. Ray Doull looked like a cop, he smelled like a cop and he spoke like a cop, but it had been years since he had behaved like one. "How did you know Kratos would leave that hotel?"

"Every night this week Charlie's pigged out at the same five star restaurant, nine o'clock, regular as clockwork. He always loved his seafood."

"Where'd you score the cabs?"

"Got a panelbeater mate on the south side. Does a lot of fleet business."

Dedovic looked at the hole in the cab roof and the cracked rear window. "Let's get this over with," he said.

At the intersection they swung west along Foreshore Road. Trucks flowed past and semitrailers crawled along the slow lane, engines whining under the weight of their container loads. The sky was filled with the roar of jets landing and taking off from the international runway. On a dark stretch of highway Ray Doull flicked his indicator on and steered the cab off the flat bitumen into the shadows of a group of spindly banksia and thick-leaved shrubs. A sandy track led down through the dunes to Botany Bay. Doull killed the engine and they waited in the darkness for the two other cabs to park alongside. A semitrailer trundled past and then it was quiet for a long moment. There were no cars parked anywhere. Dedovic got out and stood by the edge of the highway staring across at the dark reserve on the other side. The hair rose on the nape of his neck. If he had tried to, he couldn't have chosen a better place in all of Sydney to dump a corpse. Doors slammed behind him and he turned to see the Tangaluka twins and Steve Bia, their hands cuffed in front of them, being marched down the narrow sandy track by Dwyer and McJannett carrying two spades while Dennis Hargraves kept watch. Ray Doull whistled at him and they went to work, unbuckling the safety belt and easing Kratos's fat gurgling body out into the bushes and propping it against a termite-rotted fence post. Doull tapped the soles of Kratos's black shin-high boots. "Look at that stitching, Terr. Italian calf. Beautiful workmanship. What size are they, look like twelves?"

"Get the other arm, Ray. Hurry up."

"I'm a nine," Doull said. "Pity."

With a grunt they lifted the dead man onto their shoulders and half-carried him, half-dragged him down the overgrown track, his head flopping about loosely on his thickened neck. Planks had been laid down to stabilise the sand and Kratos's heels clunked on every board. Discarded oil tins and black garbage bags clung to the barbed-wire fence and Ray Doull clicked his tongue with disgust. Signs warning against dumping were fixed to the fence but Dedovic could not read the fine print in the darkness. The sand was thick and soft underfoot and the dunes, anchored down with spinifex grass, coastal wattle and wild pea, rolled out on either side. The path curved and widened and there in front of them loomed Botany Bay.

Dedovic dropped Kratos's head in the sand and stared at the view. To the east the lights of the container terminal glowed like a small city. The bay shimmered silvery blue from the reflection and a few hundred metres away, taxiing towards them, was a Qantas 747. From the shoreline it looked as if the jumbo was riding on the surface of the water, its red tail as high as a six-storey building. There was a mighty roar and then the jet seemed to leap into the air, its green and white wing lights flashing as it lifted over the dunes and the highway and then banked south towards the sea. The sky was mottled black in its wake and there was not a single star to be seen. The air smelled of hydrocarbons. Lance Bullmore and Dennis Hargraves took Ray Doull aside while Scotty Dwyer and Bill McJannett leaned on the handles of their spades. The Tangaluka twins turned their eyes to the jutting runway across the shallow water as if they entertained the idea of making a desperate swim for it. For years Dedovic had heard the rumours that a death squad operated secretly within the NSW Police, but he had never believed it until tonight. He watched the three handcuffed men in the shadowy light and wondered how in hell he had ended up here. Sometimes you took a wrong turn in life and you never got back into the lane you were on. Lance Bullmore and Dennis Hargraves were disappearing up the sandy track.

"What's happening, Ray?" Dedovic went over.

"Lance and Dennis had to leave, Terr." Doull was kneeling over Kratos's body, tugging at his high boots.

"What do you mean, had to leave?"

"They can't afford to be compromised, not in their position."

"And we can?"

With the sound of splitting leather Doull tore one of the black boots off and held it up to the light shining off the water. "Yeah, twelves," he said.

"Why did you shoot him, Ray?"

"Terr, the prick was going to sell us down the river. He would've taken our seventy-five and come back next week for another bite. He's a low-life Kings Cross squealer who's given a hot shot to three girls that I know of, raped others and sold more drugs than Souls pharmacy. He deserved to go. Now quit yer blueing and give me a hand with the fat prick."

They dragged Charlie Kratos up into the dunes and left him in a sandy hollow underneath a gnarled old-man banksia. Ants were crawling over his mangled jaw and his flattened brown eyes stared up at them. "Pity about the suit." Doull was going through his pockets. "Looks like an Armani." He removed a manila envelope and clunked a boot on the dead man's chest. "Look at this stuff." He kicked sand over the pale waxy face. "A gravedigger's delight."

Dedovic looked at the fine soft sand and then at Sergeant Doull and wondered how many other crims he'd buried in these dunes. He could hear water lapping at the shore and planes coming in over the runway and the steady sound of trucks growling behind the thick bushes. Botany Bay was where it all began. He walked across the mounds, smelling raw industrial sewage, his shoes filling up with sand, to where Scotty Dwyer and Bill McJannett were leaning on their garden spades. In the dark bluish light the Tangaluka twins were impossible to tell apart.

"You got kids, Mr D?" one of the Tongans asked quickly.

Dedovic said he had two.

"Samsun's got a three year-old boy. I got two little girls back on the island. There's a Qantas flight leaves for Fiji at 6.15 in the morning with a connecting flight to Nuku'alofa. Me and Samsun, we'd like to go home."

A wide-bodied jet lumbered overhead and its landing lights lit up the bay. Dedovic saw Ray Doull striding down the dunes towards them carrying his silver .357 Magnum at his side. "You'd never see us again," Moses said, with a sense of urgency in his voice.

"Thas right, Mr D," his brother Samsun said. "You have our word."

"Uncuff them, Scotty," Dedovic said.

"It's very unorthodox, mate. Check with Ray."

Dedovic snatched the keys off Dwyer and uncuffed the two Tongans; the steel had left white bite marks on their brown wrists. "Detective McJannett will drop you at Kingsford Smith. Don't ever set foot in this city . . ." He stopped. Ray Doull was aiming his .357 at the side of Samsun Tangaluka's shaved head. "Can't be done, Terr."

Dedovic stepped in front of him. He could see the sweat on Ray Doull's forehead, the untrimmed moustache hanging over his top lip, the broken capillaries colouring his cheeks. "You involved me in your dirt, Ray. Now I'm telling you. The Tongans walk."

He sensed Doull's finger firm around the trigger, his eyes tighten at the corners, but for the second time that evening Ray Doull lowered his revolver. He was wearing a black and gold vinyl jacket with *Tigers* stitched down the front, his cabbie's cap pushed back over his iron-grey hair and there was a palpable tiredness in his face. "Don't ever try that on again, Terr." He lit a cigarette and Dedovic realised that he had pushed him as far as he would go.

"I got kids too, Mr Dedovic," Steve Bia said.

"You got nothing, prick." Doull grabbed McJannett's spade. "Somebody's got to do the digging." He told Dedovic to march Bia up to the dunes and have him dig a large hole. "No, make that two holes," he said.

This time Dedovic didn't argue. He watched the Tongans and Bill McJannett filing up the track then walked Steve Bia up to where Charlie Kratos was lying in his fine black suit with his mouth open attracting a party of beetles and tiny-winged flies. There was a smell of petrochemicals in the air and the suburban lights of Brighton-Le-Sands were strung out along the western side of the bay. Dedovic wondered what ordinary people would think if they saw what he was doing. Would they understand how he had got to this point? Would they think he was all bad? If you didn't partake in the way things were done, you were on your own. That was the code.

He listened to Steve Bia grunting, his police bracelet clinking against the spade handle. The sand was loose and soft and shovelled easily. "I can't dig with these cuffs, Mr Dedovic."

Dedovic knew why Doull had sent him up here alone. To get his hands dirty.

"You're not going to shoot a man in cold blood are yer?"

Dedovic brought his service pistol out of its holster and aimed it at Steve Bia's head. He was going to try. "You sold my daughter drugs."

"Nah, I give 'em to her. Please. You wouldn't want me on your conscience."

Dedovic hesitated, trying to steel his nerves. Bia was right. He didn't have the pump for this kind of work. He holstered his weapon, bent down and uncuffed the man.

"Thanks Mr Dedovic." Steve Bia climbed out of the hole he'd dug, dusted sand off his shirt and brought his fist hard up under Dedovic's rib cage. Dedovic dropped to his knees and sucked in bad air. "You never shoulda loaded me up, Mr Dedovic. You never shoulda done that." He swung around and Dedovic felt the sharp edge of the spade shave his ear. He hit the dunes, right hand grappling at his holster. Something flat slammed into his back and he tasted sand. Hard wiry fingers clamped around his throat and grit stung his eyes. He threw Bia off. "Your daughter's a hot little goer, isn't she?" Bia said. Dedovic ducked under two swinging arms and slipped the pistol from his holster. The sound of the report was louder than he expected. Steve Bia stood up awkwardly as if he was drunk; his eyes widened with surprise. He tried to say something but the noise of the jets over the runway drowned his voice. Dedovic remembered the police motto – *Culpam Poena Premit Comes* – Punishment follows close on guilt – and shot Bia twice in the thorax. He watched him stagger down to the shore as if there was a chance he might survive and then flopped face-down in the low muddy tide.

Dedovic stared out over Botany Bay.

Scotty Dwyer and Ray Doull came up out of the darkness behind him as if they'd been standing there all along and handed him a fresh spade. "It's a dirty job, Terry," Doull said. "That's what people don't realise."

# 37

She rushed around the house locking windows. Found one of Garth's cast-off shirts in her linen cupboard, ragged at the collar, paint-stained. She grabbed the Chinese detective's notebook, the list of names and addresses of all employees from the South Pacific International College of English and slammed the front door behind her. Her old mustard Corona hiccuped when she pressed the ignition, the engine groaned as if it was half-asleep then reluctantly turned over. With a squeal of rubber she pulled out onto the Princes Highway, heading south. Cabs shot past in the night. She wondered if he had stumbled onto something. She'd never heard that much emotion in his voice before, the mobile batteries fading. What was he doing out near the airport? What was he up to? He was so damned secretive. If only he would learn to be more trusting. She turned into Canal Road, brakes grinding as she nearly clipped the back of a cement truck that cut across her lane, the driver giving her the finger when she sounded her horn. She sped past him. Men were such bad drivers. Road ragers. Industrial estates sprawled out on either side of her, fenced off, padlocked. On General Holmes Drive she slowed down, circling the perimeter of the airport. She pulled off onto the shoulder and reversed back to where he was standing under a street lamp. A wave of nausea enveloped her when he got in. She rolled down her window. "God, what's happened to you?"

"Police work," he said. "I can't talk about it right now."

He was covered in sand and dirt, his right ear was bleeding, his jaw was bruised and he stank of blood and bone.

"That smell – what have you been doing?"

"I've been down in the sewer," he said. "Did you bring any clean clothes?"

"Only a shirt. No-one's ever left me their trousers." She watched him remove his jacket and tie. The knuckles on his right hand were skinned and swollen.

"You'll have to take me to my unit. It's on Broadway." He started removing his holster and unbuttoning his shirt. She glanced across at his chest and accelerated onto the loop road. "Has something bad happened?"

He tossed his jacket down between his stained shoes and pulled Garth's shirt on over his Bonds singlet.

"I want to know, Terry." The blood and bone smell filled her car.

"I killed a man tonight."

She looked across at him. "God," she said.

"A drug dealer."

"Don't you have to report it or something?"

"It's been taken care of."

She knew without asking that it was Steve Bia, the man his daughter had talked of. A truck horn blared alongside and she steered the Corona back into its own lane, trying to concentrate on her driving, suspicions whirling about in her head. "Was it self-defence?" she said.

"He tried to kill me with a spade."

"A garden spade?"

"That's right." He touched the deep cut on the fleshy part of his ear. "I want to thank you for responding so quickly tonight."

Nickie squinted into the traffic lights. Now she was an accessory after the fact. She pressed her foot down. The engine spluttered and steam hissed from the radiator grille. Nickie turned down a side-alley, watching her temperature gauge flash red. "I just bought a new water pump." She stopped outside an unlit scrapyard.

"Let me take a look."

He climbed out of the front seat and she popped the catch. He bent underneath the hood and she could feel his big hands pulling and twisting on the engine block. The car rocked on its wheels.

"Radiator hose's blown," he said.

She jumped out and stared at the barbed wire fence surrounding the metal recycling yard. A black dog watched them silently from behind the gate. "Where's your car, Terry?"

"At the Cross." He flipped his mobile open.

"So how'd you get to Botany Bay?"

"A friend drove me."

"Is this the truth?"

"Have I ever lied to you?"

"Yes," she said.

"Those two dead students? That wasn't a lie. I didn't want to alarm you. Two passengers," he said into the phone. "Ready now."

"What about my car?" Nickie said. "I can't leave it here."

"Why not?"

"Someone might steal it."

"You'd be lucky." He stepped out onto the road

and waited for the cab. When it came he held the door open for her while she slid in. "Sorry about the stink," he said to the driver, "I slipped over on a sewer pipe."

The cabbie grunted, wound down his window.

"The spade," Nickie said. "Where'd he get the spade from?"

"Had it with him," Terry answered.

"At the airport?"

"No, at Botany Bay. We met on the foreshore."

She wanted to believe him. She really did. But she was out of her depth. He had been in some sort of fight, that was for certain. Out of the corner of her eye she watched him going through his pockets, taking out his wallet. "Turn down here," he said. The driver pulled in behind a converted warehouse in a narrow Chippendale street. Terry balled his dirty jacket and shirt in his big raw hands, took his change and slammed the door. "We picked up a man for questioning this evening over the Asian killings."

Nickie followed him across the dug-up street, stepping between witch hats and concrete pipes. When he keyed in his code the security door whirred its approval. "So who is it?" she said.

"No-one you know. Some Chinese gangster."

She looked at him in the lift. "But you don't think he did it?"

"Try telling my CI that."

The corridor smelled of Chinese herbs. Terry opened the door to his bachelor unit. The furniture was shiny and rudimentary, like a highway motel's. A colour brochure on the dining table proclaimed *Real Estate for Offshore Investors*. A large window overlooked the street. When he came out of the shower in his boxers and singlet the fertiliser smell was gone. The cut in his ear needed stitches. She watched him stuff his dirty brown suit into a garbage bag, tie it with an aluminium clip and dump it in the kitchen bin.

"Won't there be an inquiry?" she said.

"There's bound to be. Cops are always being investigated." He picked up the phone. "You didn't find any money in that front room of yours?"

"Money?"

"Yeah, a wad of fifties on the floor."

"There was no money on my floor."

"Christ." He shook his head and massaged his jaw with a hand. Water glistened in his hair and he'd splashed on fresh cologne. She'd never been with a man who had killed somebody before. She wondered why it didn't bother her more. Chinese music was playing in the flat next door. She sat in a chair with her hand on her belly while he talked to some policeman called Dick. "You're kidding!" He put down the phone.

"What is it?" she asked.

He went into the bedroom and came out wearing street clothes. His forehead was wrinkled like a walnut. He laced up his Rivers. "Looks they're going to drop a charge on this Asian gangbanger. The boss is getting a lotta pressure from above; he's desperate to wrap the case up."

"But you don't think he's the killer?"

"I know he's not."

"How can you be so sure?"

"You do a job long enough and you can feel it in your blood. If this was a simple extortion bid, the victims might be missing a finger or two. That's the way these gangs work. But there's no evidence of any ransom demand. This isn't about money and it wasn't any Chatswood Triad that did these three girls. The Chinese hatchet that Chen got swiped with, the plastic chopsticks inserted in Ling Ling's uterus and the strips of flesh cut from the other girls' thighs. This guy's sending us a message loud and clear."

"What is it?" she said.

"You work it out."

Nickie looked at him. "Okay, but why choose foreign students?"

"They don't know Sydney, they're more likely to talk to a stranger and they're easier to grab. Chen was spot-on about the area in which he operates. In a big city the average guy is only familiar with a handful of suburbs at most. The AK seems more comfortable on the northside. We know that."

"So who is he?" Nickie was impressed. Underneath that laconic exterior Terry was really quite an intelligent detective.

He moved over to the window and stared down at the well-lit street. "Chen's profile is the best bet we have so far and the fact that she flushed him out at Artarmon station."

Nickie said, "I went through the addresses of all the college staff this evening. There are only three South Pacific employees who live on the north shore. Mr Lipmann, Duc Vu Trinh who is head of our Asian Languages Department and Mona."

"Uh huh," he said.

She walked over to the window to see what had stolen his attention. A late model sedan parked outside the building with its headlights off. Two shadowy figures in the front seat. "Are they police?" she asked.

"Something like that." He pulled the blinds shut. "Feed me those names again."

She could tell that he was having trouble focusing his thoughts. The enormity of taking a man's life seemed to be weighing on his conscience. "Mr Lipmann," she said. "Duc Vu Trinh and Mona."

"Rule out Duc Vu Trinh for a start and Lipmann's too old, doesn't fit the profile. Chen's right. The AK's in his late twenties, early thirties. That leaves Mona and I know she didn't do it.

"She picked you up in a bar didn't she?"

"Nothing like that. We met at this gym where I train."

"You don't have to explain," she said. "I talked to Mona today. She said that she didn't have a lot of confidence in your investigation."

"Thanks for the tip. What else did she say?"

"Just that she was worried about her husband."

"I didn't know she has a husband."

"Ex-husband, but he still gives her a hard time."

"Where's he live?"

"That's the funny thing," Nickie said. "When they split, Laurie moved into the block of flats right next door." She saw the muscles at the corners of Terry's eyes tighten.

"Blond guy with a pie-shaped face?"

"You know him?"

"When I was at Mona's there was a fellow at the window watching us on the couch."

"What were you doing?"

"Talking. How old is he?"

"Twenty-eight, twenty-nine. He has his own plastering business."

Terry picked up the receiver and dialled. She heard him say, "Criminal Records Unit" then give his name and number. He put down the phone. A moment later it rang and scooping it up he said, "Detective Senior Constable Dedovic attached to Task Force Jarrah. I want to run a check on a Laurie Limacher. DOB mid-sixties. Current address, Crows Nest, Sydney."

Nickie waited. She had been to Laurie's wedding. She

had seen him come into the college to meet Mona. Apart from his looks, he never struck her as anything special. Only the stories that Mona had related about him.

"Uh huh," Terry was saying into the mouthpiece. He came off the phone and grabbed his brown leather jacket hanging over the back of a chair. "Limacher's got form. Two sexual assault charges in '91. Want to know what vehicle he drives?"

She tried to recall if she had ever seen Laurie's *veekle*. She took a guess. "Mitsubishi van?"

"The AK," Terry said.

She gripped his arm as they headed for the door. "What's an AK?"

He gave her a heavy-lidded stare as if he was surprised she hadn't figured it out. "That's what we nicknamed him in the squad," he said. "The Asian Killer."

# 38

They sat in the darkness, alert, staring out at the three-storey block of sixties flats opposite: a concrete balcony and white iron rail marking off each floor. The glass doors at the front of the building were well-lit; gunshots and a car chase blared from a TV behind yellow-curtained windows on the top floor. Terry cracked his door open. She watched him slip across the lawn and lose himself in the shrubbery. Waiting in the Commodore, frightened and excited in the same breath, the lines of a song speeding through her mind. Helter Skelter. The driver's door popped open and her heart jumped.

"He's up there alright," Terry said. "Third floor. There's a back entrance. The residents park underneath the building. So I'm going to take a look at his vehicle. I'll need you to keep watch."

She stepped out onto the quiet Crows Nest street. The night was warm and sticky and a full round moon glowed low in the sky.

Terry gazed up at it. "Every cop on the beat knows that spells trouble." She followed him to the rear of the apartment building. Black Sulo bins lined the footpath. "For Chrissake, don't stand out there," he said.

She moved out of the arc of the street lamp, watching the back stairs and the yellow curtained windows on the top floor. In the distance the bridge traffic droned along the highway. Laurie had always struck her as an ordinary bloke. Hot-tempered perhaps, but certainly no psychopath. What if Terry had got it wrong? He'd already killed one man tonight; she knew he was armed. Across the bitumen car park she saw him waving at her. She crept around the base of the salmon-brick building, slinking between the columns of the numbered car ports. A hand gripped her arm and pulled her in. "Look at this," he whispered in her ear. She saw the dented white van in the narrow space, the tinted windows and black spidery lettering on the doors: *Commercial Contractor. All types of Plastering* .

She bent over to check the plates. GNJ 677. This was the same van she'd seen outside the college.

"I can smell him," Terry said, "I can smell this fucking guy."

"Are you sure?"

"It's the AK. I gotta take a look in his apartment."

"But he's up there isn't he?"

"Yeah, but you're going to get him out."

"Me?" Nickie went.

"You wanted to get involved."

"Hold on, hold on," she said. "How am I going to do that?"

"You're a woman. Use your charms."

"That's very considerate of you, Terry." She couldn't believe this guy. First he didn't want to tell her the time of day and now he wanted to use her as sexual bait. "Why don't you just go get a search warrant?"

"Want to know how difficult it is to get a warrant these days? They're not like hamburgers. You can't send out for one when you feel the urge. You need something solid."

"What about the notebook?"

"So I front up with a scrap of paper scrawled in Mandarin that says *three diamonds white van* and tell the magistrate that's all I got. My Inspector is set to drop a charge on somebody else. Look, I wouldn't be asking you if I thought there was any risk. I like you too much."

"That's the nicest thing you've said."

"This guy only carves up Chinese girls. You're seventy-five per cent safe."

"Thanks."

He peered in the driver's window to check the odometer, his big hands splayed against the side of the van. "Fits the bill alright, high mileage, blacked-out windows. A mobile killing unit."

Nickie studied Terry's face in the shadows. He had an unorthodox approach to policing, but she didn't doubt his commitment. She wondered how much he had influenced her in their short time together. She had the strange feeling that she was becoming more like him.

"We gotta hope there's some residual fibres in there," he said, "from Ling Ling's skirt. First we need something concrete to justify an arrest."

"I'll ring from Mona's flat."

"I don't want her in on this."

"But it'd be much easier for her to entice Laurie out. He's obsessed with her."

"What else do you know about this guy?"

"When they broke up, Laurie moved into the apartments next door just to bug her. He went off the rails and started ringing her constantly. I think she took out a restraining order in the end. They got married too quickly."

"Why'd they split?"

"Mona grew sick of him. She has a high turnover rate."

"I can believe it."

"She dumped you too?"

"I wouldn't say dumped," he said.

Furtively they crossed the car park and stood outside the adjoining block of 1930s red-brick units with white wooden windows. "Least she's got better taste in apartments," he said.

Nickie knocked on her ground-floor unit. Footsteps echoed on wood and Mona appeared around the door, clad in a silky green dressing gown, her face puffy with sleep. She looked at them sharply. "What do you two want?"

Nickie started to explain. She heard the security chain clink and then Terry pushed straight past Mona and strode down her hall.

"What the hell do you think you're doing?" Mona called out.

Nickie followed them both into the lounge. "He's a policeman, Mona," she said.

"That doesn't give him the right to burst in here. Do you know what time it is?"

"Shut up and listen." Terry pulled back her curtains to reveal the ugly block of flats next door. A yellow light burned on the top floor, directly overlooking Mona's window. "We believe your ex-husband may be responsible for the deaths of three foreign students and the attempted murder of a police officer."

"Laurie?" Mona laughed. "That's ridiculous. Is that the best you police can come up with? Where's your evidence?"

"We can't reveal our evidence yet, *Mz* Limacher, but we wouldn't be here if we weren't serious."

Her gown had slipped off one shoulder and Nickie caught Terry staring at her pale skin underneath. "He's right," she said, "Laurie's van fits the description of a van seen outside the college around the time Ling Ling disappeared." She couldn't understand why Mona was suddenly so protective.

"Laurie's a selfish bastard and I wish I'd never laid eyes on him, but he's not a killer."

"I didn't believe it was him either," Nickie said, "but he fits the police profile."

"Does he have any emotional or physical defects?" Terry said.

"Laurie has lots of defects." Mona tossed back her hair, the swelling of her breasts visible through the gap in her gown.

Nickie remembered talking to Laurie at their wedding. The way he stumbled over particular words. "Doesn't he have a fluency disorder?"

"He used to have a slight stutter," Mona said. "So what?" A breeze blew in from the street and the front door banged against the latch.

Terry picked up the phone on a blue Ikea table and held it out to Mona. "Get him out of that flat and we'll find out one way or the other."

"You don't have any evidence do you? This is all just bluff and bluster." She turned to Nickie. "And what are you playing detective for? Haven't you got a life of your own?"

"I'm trying to help," Nickie said.

"Help yourself you mean. It's pathetic to watch you chase after this cop."

"We can do this with or without you, Ms Limacher." Terry's voice hardened. He was holding the phone towards her and she snatched it out of his hand like a bad actress. "Before you ring," he said. "I'll need to borrow a torch." Mona stalked down the hall to her kitchen. Terry came over and squeezed Nickie's arm. "You alright there?" he said.

"I'm fine, I'm fine." Nickie lowered her eyes. She'd never realised she was so obvious. But whatever Mona said, this was something she had to do.

"Give me ten minutes. When he gets here, keep him in this room. That way I can watch you from his apartment. Stay on the chaise longue, if I see you sitting there I'll know everything's alright."

Mona came back with a pencil-thin torch and tossed it over to him. She crossed her thin bird legs, picked up the phone and dialled.

"Be careful, Terry," Nickie said in the hallway.

He squeezed her to his chest and she smelled his skin, felt the strength of those big swollen hands pressing her ribs. "You want to know something?" she said.

"What?" He moved towards the door.

"I'm glad I was wrong about you."

Dedovic flattened himself against the smooth trunk of a scribbly gum, watching the stairwell next door. Thick black cables were strung overhead and a colony of flying foxes flitted across the face of the moon. He listened for footsteps, hoping Mona hadn't tipped the guy off. He'd seen it happen in domestics, the ex-wife changing sides. If Limacher was that obsessed, he should be down here like a shot. So where was he? The light went off in the third-floor window. Got him. The guy coming down the back stairs, dressed in black, wearing shiny new joggers. Trying to get an ID in the moonlight: Caucasian, late twenties, short blond hair, hundred and seventy-eight cm, seventy to seventy-five kilos. From the size of him, nothing to worry about unless he was tooled up.

Dedovic watched him go through the doorway of Mona's ground-floor unit, then took the stairs, moving fast for a big man. On the third floor he leaned against the door of the flat and listened. Silence. This had to be the one. Two other apartments down the corridor, TVs spitting out toothpaste ads. He knocked and waited. Nothing. He shouldn't even be thinking of doing this, but it had been a long time since he'd followed the rulebook. He cocked an ear then hit the door with the meat of his shoulder. Pain ran up the side of his neck and along his jawbone. He took a deep breath and gave it everything. Wood splintered and the striker plate bent inwards. Thank God for cheap building materials. He jammed the broken door shut behind him and ran the narrow beam of her torch over sticks of furniture.

Moving through the small neat apartment, eyes adjusting to the dark, the torch kept low. He turned over cushions, peeled back the edge of a Mexican rug. Got down on his hands and knees, checked under chairs, a table, ran his fingernails along the cracks in the skirting boards. Imagining himself in the shoes of a killer. An intelligent predator; someone who's careful not to get caught, who leaves no prints, no body fluids. Every tool he uses is non-specific, nothing that can't be bought from a chain-store. His methods are well-rehearsed, reliable. At nights he recalls the finely-boned Asian girls trapped in the back of his van, the way they kick and struggle as he applies the knife. With each victim he retains a lock of hair, a tooth, a patch of skin. The memories are enjoyable and the enjoyment reinforces his desires. But he has to be careful, above all he has to be very careful.

Dedovic kicked open the bedroom door and shone the thin blade of light over a white chipboard wardrobe and a raw pine bed. He up-ended the mattress, shook out the pillow, searching for hidden keepsakes, tent pegs, duct-tape. His torch lingered on a gold spine lying on the bedside table. He picked up the book and saw stamped across the opening page: *Medical Library, University of Sydney*. Flicked through graphic colour plates of bodies in various stages of decomposition: *The Handbook of Forensic Pathology*. In a drawer three more well-thumbed texts: *Practical Homicide Investigations, Interpretation of Bloodstain Evidence at Crime Scenes* and Polson, Gee and Knight's *The Essentials of Forensic Medicine*.

Slowly, Dedovic backed out of the bedroom and clicked off the torch. It was not courtroom proof, but it was confirmation. He could smell death in this apartment. The pale light from the moon shone through the curtained window and he could hear the city breathing outside. He checked the luminous hands of his watch, pulled back a corner of the yellow curtain and looked down into next door's ground floor flat. Laurie Limacher arguing at the window with Mona in her green dressing gown. But Nickie, where the fuck was Nickie? He'd told her to stay on the chaise longue. So where had she got to? The phone rang by the door and he flicked the torch on, sweeping it in the direction of a white metal table. Get out now, a voice was telling him. Call in back-up. You've done enough already, let the sniffer dogs take over. The phone kept ringing, loud and persistent, and he hesitated in the doorway. What if it was Nick? Warning him. He had to take a chance. He grabbed the receiver off the hook, pressed it against his ear without speaking.

"He knows you're up there, Terry," Nickie said.

And the line went dead.

# 39

He went up the back, through a wild tangled garden, ducking under bougainvillea spines, the vicious thorns of a coral tree tearing at his hair. The French doors were open and he stepped into Mona's kitchen, his Glock pistol drawn, running his eyes over a set of German chef's knives mounted on her wall, at the gap in the steel rack, wondering what Limacher had taken, the boner, slicer, cleaver? He had a bad feeling about this. He was dog-tired, his jaw ached, but the thought of Chen lying in an ICU bed drove him on, and Nick, there was something special about his little Greek-Australian friend. She'd grown on him like a vine and he had the strange impression that he was becoming more like her. He moved down the hall on the balls of his feet. Maybe when this was finished they could start afresh. He was tired of being a cop. Voices were arguing in the lounge room. He counted to three and threw himself into the doorway, crouched low, pistol raised to eye level, hands as steady as a rock. Laurie Limacher and Mona were grappling with each other by the window; a length of steel flashed near her throat.

"Police," Dedovic said. "Drop the blade!"

Limacher jerked back her head and brought the razor-sharp edge of the German boning knife up against his ex-wife's carotid artery. Her silky green gown had torn open to reveal the flat bed of her stomach and she yelled abuse at him, arms flailing in the air. Limacher ignored her, his slate-blue eyes locked on Dedovic. He was young with a clock-shaped face and blond surfer's hair. When he opened his mouth the words had trouble coming out. "You b-b-itch," he said, "you've set me up." He held her tight against him, exposing her neck.

Dedovic raised his pistol, looking to drop Limacher with a clean shot, but Mona was too close. He couldn't risk it. Not with a handgun. "Put the knife down, Laurie, walk away from her and we can talk."

"You're a cop," he said. "You'll shoot me."

"No. I give you my word."

"I n-n-never touched those girls." His stutter was faint, a slight impediment, and Dedovic wondered whether that was the reason Limacher had sought out non-native speakers. "I only talked to them, that's all. Somebody's trying to stitch me up."

Dedovic knew the guy was lying. "Where's Nickie?"

" . . . the bedroom," Mona stabbed two fingers at the doorway, her voice distorted by the boning knife clamped firmly against her windpipe.

Limacher stared at Dedovic. "I saw you f-f-fucking on my couch, I paid for that couch."

"Cool it, Laurie." Dedovic had his pistol fixed on Limacher's forehead. Adrenalin was pumping through his veins; he wanted to take him alive if he could. The sounds of the city blew in through the open window; tyres skidded on a road. Dedovic had to admire Mona's nerve; even with a chef's knife at her throat she continued abusing her ex-husband. "You're an idiot, Laurie," she said, "you always were."

"I know what's going on." Limacher's eyes popped. "I'm not stupid. You're in this together. You stuffed them snuff books in my m-m-mailbox—"

Dedovic heard the shot. Limacher's head reared back as if attached to a wire. Mona clutched at her throat, a fine trickle of bright red blood seeping through her fingers. For an instant Dedovic thought his pistol had misfired; unlike his old Smith & Wesson .38, there was no thumb safety. He sniffed the barrel; it was cold. Limacher took two steps forward, the chef's knife slipping from his fingers. "You gave me your word," he said, and tumbled over the chaise longue he'd paid for, a small purple entry wound like a bee sting at the back of his head. Dedovic ran to the open window, looked out into the moonlight at the thick-chested figure standing on the concrete path.

"Ray," he said.

"Mate." The lines on Doull's face were like grooves in a rock. A small stainless steel revolver sat up in his hand. He squinted through the window. "He was about to carve her up, Terr. You're a witness."

Dedovic could hear him ironing out the story; he wanted to ask his former sergeant how he knew that he was here, but there were more important considerations. He stepped over Mona gurgling on the floor and went into the small dark bedroom next door, his imagination careering ahead. He promised himself if Nick was unharmed he'd make a clean break with the past. Her body was foetalled on the double bed, hands and ankles bound tightly with pantyhose. When he called her name, she didn't move. He pulled a silky garment from her mouth, untied her joints and slid his thumb and forefinger down her wrist searching for a pulse. "Nick," he said. "You okay?"

She looked at him from the bed and then her arms shot up around his shoulders. She hung there for a moment squeezing him so hard he could feel her heart ticking against his chest. "I thought he was going to strangle me," she said, "but he just tied me up with Mona's underwear." She fingered the camisole. "Pure silk."

He helped Nickie off the bed and led her back into the lounge where Mona was down on one knee, hands cupped around her throat to stem the bleeding. "Oh God," Nickie said and ran over to the younger woman. Blood was splashed over Mona's green gown and lay pooled on the floor.

"I'm not going to die," Mona said. "Am I, Nickie?"

Dedovic prised away her fingers and examined the horizontal incision. The blade had cut through two layers of skin and some minor blood vessels, but avoided the main cables. "You'll need stitches," he said, "and most likely you'll carry a scar, but you're going to live."

"That bastard." Mona turned her head slowly to where the body of Laurie Limacher was lying face-down on the floor. When she saw him, her top lip quivered and she let out a whimper. "He's not dead, is he?"

"Miss," Ray Doull said, "he was about to slit your throat."

"You didn't have to kill him. You could've reasoned with him."

"It was a high-stress situation." Ray Doull patted down the pockets of Limacher's black Levis with a gloved hand.

"Who are you?"

"I'm a police officer," Doull explained. "Did you see what happened?"

"No," Mona whispered. "All I heard was a shot."

"What about you, Miss . . . "

Dedovic knew where this was going. Nickie shook her head rapidly, looking up at Dedovic with wide brown eyes. Telling him in a single glance of her suspicions. Blood began to flow down Mona's neck, bright red against her pale blueish skin. Dedovic stared at it seeping down her green gown and between her small, veined breasts, thinking there was nothing more tangible, more real, than blood. Mona fastened her white fingers around her throat. "Terry," Nickie said, "we need an ambulance." She was holding Mona in her arms. "Take her into the bathroom," Dedovic said. "Tie a towel around her neck and I'll call it in." He helped Nick carry Mona to the doorway and fished the mobile out of his pocket, not taking his eyes off Doull for one second. "What are you doing, Ray?"

"Mate, I'm covering our arses."

"You're fucking up the crime scene."

"Leave it with me, Terr, I know what I'm doing here." Doull dragged Limacher's body onto the floor and pressed the butt of his stainless steel revolver against the thumb and forefinger of the dead man's right hand.

"So the guy shot himself in the back of the head?"

"He didn't shoot himself, Terr." Doull straightened his back. "You did."

Dedovic looked at the Ringmaster standing there in a brown cardigan, wheat-coloured trousers and police work boots. "You gotta be kidding."

"Listen, it's got legs. He comes in waving a gun about, but you wrestle it off him, then he pulls a knife, threatens to slice the redhead, so you shoot him . . ." Doull dropped the stainless steel revolver onto the floor with a clunk.

"There isn't a coroner in the country who would swallow that."

"They'll buy it, I'm telling you. They're not looking for holes in the woodwork, they're looking to wrap this case up. You know how the brass think – PR. You'll be a hero, Terr, everyone wants a fuckin hero, the papers, the punters, the politicians. They'll probably make you Chief Inspector."

"It won't wash, Ray."

"Terr, I'm giving this to you. Can't you see?"

"It's too late for that, I'm calling it in." Dedovic switched on his mobile.

"Mate, we stick together, we're set. They divide us, we're gone." The ends of Doull's thick moustache were moistened with sweat, his breathing came slow and heavy. "I can't be involved, I'm off the job."

Dedovic stared at the older man's bloodshot eyes, his skin was cracked and scaly. He looked tired and haggard as if the city had worn him down to the bone. The sounds of traffic rolled in from the highway like waves on a beach.

"I gave you your start," Doull was saying. "Took you under my wing."

"You corrupted me, Ray."

"That's a load of shit. Without me you'd be living in some poky little flat somewhere."

"I am."

"Driving a piece of Jap crap and happy if you took your kids out for Yugoslav meatballs once a month."

"How'd you know I was here tonight?"

"I followed you." Doull wiped sweat from his lips. The buttons pulled against his nylon shirt. "Came over to give you this." He reached into his trouser pocket and brought out two rolls of fifties.

Dedovic took the money; it was wet and sticky with blood.

"That'll wash off," Doull said. "I parked out front of your unit when I spot that green Camry. A minute later you appear with the little Greek piece in tow, dive into a cab. I can tell you're on the trail of something big when you get to the Cross, you don't even see the dogs following yer. So I sit on their bumper bar all the way over. They're that fuckin useless, they don't know I'm here. They're out front now."

"I can't cover for you, Ray." He trousered the fifties.

"Call 'emselves cops," Doull said. "Whatever happened to the code?"

Dedovic shook his head. Sometimes you saw people in a different light, people you knew, heard them talking and you wondered how you'd ever got close to them. It was hard to believe there was once a time in Darlinghurst Station when he'd admired Ray Doull and wanted to be just like him. He started keying in the number of the Task Force Commander.

"If I have to shoot you, Terr, I will."

Dedovic looked up at the silver .357 Magnum cocked in the palm of Ray Doull's hand, its black snout pointed directly at his sternum.

"I was one of the best cops this city ever had," Doull said. "We ran the place. It was our town and business only got done if we let it. Crims respected that. They knew where they stood. Guns were out of order for a start. That's all gone. That respect."

"Save it for your memoirs, Ray." Dedovic looked to the doorway and saw Nickie standing there, her large brown eyes flickering uneasily. Doull waved her inside with the barrel of his Colt. Dedovic admired the way she didn't ask any questions. Like a real detective. Her arm went around his waist and he hugged her to him. She was small and warm and her hair was speckled with Mona's blood. He said to Doull, "You going to shoot both of us now, or you going to put down that revolver?"

"You're not going to ruin my career, Terr."

Dedovic laughed. "You don't have a career. You're suspended from the service and you killed two men tonight."

"Either you pick up that .32 from the floor and take the credit for this pinch or I'll make it three men and a woman."

Dedovic could feel Nickie trembling against his arm. He'd never thought of himself as a brave man, but he felt a lot braver with her close to him. He pushed Nickie to one side and stepped in front of the silver .357 Magnum. Moonlight played through the window behind and a car revved in an alley, but Dedovic knew that no-one was going to intervene now. "You set me up with Steve Bia didn't you, Ray? Got me to help you load him when he was never talking to the investigators in the first place."

"Why would I do that?" Doull said.

"Because you wanted him coming at me. You stuck that fit in my garage, then got Bia to sell dope to my daughter. You told him it was me who loaded him up. It always bothered me how Bia didn't know you were involved."

"Keep talking, Terr, if it makes you feel good."

"You figured I'd settle up with mad Stevie, that I'd get my hands dirty and then you'd be certain I would never roll over. You did a job on me."

"The Leb copped his right whack. He deserved to go."

"For all I know, you probably set this poor dead prick up too." Dedovic looked at Limacher lying face-down on the floor. "Shot him in the back of the head. Maybe it's you been knocking off Asian students."

"You think I'm going to cut up little Chinese girls for nothin'?"

"You told me yourself, Ray, there's nobody in this world you can't load. Be easy enough for a smart cop. One who knows his profiling."

"This bloke's done it or else he's as good as done it. Either way you can wrap this case up, make a name for yourself."

"Give me the revolver, Ray." He held out his hand.

"The trouble with you, Dedovic, is you never had any real backbone. You were never one of the elite."

"Give it to me, and I'll stall 'em for an hour."

"Mate." Doull shook his head slowly.

"The old days are gone, Ray. Finished."

"This used to be a great little city," Doull said. He looked down at his gun. He uncocked the hammer with his thumb, released his grip on the trigger and handed over his silver .357 Magnum, the same Colt Python that he'd seized from a gang rapist and heroin dealer all those years ago. Nickie made a noise of relief in her throat. Dedovic unloaded the revolver on his knee. "Go out the back way. They'll be here any minute." He went over to Nickie and took her in his arms. They listened to Doull's footsteps fade down the hall and out through the kitchen into the overgrown garden.

From the window came the soft heavy breathing of late-night traffic. "I really thought he was going to shoot you," she said.

"So did I."

"I never want to go through that again. I'm glad it's over."

"It's not over. It's only beginning." He looked into her brown eyes and touched the faint line of silky hair on her upper lip with the ball of his finger and then with his mouth. They kissed long and hard before she broke away.

"Mona – I left her in the shower bay. Have you rung an ambulance?"

Dedovic threw her the mobile. "You call 'em." He could hear shoes on the path out front and then a fist banging loudly on wood. He stepped over Limacher's body and walked down the hall, taking his time as the knocking grew persistent. He opened the door and saw them standing on the porch like two Mormons in coal-black suits. Young, clear-eyed, clean-shaven and as fit as bulls. "Detective Senior Constable Dedovic?" one of them asked.

"Come on in," Dedovic said. "I've been expecting you."

# 40

She clutched the metal rail and watched the ferry slice through the choppy waves. Standing on the prow of the main deck, listening to the thrum of the engine and the swish of sea water. The ferry rolled from side to side and the Swedish and German backpackers hugged the red wooden seats behind her. She held on tightly, tasting the spray on her lips, feeling the August wind burning into her skin. Her head was spinning from the glare, the long heavy lunch. Thirty-five. Tourists were staring at her, but no-one offered her a seat. All of them wearing rope sandals that she never saw any Australian own; bright-coloured shorts, copper-tanned legs. She wondered how they viewed her. Mona saying in the restaurant, "You're looking terrific, Nicola, a real glow."

"A touch of sun," Nickie said.

"You know what I mean."

And she did know. She had to admire Mona's resilience. The way she bounced back. She hadn't changed at all, apart from the silk scarf she wore around her throat. They didn't talk about Laurie, or the collapse of the college, or any of it, just the new job Mona had found, managing a seafood cafe on The

Corso, and the man she'd met at a Manly gym, a little older, something in television, she said, mimicking his self-importance. She was good company: abrasive, acerbic, but never dull. They'd been through a lot together. Nickie stared at a sailboat dipping into the wind, the waves crowned with foam. The ferry passed between the heads, tourists roaming the deck taking photographs of seagulls, the coastal headlands, one another. She had the feeling she was the only native on board. Leaning against the green rail, the city outlined in the distance.

She'd seen Detective Chen's name mentioned twice in the newspapers in the past six months. Wai Yi Chen had fully recovered from her head injuries, Terry said, though she retained no memory of the attack and was unable to provide police with a description of her assailant. Detective Sergeant Chen was now attached to a Joint Task Force investigating Asian gangs in the south-western suburbs.

There had been nothing in the papers about Detective Sergeant Doull, no mention of his funeral. Terry had wanted to attend the service, but the authorities would not allow it. He told her that Ray had "necked himself" in the garage of his North Ryde home. No evidence was found linking Doull to any of the Asian killings. At least once a week Terry rang her. The situation was delicate. They'd offered him a qualified indemnity against prosecution under New South Wales law for offences he had admitted apart from murder. He did not know what proceedings would be taken against him over the death of Steve Bia or what his tax situation would be. He told her he was hopeful of some light at the end of the tunnel. Investigators had swooped on his Meadowland Avenue house and despite initial protestations from his wife, his family had been whisked away from their home, taken out of the country and given new identities. When this was over, Terry said, he wanted his daughter to come and live with them. Nickie hadn't asked him which daughter. She got the impression that he was lonely. Whenever he rang he did most of the talking. They kept switching him from place to place. She hadn't told him about the five thousand dollars she'd found on the couch in her front room, money that she was using to live on. She hadn't told him of her news. Some nights she saw his hands in her dreams, but never his face. She'd forgotten what he looked like. She had no idea if it would work out between them.

The ferry rounded a lighthouse on Bradleys Head and she saw the grey ribs of the bridge, the sharp white shells protruding from Bennelong Point. A Japanese tourist was viewing her through his video camera. The wind blew in her face. She held onto the sides with both hands, the ferry rolling in the swell, the twin engines grinding below. She felt enormously happy. She didn't know why. She suspected it was because she had come through it all unscathed. There had been no further murders of foreign students since the death of Laurie Limacher. When police units tore his apartment apart – ripping out floorboards, walls, ceilings – they found nothing incriminating other than four stolen medical textbooks. Witnesses remembered seeing a white van outside the college on the day that Ling Ling disappeared, but no forensic evidence was found inside Limacher's Mitsubishi, no hair, no blood, no DNA. Terry was convinced that if Ling Ling had been dragged into that van there would have been some transference of fibres. Sometimes the truth was hard to find, he said. Sometimes there were no easy answers, that not every case was wrapped up neatly and that a detective had to learn to let go. In his opinion the AK was still out there, living on his fantasies, getting sexual gratification from what he had done. It was only commonsense to say that it could happen again, but it was out of his hands now. His career was over.

Nickie looked up at the concrete and glass towers growing closer and wondered where they were holding him. He said he could see the Cahill Expressway from his window. Tonight he was ringing her on her birthday. They were moving him soon to a new location. The ferry straightened and slowed as it approached the quay, the waves around the steel hull frothing and foaming and she could feel the city pulling her in like a magnet.

# Also by John Dale and published by Serpent's Tail

## *Dark Angel*

Jack Buturov is a bouncer in a Sydney casino. He's in hiding from life, his ex-wife and his chronically ill son. Damian was a rent boy hustler, who got in over his head in some bad political business. Despite himself, Jack loved Damian, and when someone guns the boy down, he has to investigate. Along the way he runs into the Vietnamese mafia, corrupt cops, psychotic bikers and, best and worst of all, Damian's sister Angie — a woman as burnt out as Jack Buturov. An outstanding debut, *Dark Angel* is an Australian thriller that crackles with the same white lightning as a James Ellroy, or a James Crumley.

"Confident Sydney thriller, which recalls the reductive world of Jim Thompson... stark urban imagery, emotional ambush, balletic violence, and a cast of speedballs" *Guardian*

"Succeeds in turning the well-tended streets of Sydney into something resembling the seedier parts of Los Angeles" *Sunday Times*

"Love, loss and low-life in this provocative Australian thriller" *New Woman*

"Great energy, dynamic story-telling, a winning fondness for the genre... Intense entertainment" *Kirkus Reviews*

# Also published by Serpent's Tail

## *The Crust On Its Uppers*
**Derek Raymond**

"It's a tale of someone who wanted to go and go – who was sick of the dead-on-its-feet upper crust he was born into, that he didn't believe in, didn't want, whose values were meaningless, that did nothing but hold him back from his first nanny onwards. I wanted to chip my way out of that background which held me like a flea in a block of ice, and crime was the only chisel I could find."

First published in 1962, *The Crust On Its Uppers*, Derek Raymond's first novel (written when he was Robin Cook) is a gripping tale of class betrayal. With ruthless precision, it brings vividly to life a Britain of spivs, crooked toffs and bent coppers – in fact, a Britain that in its bare essentials has changed little over the last 30 years.

"Best place to start is the slangy baroque of the re-issued *The Crust On Its Uppers*, Raymond's autobiographical account of the dodgy transactions between high class wide boys and low class villians. You won't read a better novel about '60s London..." *i-D*

"Tremendous black comedy of Chelsea gangland, written and set in the early Sixties, on the cusp of swinging London" *The Face*

"A breathlessly good read, as funny, relevant and resonant as it was thirty years ago" *Literary Review*

"Peopled by a fast-talking shower of queens, spades, morries, slags, shysters, grifters and grafters of every description, it is one of the great London novels" *New Statesman*